SHE'D FORGOTTEN
WHO SHE WAS...
WOULD A STRANGER'S
LOVING LIES
KEEP HER FOREVER
IN THE DARK?

"A Woman Shouldn't Be
Asking a Man to Kiss Her."

She smiled as her fingers slid sensuously over his shoulders, then trailed on down his neck. She watched his expression change to one of growing desire. "This woman has no pride when it comes to you, Tom Lannigan."

He moved against her in an attempt to warn her that this was not a game they were playing. She was a very desirable woman at his mercy, and he was a man, a hungry man. "You do this to me, and you have no shame." His eyes gazed deeply into hers. "What if I took you right here, right now?"

"I know it would be sinful, but in my heart I know that it is something I would welcome." Her hands gently cupped his face. "If you're trying to scare me, you might as well stop. It's time you knew, Tom Lannigan." Gideon smiled, and Tom discovered he was lost. "There isn't anything you could do to me that I wouldn't be in full agreement with."

"Look . . . I don't want you to say that—"

"Why not? It's true. If you want to ravish me—"

"I'm sorely tempted, lady."

She smiled up at him as his mouth slowly lowered to meet hers. Soon he would love her as wildly as she loved him. . . .

Fool Me Once

LORI COPELAND

A DELL BOOK

Published by
Dell Publishing
a division of
Bantam Doubleday Dell Publishing Group, Inc.
666 Fifth Avenue
New York, New York 10103

The trademark Dell® is registered in the U.S. Patent and Trademark Office.

ISBN: 0-440-20564-6

Printed in the United States of America

Published simultaneously in Canada

April 1990

10 9 8 7 6 5 4

OPM

Every writer is dependent upon research he has either read or experienced. Sometimes I found it impossible for me to accurately describe what a logging camp was like a hundred and twenty years ago, so I wish to gratefully acknowledge four sources I've relied heavily upon in creating the background for *Fool Me Once*. *When Pine Was King* and *Incredible Seney*, by Lewis C. Reimann; *Logging the White Pine in the Saginaw Valley*, by Harold M. Foehl and Irene M. Hargreaves; *Memories of the Minor Lumber Camps*, by Carl B. J. Minor.

In the summer of 1988, my husband and I spent a week in beautiful Michigan, visiting the old logging towns and researching how the lumberjacks lived in the eighteen hundreds.

I came away with a new respect and gratitude for those men.

I dedicate this book to the lumberjacks of old, to all the Toms, Andres, Shots, Jims, Herbs, and Rays who've made my life easier.

Thanks, guys, I appreciate it.

Fool
Me
Once

1

The door of the post office flew open, and a tall, powerfully built man stepped outside. Moments later, Tom Lannigan was striding angrily down the planked sidewalk.

The arresting sight of the six foot three, two hundred twenty-five pound foreman of Wakefield Timber hurrying in his direction made Paddy Morelock drop what he was doing and scramble to his feet.

"Mornin', Mr. Lannigan," Paddy said quickly.

Lannigan nodded curtly, never breaking stride.

"What say you and me share an eye opener?" Paddy asked hopefully.

"Not this morning, Paddy." Tom's refusal seemed uncharacteristically sharp, but his mind was on other things.

Gideon Wakefield—that damn Gideon Wakefield—had his full attention today.

Tom's handsome features were knit in an

angry scowl as he strode briskly down the planked sidewalk. He found it incredible that Rutherford Wakefield would be foolish enough to leave his vast logging empire in the hands of a willful, misinformed, imbecilic adolescent!

But that's exactly what Rutherford had done. He'd left Wakefield Timber and everything else he owned to his granddaughter Gideon.

The familiar jangle of harness filled the air as more wagons pulled into town loaded with men looking for work. Tom made his way across the busy street, oblivious to the commotion. A new timber season had begun and with it, another merciless slaughter in Michigan of the white pine. Tom knew that half the greenhorns—inexperienced lumberjacks—arriving here today had no idea what they were getting into. Come spring, most of them would be eager to move on.

Tom wondered if his life would have been different if his grandfather J. Basil Lannigan had not been one of the first eastern timber speculators to come to the upper peninsula back in the late eighteen forties. In those days, men and women had come by canal boats, paddle steamers, sloops, wagon trains, and clipper ships, looking for limitless stands of the coveted *Pinus strobus*—that lofty, graceful, aromatic evergreen known as the Canadian white pine.

Still a young man, Basil had been barely eking out a living for his family on a small piece of land in the Midwest when timber fever spread across the eastern states like wildfire.

The Gazetteer, a popular tour book of Michigan in the eighteen hundreds, had sounded the news that stands of white pine on the Penobscot and Kennebec rivers in Maine were being depleted and that dry lumber was in great demand. Maps of the mysterious western lands were passed around to encourage the brave to seek their fortunes.

J. Basil Lannigan had heard that the Michigan Territory was a virtual swamp, infested with hostile Indians, miasmatic marshes and bogs, and mosquitoes so large they could carry a man on their back. But despite these warnings, he'd packed up his wife and two young sons and had headed for the upper peninsula of Michigan in search of his fortune. Land could be purchased cheaply, from sixty cents to a dollar and a quarter an acre. And the white pine was desperately needed for houses, barns, sheds, wagons, fences, bridges, boarding houses, saloons, steamboats, railroad ties, and trestles.

A fortune could be made in timber, and J. Basil Lannigan was not a man to let opportunity pass him by.

Almost overnight, the rapid influx of new settlers into the upper and lower peninsulas of Michigan had spawned a string of hell-raising, lawless lumber towns. The timber boom had begun, and would continue, it was said, as long as man existed.

But as young Tom Lannigan had watched the destruction take place over the years, he'd gradually begun to realize the truth: The timber was running out. He could see it, and it worried him.

For sixteen years he'd taken part in the desecration of the land, and he wasn't proud of it. When he was a boy of fourteen, his father had set him behind a pair of Percherons, and he'd worked as a teamster, dragging logs out of the woods to the skidways. He was taught how to build roads and how to use an ax and a crosscut saw. He'd worked at every job there was, from pin whacker to ink slinger, and he had learned his job well.

A quiet, unassuming man, Tom was known to avoid trouble. For years, he'd kept his fears about the land's destruction to himself. He'd worked as hard as anyone, saying little, trying to ignore what was being done to the land. It was clear to him that no one else cared what was happening, certainly not his father or the men whose livelihoods depended on the pine.

But the day came when Tom took a long, hard look around him, and could no longer avoid the appalling truth.

The land was being raped. It was a cold, callous, premeditated rape. Tom knew he could no longer, in good conscience, ignore his responsibilities to his future children, and their children, and their children. He knew he had to do something to offset the madness that was systematically destroying the countryside.

Greed had blinded the timber barons. They'd ruthlessly slashed their way through the stands of pine in order to make quick fortunes, callously adhering to their slogan: "Wealth is for those who know how to get it."

Over the last few years, Tom had tried to get his father to understand what was happening, but he had to admit that he'd failed. His father wouldn't be convinced.

Still clinging to the hope that he could persuade just one timber baron of the madness of the destruction, Tom had left Lannigan Timber to accept a job as foreman of Wakefield Timber.

Tom was convinced that new trees had to be planted or there would be nothing left for future generations. The decision to leave his father's business a year ago had been a painful one, but Tom considered Rutherford Wakefield to be his only hope.

And, thank God, Rutherford had taken the time to hear to what Tom had to say.

Tom could still remember how the wizened old man had sat before the fire, quietly listening as Tom explained his dream of planting millions of acres of young pine to give new life to a dying land.

When Tom finished, Rutherford had

knocked the ashes out of his pipe before absent-mindedly repacking it from the can of Peerless tobacco beside his chair. "What you want, son, would be a mighty big job."

"I know, sir, but it can be done."

Rutherford had studied the tall, brawny young man sitting before him, and a smile formed at the corners of his mouth. "I don't doubt that you can." He'd liked this honest, God-fearing, hard-working young man. 'Twas a shame, he thought, that his granddaughter, Gideon, couldn't find a man like Tom Lannigan.

Tom could recall the sense of relief he'd felt after Rutherford's quiet acquiescence. For the first time in years, Tom had felt a resurgence of hope that the madness might begin to subside. Surely, when others saw the farsighted concern for the forest's future that men like Rutherford Wakefield had, they, too, would follow suit.

"Then you'll authorize me to begin replanting?" Tom had asked.

The old man nodded. "I've taken more than my share from the land. You and I will see to it that the pine lives on. Once a stand is cut, you put a crew to replanting what we've taken."

Tom beamed with joy, and together he and Rutherford had started to form a schedule for replanting.

But one afternoon, while trying to bring a skid of logs out of the woods, Rutherford had keeled over dead. At that instant, Tom's hope for the future had dimmed.

And now it was totally gone.

With renewed anger, Tom stepped up onto the porch of Menson's Camp Store and opened the door. He glanced around, his eyes searching for his friend, the Frenchman, Andre Montague.

Smoking a stogie at a table drawn close to the pot-bellied stove, the burly Andre was playing poker with three other lumberjacks. He glanced up from his hand and lifted a dark brow expectantly in Tom's direction. "Well?"

"She's going to sell," Tom said bitterly.

Andre shrugged and looked down at his cards. "Doesn't surprise me."

Tom took a deep breath, telling himself he no longer gave a damn what Gideon Wakefield did with the business. He'd done all he could. The land was Gideon Wakefield's now to do with as she pleased. He had no choice but to accept her decision.

But he damn well didn't have to like it.

As he reached inside his jacket and pulled out a sheaf of letters, Tom's anger flared anew as he thought of the time he'd spent corresponding with Gideon over the past few months, trying to persuade her to replant the forests and refrain from selling Rutherford's timberlands. *Her* timberlands, he corrected angrily.

With a flick of his wrist, Tom snapped open her first letter.

Dear Mr. Lannigan,

My, my, the budget increase you suggested for planting seedlings seems rather substantial to me. Couldn't you cut the seedling purchase in half and just plant them farther apart?

You are running a business, you know, not a charity. While planting little trees sounds like a worthy cause, we must show a profit or sell. I have started a project here in Philadelphia that has always been close to my heart, so it's crucial that we trim the waste at your end, don't you see?

Sincerely,
Miss Gideon Wakefield

Tom cast the letter into the pot-bellied stove. With a small measure of satisfaction, he watched the fine-grained parchment with the ornate handwriting writhe for an instant then burn to ashes.

Charity? She dared to call planting trees charity?

The word gnawed at him. Tom Lannigan had never asked anyone for charity in his entire life. Replanting the forests was not a philanthropic venture; it was a necessity, pure and simple. He had the foresight to know that if life wasn't given back to the land soon, the time would come when nature would simply refuse to provide. And he had repeatedly told Gideon Wakefield this in at least four different letters, but what did he get as an answer?

Dribble. Pure, unadulterated dribble!

Andre glanced up from his cards to see Tom slam shut the stove door and take another letter from his coat pocket. Without comment, Andre returned to his card game.

Mr. Lannigan,

How nice to hear from you again. My new millinery shop is causing quite a stir in Philadelphia. Everyone is commenting about my creations! The replanting you keep suggesting will just have to wait because, you see, I need to raise the capital to open another shop, and I simply must import that lovely English lace and expensive Chinese silk, which, as you know, is quite the rage in ladies' hats.

Gideon Wakefield

Tom jerked open the stove door and tossed her letter to the greedy flames. His intense gaze circled the room. Here were men who'd dedicated their blood and sweat to Wakefield Timber. Now Gideon Wakefield wanted to forfeit their futures for some damn *hats*?

But of course! How could future generations possibly matter when the little woman in Philadelphia wants to invest in hats? Every lady

9

simply must *have hats made of lace and English silk!*

Andre caught a glimpse of his boss's flushed face, and said nothing as Tom angrily flipped open the letter he had just received.

Mr. Lannigan,

I found your plea for more time compelling; but my millinery shops are simply booming, whereas, Wakefield Timber is presently a terrible drain on my resources. Although you've insisted that Grandfather's business will show a profit at the end of the season, I think my fiancé is right: I must cut my losses and reinvest in something else entirely.

Therefore, I must inform you that I am selling my logging business to Mr. Sven Templeton. I will be arriving in a few weeks to sign the papers and settle accounts with you. I'm sure you will join me in making this a smooth transition for everyone.

G. Wakefield

Tom wadded the paper in his powerful fist and flung it into the fire. With a shove, he closed the cast-iron door with the heel of his boot, the angry clank echoing throughout Menson's Camp Store.

Sven Templeton—he was the most ruthless competitor in the timber industry! No doubt he would continue the destruction that Tom found so deplorable.

Gideon Wakefield didn't care a tinker's damn about anyone but herself.

The little twit has a heart of stone, Tom fumed. She was nothing but a coddled, selfish brat. If he hadn't already known it, he could easily have seen it in her picture in last month's newspaper.

She'd looked as rotten as last week's fish.

Her face had been all smiles as she'd gazed adoringly into the eyes of Talbot Wellington-Kent, that fancy-talking high-brow Philadelphia carriage maker she was engaged to marry.

Andre glanced up from his cards as Tom made a disgusted sound deep in his throat.

"Somethin' wrong?"

"Nothing's wrong," Tom snapped with a murderous glare. "Miss Wakefield will be paying us a visit."

"Oh?" Andre was grinning as he laid down three ladies and a pair of deuces. "Mighty touchy this morning, aren't we?"

Tom ignored the good-natured jibe as he continued to brood. Talbot Wellington-Kent, what kind of a name was that to stick on a man? he wondered irritably.

"So, when is our little flower from the East arriving?" Andre asked as he shuffled the cards. Cocking an eyebrow at Tom, he proceeded to deal a new hand.

"The 'little flower' didn't say exactly."

Andre chuckled again, amused that one tiny

11

woman could get big Tom Lannigan all riled up. And it seemed that Rutherford's grand-daughter had gotten the job done without half trying. "Maybe we ought to throw some sort of a welcoming party for her," Andre suggested, watching out of the corner of his eye as Tom's face grew more grim.

"You do that, Andre," Tom said curtly. "But don't expect me to show up."

Just then, the pair of cats Henry Menson owned to curb his store's rat and mouse popu-lation began racing around the store crazily. Yowling and spitting, they bounced noisily off the shelves, sending canned goods clattering loudly to the floor.

"Somebody throw those cats outside!" Henry called as he leaned closer to the light, squinting to read the handwriting on Florabelle Melton's grocery list.

One of the cats came hurtling past Tom, and he reached to grab it. The cat hissed and clawed at him as Tom gently removed the wooden clothes pin someone had clamped onto its tail.

"Now, I wonder how that got on there?" Nate Waltrax asked, struggling to keep a straight face, as the second cat yeooowwed and sprang headlong into the flour barrel.

"Get the pin off that cat's tail!" Henry de-manded as flour fogged the air.

Chairs scraped against the wooden floor and bedlam broke loose as the men scrambled to

12

catch the white streak darting wildly around the room.

The front door opened and into the midst of the fracas marched Berniece Trunksmore, a tall, raw-boned woman who served as head of the school board. Spotting Tom, she sailed across the room like a clipper in a high gale.

Tom grabbed the cat as it lunged between his legs, then braced himself for one of Berniece's routine tongue-lashings, which was never long in coming.

"Have you heard from the new teacher?" Berniece demanded.

"Now, Berniece—"

"Don't 'now, Berniece' me, Tom Lannigan!" she warned. "When is Fedelia Yardley arriving?"

"Soon."

Berniece narrowed her eyes ominously. "When? Monday? A week from Monday? Two weeks from Thursday? And what have you hooligans done to that poor cat?"

Tom quickly removed the pin from the cat's tail and let the animal drop to the floor. Flour clogged the air again, and Berniece rummaged blindly in her purse for a handkerchief. "No *wonder* the children of this town are such heathens!"

Tom and Andre exchanged a pained look.

Berniece promptly returned to the subject uppermost on her mind. "When is Miss Yardley arriving?"

"Berniece, I can't say—"

"*Why* can't you say?" Berniece interrupted. "It's your job to say—are you no longer capable of doing your job?"

"My job is to run Wakefield Timber, not—"

"I don't want to hear excuses!" she snapped. "I just want out! Is that clear, Thomas?"

"Berniece." Tom's eyes grew steely hard. "I'm doing my job. I have made arrangements for a new teacher, but you're going to have to be patient long enough for her to get here!"

"Hogwash. I've been patient as long as I'm going to be. The party's over, Tom Lannigan. There'd better be a teacher here Monday morning, or you'll be up that well-known creek!"

"Now, Berniece—"

"You stop it with the 'now, Berniecing,' Tom Lannigan! You tell me when Miss Yardley is coming!"

Tom glanced at Andre for help, but from the way his friend was grinning from ear to ear, Tom knew he was in this one alone.

"I can't say exactly when Miss Yardley will arrive. Her letter just said that she'd arrive here within the month."

Berniece jerked the strings of her bonnet as if they were her enemies, and her snapping blue eyes riveted Tom to the spot. "Well, I'm giving you fair warning: she'd better be."

A dimple worked at one corner of Tom's mouth, but since he valued his life, he smothered the urge to grin. "The children giving you trouble again?" he asked innocently.

Berniece blew up. "They're nothing but ill-mannered heathens." She edged closer to wag her finger under Tom's nose. "I will *not*—listen to me—I *will not* spend another week in the classroom with those fiends, do you hear me? If Miss Yardley is not here on Monday morning, this *coming* Monday morning," she emphasized, "the school will be closed. Do I make myself clear?"

"Yes, ma'am. Perfectly clear."

Convinced that Tom finally understood the urgency of the matter, Berniece whirled on her heel and marched to the door. "Monday morning," she called over her shoulder. "Not one moment longer!"

She left, slamming the door behind her and rattling every tin and glass jar on the shelves.

Henry Menson looked up from his task of dipping pickles from the crock of brine. A frown creased his forehead. His little girl, Modeen, would be without a teacher again if Berniece carried through with her threat. Berniece would be the eighth teacher to resign in as many months, and it was becoming impossible to fill the position. They'd already been through every woman in camp.

"Berniece sounds like she means it this time, Tom," Henry fretted.

Tom turned back to warm his hands at the stove. Few men chose to subject their families to the isolation of a logging camp. But Watersweet was larger than most operations, and Tom had sixteen families to look after. Sixteen families—with nine children to educate. If the five boys and four girls behaved like normal kids, it would've made Tom's job considerably easier.

But they were hellions, and Tom knew it.

"She's just upset because Pud Wilkerson took the screws out of her chair," Tom dismissed absently.

Andre chuckled. "Yeah, and he forgot to mention it until after Berniece sat down."

"Serves Berniece right," Henry put in. "She should have let Hubert build the schoolteacher's chair outta nails instead of making him use those fang dangled screws she insisted on."

Nate Waltrax chewed on his cigar as he shuffled the cards for another game. "Can't really blame Berniece for wanting out. I wouldn't put up with those kids if it were me."

"Now, wait a minute, Nate," Henry protested. "My little Modeen—"

"Is part of the problem. She swears like a man, bullies anyone who gets in her way, and has a mean streak a mile wide," Nate finished. He bit off the end of his cigar and spat it on the floor.

"Nate, how many times have I warned you about spittin' on the floor," Henry complained as he replaced the lid on the pickle jar. "Now,

16

my Modeen is a little high-spirited, but she can be controlled."

"With a whip and a chair," Andre muttered under his breath.

"Well," Sy Melton said, picking up his box of supplies and looking at Tom, "we'd all better hope that the new teacher makes it by Monday. If Berniece quits before she gets here, the womenfolk will be real upset."

Tom reached up to rub the back of his neck wearily. After his hand fell away, the imprint of five fingers was left behind, outlined in a fine dusting of flour.

He figured he had as much of a chance of meeting Berniece's Monday morning ultimatum as the white pine had of avoiding Sven Templeton's crosscut saw—all thanks to Gideon Wakefield.

All Tom could do was hope Fedelia Yardley got here.

And soon.

2

"**N**ext stop, Watersweet!"

Gideon's head snapped to attention at the sound of the conductor's call. Aware that she'd been caught dozing again, she glanced sheepishly at Fedelia Yardley, sitting across from her.

Fedelia never dozed. In fact, Gideon could have sworn that the woman sharing her coach hadn't shut an eye from the moment they'd left Philadelphia. For days, the two young women had sat opposite one another as the train rattled and swayed its way across the countryside.

Though pleasant enough, Fedelia had done little to reward Gideon's periodic attempts to draw her into conversation. She seemed content to thumb methodically through textbook after textbook, enduring the tedious journey with as few distractions as possible.

Sighing, Gideon readjusted the folds of her heavy woolen skirt. With more than a touch of pride, she reached to adjust the creation adorning her head. With ostrich plumes, coils of silk and rows of fine English lace, she had to admit, she had fashioned a hat fit for a queen.

Gideon felt a warm glow as she thought of her lovely little hat shops in Philadelphia. They were her pride and joy. While she sketched her breathtaking creations, two seamstresses brought her ideas to life. It had all been such wonderful fun. And Talbot was so proud of her! She could hardly wait to get back to her little shops; her mind was simply brimming with new ideas for the fall season.

The train whistle sounded another warning, and Gideon sat up straighter and began to replace the pins that had fallen loose from her hair. Wisps of dark, springy curls fell haphazardly to her shoulders as she swept off her hat.

"I'll be glad to see this trip end," she confided to Fedelia as her fingers nimbly worked the thick mass back into a soft cluster atop her head.

The journey had been uncomfortable, and Gideon longed for a hot bath. She planned to go straight to the hotel and soak for hours in a tub of steaming hot water before she went in search of a decent meal.

Fedelia murmured something distractedly, and continued reading.

It was Fedelia's hairstyle, Gideon decided, that bothered her about the woman. She really should do something about it. The dark

20

brunette mass was tidy, but it looked too severe pulled back from her face in that tight, restricting bun.

Gideon glanced lovingly at her elaborate creation on the seat beside her. What a hat like that could do for a woman! Gideon was certain that one of her designs would indeed perform a miraculous transformation for this girl.

Gideon found it disturbing that she and Fedelia bore a slight resemblance to one another. The conductor had assumed they were sisters until Fedelia stiffly informed him that she had no family.

Gideon conceded that Watersweet's new schoolmarm, though not overly friendly, was pretty in a modest sort of way, but the serviceable brown traveling suit she wore and the equally uninspired brown hat anchored firmly atop her pragmatic bun just cried dull, dull, dull. Gideon sighed again. Oh, that hat! Dreadfully uninspired.

"I don't plan to be in Watersweet long," Gideon remarked as if Fedelia had inquired—or was concerned about the length of her stay.

Fedelia's eyes remained on the passage she was reading.

"My," Gideon drew in another long, weary breath as she leaned back against the seat and gazed wistfully out the window at the passing scenery. For hours, the train had been winding through an unending forest of tall Michigan pines.

She had been studying the trees with rapt attention. She had never seen such trees!

The branches towered sixty to eighty feet above the ground, and the pine grew so thickly in the forests that the sunlight never reached the ground. Though her grandfather had lived his entire life in these forests, Gideon had not been to visit him since she was a small child. "It is lovely, isn't it?"

Fedelia finally looked up. A cold north wind was pelting a heavy rain against the side of the coach. At times, the rain mingled with sleet. To Fedelia, inclement weather was anything but lovely.

Gideon smiled, aware of Fedelia's lack of enthusiasm for the raucous logging town that they were approaching. They'd briefly discussed the stories they'd heard circulating through the train about Watersweet.

The description of the rough, lawless town of three hundred clearly horrified Fedelia. But Gideon, who had always been safely protected from anything remotely dangerous, couldn't wait to get there.

Although she'd been instructed to complete the sale of Wakefield Timber as quickly as possible, she was secretly coveting the freedom she'd been enjoying ever since Talbot placed her on the train three days ago.

In all of her eighteen years, Gideon Wakefield had never been allowed to go anywhere alone, and with the exception of opening her own millinery she had never been allowed to make even the smallest decision for herself. She was reveling in her newfound independence, and she had to admit that she would experience a certain letdown when it came to an end.

Sighing, Gideon thought about the changes that had come into her life recently. Her mother had died some years ago, and now Grandfather Wakefield, so she had no one left . . . no one but Talbot, her former guardian.

Gideon smiled as she thought about her fiancé. Talbot had been adamant that she make a swift journey to efficiently dispose of her grandfather's timber business. He would have come with her, but he'd had previous commitments that could not go unattended. After hours of pleading, she'd finally convinced him she was capable of making the trip alone.

Though she'd been a bit frightened at first, she'd relished her little adventure, and it wasn't over yet. Talbot had said she could take as long as she needed to finish her business in Watersweet.

"You're so lucky." Another wistful sigh escaped Gideon as the train clattered nosily down the uneven tracks.

Fedelia lifted her brows questioningly. "Lucky?"

"Yes," Gideon whispered, taking care not to awaken the boisterous set of hooligans who had boarded the train at the last stop.

23

The men were woodsmen traveling from the east to work in Seney, another crossroad settlement in the upper peninsula of Michigan that boasted twenty-one saloons and three brothels. Becoming upset because their dinner wasn't to their liking, they had proceeded to kick out the windows of the coach, then they'd picked up the stunned conductor and pitched him headlong out of the train into a snow bank.

The train had been delayed nearly thirty minutes while Fedelia and Gideon had moved to another coach and waited for the harried conductor to reboard.

Fedelia had been appalled by the ruffians, but Gideon, who'd remained wide-eyed throughout the fray, had found it all very exciting.

"Why would you think that I'm lucky?" Fedelia asked.

"Because you are completely on your own," Gideon said.

How wonderful it must be to have no one to tell you where you may go, when you must smile, what you must say, she thought.

Gideon was grateful to have a man of Talbot's position in the world to look out for her, yet how nice it would be to be on your own. Your very own.

Of course, she didn't envy Fedelia her reason for going to Watersweet. Though she'd been schooled at the most prestigious establishments, Gideon knew that she'd be ill-suited for teaching young children. Her teachers had been candid with her parents when she'd first started school.

Their raven-haired daughter, though extremely personable, was, sadly enough, not overly gifted where scholarly pursuits were concerned. But she supposed that it didn't matter whether she was considered brilliant or not. In a few short weeks, she and Talbot would marry, and then her future would be secure.

Gideon smiled as she thought of Talbot Wellington-Kent. She had a large trust fund, but Talbot was a wealthy man, born into a family that had already made their fortune. Wellington-Kent had produced the finest Philadelphia carriage available for over seventy-five years. But it wasn't Talbot's money that Gideon found attractive, because she would soon be wealthy in her own right, with the sale of her grandfather's business. No, it was Talbot himself. She felt comfortable with him, though he could be a bit stuffy at times. But he was awfully dependable, and Gideon knew that this was important in the man she married, since she herself tended to be flighty sometimes, or so she'd been told.

Still, these glorious few days of freedom had made her wonder if she could make it on her own. . . .

Laying her book aside, Fedelia shook her

head and sighed. "I must admit I wish I shared your feelings."

"You don't feel lucky?"

"Only apprehensive."

Gideon laughed. Old Walter Fedderson, the elderly gentleman sitting across the aisle, stirred, cleared his throat loudly, then dropped back to sleep. "Oh, don't let all that talk about Watersweet upset you. I'm sure the town can't be all that bad," Gideon whispered.

Fedelia appeared skeptical, but continued, "I should think you would want to keep the logging interest your grandfather left you. The timber business is quite lucrative," she pointed out.

"I know." Gideon's smile faded as she turned back to watch the passing scenery. "Actually, I was in favor of keeping it and letting grandfather's foreman run the business for me."

"Why did you change your mind?"

"Talbot thinks it would be best to liquidate my assets and invest in something more promising. I've opened my own hat shops recently. This is one of my creations." Gideon smiled as she lifted her hat from the seat and held it out to Fedelia. "Would you like to try it on? I wouldn't mind, you know."

Fedelia recoiled. "No," she said flatly. "No, thank you," she added as if remembering her manners. "I couldn't, really."

Gideon saw the mixture of awe and revulsion in the girl's eyes and understood that Fedelia was probably not accustomed to such finery. "If I'd brought another with me," Gideon said apologetically, "I'd be happy to give it you. But since this the only one—"

"That's quite all right," Fedelia interjected. "What were you saying before?"

"Oh," Gideon said, placing her hat on her own head, noting the look of relief that entered Fedelia's eyes. The poor girl, Gideon thought, she might have plenty of book learning, but she knows nothing about current fashions. "Well, as I was saying, my fiancé's broker says the timber business has been on the decline in recent years."

"Is your grandfather's foreman trustworthy?"

"Oh, I think so. Mr. Lannigan and I have corresponded over the past few months, and he seems to know the business," Gideon mused. "But he has this crazy idea of wanting to replant trees for future generations. Can you imagine?" Her gaze returned to the seemingly endless rows of pine flashing by the window. "I've heard it's estimated that there is enough timber to last for *hundreds* of years."

"Yes, I've read the same," Fedelia agreed thoughtfully. They were beginning to catch an occasional glimpse of fallen pines. "But I have heard that logs with the slightest blemish are sometimes left on the ground to rot."

"Surely not!" Gideon viewed the landscape.

"They won't leave it like that. They're probably just not finished here yet."

"One would hope not." Fedelia shook her head sadly.

"I'm sure this sort of thing never happens in my grandfather's outfit," Gideon said again, watching as the countryside grew more barren.

"I'm sure it doesn't."

Gideon settled back against her seat to pass the final few minutes of the journey as the train picked up speed. "Anyway, Talbot feels I shouldn't be burdened with owning a business in the wilds of Michigan."

"You're to be married soon?"

"Sometime in April." Leaning forward, Gideon proudly displayed the ring Talbot had given her. "See?"

An almost envious look came into Fedelia's eyes as she gazed at the cluster of precious stones. "It's very lovely."

"Would you like to try it on?" Despite Fedelia's soft gasp of protest, Gideon removed the ring and handed it to her. "Don't worry, Talbot will never know."

Fedelia slipped the ring on her finger and moved her hand back and forth, admiring the way the diamonds caught the light from the window.

A sadness entered her eyes, and Gideon saw it. "Is there someone you care for deeply?" she asked.

"There was . . . once," Fedelia returned softly. "But he died before I realized how much I loved him."

"Oh." Gideon reached out to touch Fedelia's hand gently. "I'm so sorry. Was it long ago?"

Fedelia smiled. "Sometimes it seems like it was a hundred years ago . . . but it was only a few months. I'm afraid I've lost track of time. That's why I accepted the teaching position in Watersweet. I thought perhaps . . ." Her voice trailed off as pools of tears began to well in her eyes.

Clearing her throat, Fedelia quickly returned to their earlier subject. "This Mr. Lannigan you spoke of . . . how does he feel about your selling your grandfather's business?"

"I'm not sure." Gideon frowned. Actually the foreman had never replied to her last letter. She wasn't surprised; from his letters, she'd gathered that Mr. Lannigan was a stubborn man who could be quite rude when things didn't go his own way. "But I don't care. I just want to please Talbot, and he feels we can invest my money more prudently."

"And how do you feel?" Fedelia prompted.

"Actually, I have better things to do with my money than plant trees—"

Gideon grabbed for support as she felt the train suddenly lurch violently sideways.

"My goodness!" Fedelia's stunned exclamation was interrupted as she came sailing out of her seat onto Gideon's lap.

The high-pitched squeal of metal grating against metal signaled that something was terribly wrong with the train. The two women scrambled to regain their balance while the engineer tried desperately to bring the train to a halt.

Walter Fedderson was wide awake now. The jolt had thrown him out into the aisle, and he was trying to pull himself back up on the seat.

"What's going on?" he demanded, glaring at Gideon as if she had unseated him.

Suddenly, the whole world turned upside down. In the blink of an eye, the coach tilted upward, left the track, and became airborne.

Gideon was helpless to understand what was happening as she struggled to hang on. The passenger car rolled over and over as it tumbled down a steep incline, hurtling toward a body of muddy, swift-running water.

Fedelia screamed. Gideon reached out to grab onto her, but her hand met thin air.

"Grab my hand!" Gideon shouted frantically as the side of the rail car ripped away. Fedelia screamed Gideon's name as she went flying out the gaping side of the coach like a rag doll.

"Dear Mother of God," Gideon murmured as she saw Walter Fedderson go next.

She could hear her screams blending with Fedelia's as the young schoolteacher fell headlong into the icy waters. The turgid river lay claim to her flailing body, picking it up and carrying it swiftly along the icy current.

"Fedelia! Grab onto something!" Gideon shouted, trying to hold on as the car bumped and slid its way down the frozen hillside. After what seemed like an eternity, it finally tumbled into the glacial waters, trapping Gideon inside the wreckage.

Bitterly cold water rushed into the cavity, engulfing her, stealing her breath away. Heart pounding, she tried to gather her bearings. Her lungs already felt like they would burst as the water poured in around her.

She didn't want to die. She'd only begun to live. There was so much left that she wanted to do—she wanted to marry, to have children. . . . She had yet even to bake a pie or read an entire book . . . and her hats . . . her lovely, lovely hats. . . . She struggled more fiercely to free her body, imprisoned in the frozen bowels of the debris.

Mr. Fedderson—where was Mr. Fedderson? Had she only imagined that he'd been thrown clear, or was he trapped somewhere below, fighting for his life? Her hands reached into the freezing water, searching frantically for the older man. Her hands were growing numb. She realized she couldn't feel anything now, just a vague tingling where the tips of her fingers were supposed to be. She grasped the window frame, trying to brace herself against the swift current. Her lungs were aching for breath.

Oh, dear God, help me, she prayed, finally accepting the knowledge that she was about to die. Where were those bad-tempered woodsmen? Had their car derailed too? she wondered. They were strong; they could help her. . . .

Don't let me die like this—don't let me die like this—she could feel herself losing consciousness, but she continued to pray as a terrifying blackness began to devour her.

"Please, God, I don't want to die," she sobbed. "I want to live. . . ." Her words were a mere whimper now as her head pounded unmercifully. The mounting pressure in her chest seemed to sap what strength she had.

She was truly alone now, a thought that only an hour ago she'd found so exhilarating. Now it made her feel terribly afraid.

Her hand began to lose its grip on the window frame, and she could feel her body growing lighter, almost weightless.

Please, God, if it must be the end, let it be merciful and swift. . . . Take care of Talbot. . . .

Then she could hear nothing but the sound of the cold, rushing water . . . pounding . . . pounding . . . ever pounding. . . .

3

"*T*wo dollars a day?" Hugh Burton sat in Tom's office, rubbing the dark stubble on his chin.

Tom wished he could offer Hugh more. A river driver with Hugh Burton's experience was hard to come by. The river hog's work was not only hazardous, but the working conditions were rugged.

Agile, fearless, and skillful, a river driver drove the logs from the rollways to the booming grounds, working from twelve to fourteen hours a day before facing the long walk back to camp each night.

But two dollars a day, plus a bed and three square meals were all Tom could offer, considering Wakefield Timber was about to change owners. And it was a sure bet that heartless Sven Templeton wouldn't be offering more.

Rumor had it that when one of Sven's river hogs had been killed in last year's spring drive, Sven had docked the man's widow thirty percent of his pay because her husband had failed to complete the terms of his contract.

"Sorry I can't do better, Hugh." Tom pushed back from his desk and reached for the pot of coffee on the stove.

"I was hoping for more," Hugh admitted.

"I know you were." Tom filled Hugh's cup before replenishing his own. "But I'm sure you've heard Wakefield Timber will soon have a new owner."

"Gossip says you're going to be leaving once the sale is final. That so?"

Tom let the question go unanswered. Although Sven had already approached him about staying on, Tom knew he couldn't. He was seriously thinking about yielding to his father's pressure to return to Lannigan Timber—then again, maybe he'd just get out of the damn timber business altogether.

After placing the pot back on the stove, Tom walked to the window, and his thoughts returned to Hugh. He'd heard that Hugh's wife was seriously ill and that he needed money to send her downstate for an operation that could possibly save her life. In hardship cases like this, Tom and his crew usually dug into their pockets to help with the expenses, but anyone who knew Hugh was aware that he was a proud man, a man who would take nothing he hadn't earned, a man who'd prefer to work eighteen hours a day if necessary to provide the care his wife and family needed.

"My Nellie's real sick." Hugh's soft-spoken admission broke into Tom's troubled thoughts.

He turned from the window, where he'd been watching the sleet that had been falling all morning grow into snowflakes the size of a man's fist. "I'd heard that, Hugh. I'm sorry. Is there anything I can do to help?"

"No, but I'm desperate, Tom. I'll take the job and as much overtime as you can see fit to give me."

"You know I'll help you all I can, Hugh."

Hugh rose to shake Tom's hand, his eyes filling with quiet gratitude. "I'm much obliged to you, Lannigan. I'll earn my keep."

Tom clasped Hugh's work-callused hand reassuringly. The man had run into a string of bad luck lately. First his wife's illness, and then his former employer's announcement at Barlow Timber that they were shutting down for good after last season.

Tom was willing to do whatever he could to help. "Glad to have you aboard, Hugh. Take your things to the bunkhouse and get settled in—"

The two men glanced up as the door to the office burst open, bringing with it a frigid blast of arctic air. A grim-faced Andre stood in the doorway. "You had better come with me, Tom."

"What's wrong?"

"There has been a train accident. It is serious."

Reaching for his mackinaw hanging behind the stove, Tom nodded his apologies to Hugh. He slipped into his heavy jacket as he followed Andre out the door. "When did it happen?"

"About an hour ago. I helped drag a woman out of the river. She is near frozen, but Doc Medifer's working on her right now. Another lady passenger and a man were swept downstream. They are still looking for the bodies."

"They'll never find a body in that current," Tom acknowledged grimly.

The two men matched strides as they braced themselves against the blustery wind blowing off Lake Huron. Watersweet lay next to a deep harbor, protected on one side by a hundred-foot limestone cliff. The scenic logging town was a top-notch operation with land covered by beech, maple, birch, and deep forests of the coveted stands of white pine. But by mid-October, natural wind breaks did little to protect anyone from the fierce bite of old man winter.

"How many were injured?" Tom asked as he and Andre made their way across the street and turned the corner. The wind stung their faces and turned the tips of their noses to an angry red.

"There were three passengers in the car that derailed. The remainder of the passengers have been put up over in Shadow Pine for the night."

"Does anyone know how it happened?"

"Engineer says he thinks they hit a deer that darted onto the tracks." The men crossed the street again and strode briskly toward the doctor's house as Andre continued. "The damn car jumped track and slid down into a ravine. I am surprised anyone got out of it alive."

Tom shook his head sympathetically. The river had been up and running for days after the heavy fall rains they'd been experiencing. A strong man swimming against a swift current on a day like today wouldn't have much of a chance of making it to safety, much less a woman.

They reached their destination and hurried inside to find a small group of townspeople gathered around the red-hot stove. They stood talking in hushed tones about the unexpected turn of events, shaking their heads amid grim predictions that the other two passengers would never be found alive.

Staring through the curtained partition, Tom could barely make out the outline of the doctor hovering over a young, dark-haired woman lying unconscious on a table.

Berniece spotted Tom and rushed over, her excited voice raised to a fever pitch. "I'm glad you're here—do you know what's happened?"

"The train had an accident—"

"And do you know who that is lying in there on that table frozen stiffer than a sheet in a January wind?"

Tom didn't, but whoever it was had Berniece worked into a lather. "Berniece, I don't—"

"Fedelia Yardley, that's who!" Berniece began wringing her hands as she paced the length of the room.

Tom glanced at Andre questioningly. "The new schoolteacher?"

Andre nodded and added in a whisper, "What information we have points that way. The conductor verified that Miss Yardley was on the train when it derailed, but he couldn't recall which car she was riding in. We think the other passenger might be the woman Burl Sutter's been expecting."

"The one from East Saginaw?"

Andre shrugged. "Can't be positive, but Burl said she was due in on the train sometime this week."

Tom glanced back at the table where the young woman was lying. "Did she have any identification on her?"

"No. We found a couple of valises with the initials FY on them near the wreckage," Andre said. "The current swept the rest of the personal belongings downstream—except for a couple of Miss Yardley's textbooks found on the bank."

"Oh, merciful heavens, *why* did this have to happen now! If that poor woman dies—" Berniece's voice grew an octave shriller as the appalling ramifications became apparent.

Slapping her hand against her forehead,

Berniece tramped back and forth across the wooden floor, picking up tempo as she went. "If that poor woman dies, I swear you will have to close the school down permanently, because I simply will *not* be responsible for teaching those—those *hoodlums!*"

Tom moved to the informal partition and parted the curtain. Doc Medifer barely glanced up as he concentrated on the stethoscope he was holding to the woman's chest.

"How is she, Doc?"

Peering over the rims of his wire spectacles, Doc shook his head worriedly. "I was hoping she would have come around by now."

Stepping into the small room, Tom had his first real look at the injured woman. He had a strange feeling as his eyes focused on the bedraggled woman lying on the table. A gut instinct made him wonder if this woman was really Fedelia Yardley.

From out of nowhere, the name of Gideon Wakefield entered his mind. No, it was impossible . . . and yet. . . . Could the woman who lay on the table looking like near death be *Gideon Wakefield*?

Tom thought of the blurry newspaper picture he'd seen of Rutherford's granddaughter. This woman *could* be her, he supposed, gazing at the mass of dark, unruly hair, the small cupid-shaped mouth, looking pouty even now, as she lay limp as a rag doll.

Tom studied the patrician features that

were characteristically Rutherford: high cheekbones, wide-set eyes, a straight nose, and the chin of iron determination. But many people possessed such features, he reasoned. And yet, there was something, something he couldn't explain, something that made him wonder if this slender creature with just a hint of nubile curves lying beneath the white sheet could possibly be Gideon Wakefield.

"She's mighty lucky to be alive," Doc said as he walked to the medicine cabinet and pulled out a bottle.

"Will she make it?" Tom asked, trying to keep his voice steady as he looked at down at her face again.

Are you Gideon Wakefield? Impossible! Well, perhaps not impossible, but certainly unlikely. Am I losing my mind? Is the strain of holding the business together finally getting to me?

"I think she'll make it," the doctor replied. "She has a few cuts and bruises, and I'm a little concerned about the fingers on her left hand. They're frostbitten, but I think she'll regain the use of them. I'm more concerned about exposure right now."

"How long was she in the water?"

"Not long, thank God. Andre managed to pull her out of the wreckage shortly after the accident happened." The doctor sighed. "I'm betting they'll never find the other two."

Both men knew the hazards of the river. At

this time of year, the current could easily propel a body straight into Lake Huron, never to be seen again.

Fedelia Yardley's body? Tom wondered. Andre had found two valises bearing the initials FY. The new teacher must have been on the train.

Suddenly, Andre poked his face through the parted curtain and asked in a hushed tone, "How's she doing?"

The young woman on the table began to stir, murmuring softly, "Please, help me . . . I don't want to die . . . please . . . my lovely hats . . ."

"Looks like she's starting to come around." Doc moved back to the table and bent over his patient. He smiled. "Yes, she's coming back to us."

"Please . . ." Slowly, the young woman's eyes fluttered open. Eyes like rich dark satin stared up at Tom.

He felt a swift quickening in the pit of his stomach. She took his breath away, with her striking dark eyes, dark hair, and soft, husky voice.

A frown gathered on Gideon's forehead as her eyes darted about, trying to bring the room and its occupants into focus. "What . . . where am I?"

"Just try to relax, young lady," Doc said soothingly. "There's been an accident, but you're going to be fine."

"An accident?" Gideon stared up at the tall, blond-headed giant looking down at her as she tried to clear her senses. "What kind of accident?"

"The train had an accident," Doc said. "And you were injured."

Gideon brought her hand up to her forehead, trying to relieve the pressure in her brain. "Train? I . . . I don't seem to recall . . ."

Doc glanced at Tom and Andre with a frown. "Her memory may have been affected, which isn't unusual. Sometimes a blow to the head will make someone feel a little vague for a few days."

From the corner of her eye, Gideon watched as the blond giant moved away from the table. She heard an incredibly deep, resonant voice coming from him as he asked, "Are you saying she has amnesia?"

The doctor lifted her eyelids to study the dilation of her pupils. "Do you know your name?" he asked.

"Why, of course . . . it's . . ." Gideon fought to clear the cobwebs cluttering her mind. "It's . . . no." She shook her head. "I'm . . . not sure."

"Well, don't be concerned." Doc patted her hand, then walked back to the medicine cabinet and took out a small bottle of white powder. "I'm going to give you something to make you rest. Perhaps when you wake up you'll be thinking more clearly."

Andre stepped into her line of vision, holding his hat in his hand. "Hello, do you remember me?" he prompted gently.

Gideon peered up at the handsome Frenchman, her eyes growing heavy with fatigue. Did she know him? Yes . . . no, then she was sure she'd never seen this man in her life. "No, I'm sorry. . . ."

Andre's smile was gentle. "You gave me quite a scare, *ma petite*. I am the one who pulled you from the river."

"Oh . . . thank you . . ." She reached out to clasp his hand weakly. "That was very kind of you. . . ."

Holding her small, delicate hand as if it were a rare treasure, Andre smiled down into the warmest pair of brown eyes he'd ever seen. "It was my pleasure, *ma chérie*. I hope you will feel better very soon."

Tom groaned. Lumber camps were a man's world, and he knew by the tone of Andre's voice that the striking new schoolteacher would bring nothing but trouble. *But is she the new schoolteacher?* an inner voice taunted him. Andre and now the others were assuming that she was.

Only Tom suspected otherwise.

The doctor lifted the young woman's head, and she took a sip of the sedative from the cup he offered. As he eased her head back onto the pillow, Gideon tried to smile at him. "Thank you."

"You're welcome. You should sleep for several hours."

Andre began pulling his woolen cap onto his head. Glancing at Tom, he said softly, "I must get back to the crew. They are still looking for the others. I will check back with you later."

Tom nodded vaguely, his thoughts occupied with the woman lying on the table.

"Lannigan," Doc Medifer said, "if I can prevail upon you to stay with Miss Yardley for a minute, I'd like to get a cup of coffee." The doctor rolled down the cuffs of his sleeves wearily. "Do you mind?"

"No, go ahead."

Reaching in his shirt pocket for a smoke, Tom watched as the woman struggled to stay awake. Moments later, she lost the fight and drifted back to sleep.

Well, hello Miss Yardley—or is it Miss Wakefield? Tom greeted her silently as he bit off the end of the cigar and leaned against the medicine cabinet to await Doc's return.

What was he going to do now? Andre and Berniece had everyone assuming that Fedelia Yardley had survived the accident. It was a logical assumption, considering the luggage found and the fact that Gideon Wakefield had never sent him an arrival date. Her last letter had mentioned that she planned to come to Michigan in a few weeks. For all he knew, she might have changed her mind. It would have been just like the flighty twit not to inform anyone. And it would have been just like her to show up without bothering to inform anyone of her impending arrival.

Tom struck a match with his thumbnail while he studied the sleeping woman's features.

If this was Gideon Wakefield, would he go along with her mistaken identity? He shrugged. How could he know for certain who this woman was?

He chuckled mirthlessly as he imagined how Miss Philadelphia-born-and-bred Wakefield would cotton to the job of trying to teach school to seven hell-bent hooligans.

Now, wouldn't that be a laugh.

His eyes narrowed as he contemplated such an unexpected opportunity for revenge. If this woman was Gideon Wakefield, then it would serve her right. He couldn't think of anyone who deserved such a lesson in humility. It was high time a woman like her was introduced to the real world. Obviously, she didn't give a damn about anyone else's welfare, so why should he protect hers? If this was Gideon Wakefield, then she was planning to waltz in here and sell her lumber company to the low-down-good-for-nothing weasel Sven Templeton, not caring in the least that she might endanger the jobs of every man who worked for Wakefield Timber.

In Tom's opinion, it was justifiable not to mention the possibility that this woman could be anyone other than Fedelia Yardley. If it turned out that she was Miss Yardley, then no harm done. If it turned out that she was Gideon Wakefield, then she had it coming to her.

Besides, what did he have to go on besides a blurry photograph and the woman's resemblance to Rutherford Wakefield? He wasn't sure he trusted his own instincts anymore, not with the stress he was under. Nevertheless, his conscience plagued him.

You can't let everyone think she's someone she's not. You might be mad as hell about her decision to sell the company, but you wouldn't deliberately perpetrate such a fraud on anyone.

Bringing the smoke back to his mouth, he shrugged. *Why shouldn't I?*

It's tempting—but you wouldn't do it. That would be a hell of a trick to pull on anyone.

A sly grin tugged at the corners of Tom's mouth as he thought about Gideon having to earn her way in the world for a change. Wouldn't that be something? Little fancy-pants Gideon Wakefield believing she was Fedelia Yardley? A pampered little rich girl, who'd probably never done a lick of work in her entire self-centered life, forced to cope with the likes of Pud Wilkerson and Modeen Henson?

The thought made Tom chuckle aloud as he imagined it.

Gideon's eyes momentarily fluttered open with the intrusion.

He quieted instantly. "Sorry, ma'am. I didn't mean to disturb you."

She smiled wanly and drifted off again.

She'd most likely regain her memory, he reasoned, but how long would that take? Long enough to show her a lesson, he figured. What if Miss Yardley's body was found? Even if that happened, it could take weeks before anyone could identify the body. Miss Yardley's application had indicated that she had no close living relatives.

And what about Gideon's fiancé? If this was she, wouldn't he be asking questions eventually? Well, we might as well wait and see what happens, Tom thought as he puffed his cigar, deliberately ignoring the little voice of warning.

Hell, it was only *his* guess that she might be Gideon Wakefield, he rationalized. For all he knew, she could be anybody. Maybe this woman *was* Fedelia Yardley, and the new schoolteacher just happened to bear a resemblance to Rutherford's granddaughter.

How was Tom Lannigan supposed to know any more than anyone else at this point? Let the town and Andre assume what they wanted.

His only regret was that this might be affecting Rutherford's granddaughter. Rutherford had been an honest, caring man. However, the old man was gone now and Tom had the welfare of his employees to think about.

For as long as he could see to it, their jobs would be safe. And in the meantime, he might even plant a few pines here and there, just to prove to someone a hundred years down the line that at least one person cared about the next generation.

The doctor returned carrying a cup of coffee, as Tom was crushing out his cigar.

"Everything all right?"

Tom smiled. "Fine."

"Good. Well, much obliged. I think I'll just sit here and drink my coffee and keep a close watch on the new schoolteacher." Doc lowered his voice. "Berniece is about to have an attack of the vapors worrying about her."

"Yeah, Berniece sure wouldn't want anything to happen to the new teacher," Tom agreed.

You'd better mention to Doc that this might not be the new schoolteacher, his inner voice demanded again.

In a pig's eye, Tom thought to himself.

As far as he was concerned, if this woman *was* Gideon Wakefield, she was only getting what she had coming to her.

48

4

When Gideon opened her eyes again, she squinted painfully against the bright ray of sunlight streaming through a small windowpane. Her hand came up to shade her eyes. She glanced around and realized she was lying in a bed.

The tantalizing aroma of hot cakes and sausage filled the air. She looked up to find a young woman standing beside her bed, pouring hot tea into a tin cup. When the girl noticed that Gideon's eyes were open, she smiled, pleased that her patient had finally decided to wake up.

"Good morning, ma'am. I hope you slept well?"

"Very well, thank you." Gideon glanced around the room, trying to clear her mind. Her head hurt. It was a dull, throbbing ache located somewhere near the base of her skull.

"I have your breakfast." The pleasant fragrance of vanilla drifted over Gideon as the

49

girl leaned over her to arrange the bed pillows. Moments later when the breakfast tray was in place, Gideon pushed herself up into a sitting position. The effort made her feel slightly lightheaded. Her eyes focused on the thick patties of sausage and the mound of golden brown hot cakes swimming in heavy maple syrup, and she felt her stomach lurch.

Seeing how pale Gideon's face had suddenly become, the young woman quickly removed the tray and said brightly, "Maybe we'd better wait until your stomach settles a bit."

Gideon nodded gratefully, trying to fight the waves of nausea washing over her. She allowed her head to drop weakly back onto the pillow, and she closed her eyes tightly. "Where am I?" she finally managed to ask.

"Watersweet. There was an accident involving the train yesterday. You were thrown into the river, but Doc Medifer says you'll be good as new in a few days."

Gideon's eyes opened slowly. Watersweet. The name sounded vaguely familiar. "I don't seem to remember," she admitted.

Actually, she couldn't remember anything except waking up in the doctor's office, then promptly going back to sleep after a strong sedative. "Were there others . . . ?" she ventured to ask.

"Yes." The girl turned to pick up a third pillow. "Two passengers were swept downstream, I'm afraid."

50

Gideon's eyes closed again. She felt heartsick. "I'm so sorry."

"The doctor don't want you thinkin' about that right now." The girl's voice brightened as she reached out and squeezed Gideon's hand reassuringly. "My name is Echo Burne. I been sent to look after you until you're on your feet again. You be needin' anything, just anything at all, Miss Yardley, and I'll come a-runnin'."

"Thank you, Echo, you're very kind." Although comprehension was a chore, Gideon sensed that she'd just made a new friend.

The girl moved lithely away from the bed to adjust the curtain at the window as Gideon studied her. She was young, maybe fifteen or sixteen, with large, expressive blue eyes and a liberal sprinkling of freckles across the bridge of her nose. The simple cotton dress she was wearing was drab and threadbare, but immaculate.

The throbbing in her head intensified as Gideon struggled to recall the events of the past few days. She could remember nothing. Even her name failed to register with her. Yardley? Somehow it just didn't seem to fit, yet it had a familiar ring to it.

"Echo, you called me Miss Yardley."

"Yes . . . oh . . ." Echo could see that Gideon was having a hard time grasping all that had happened. Moving back to the bed, Echo reached for her hand again. "Now, don't you be worrin' your pretty head about a thing. The doctor says you might be a tad fuzzy about the accident for awhile, but it's nothin' to be concerned about."

Gideon stared back at her expectantly. "That's my name? Yardley?"

"Yes, ma'am, that it is. Fedelia Yardley." Gideon noticed a slight hesitation in the girl's voice, almost as if Echo wanted to stop there, but she went on, "You're the new schoolmarm."

"I am?" Gideon frowned. Somehow *that* didn't sound right either. "Are you certain?"

"Yes, ma'am." Echo occupied herself with straightening the sheets. "The town was sure relieved to learn you were spared."

Gideon found the girl's words disturbing. Though her mind failed to register anything at this point, she still couldn't believe she was a *schoolteacher.* At the moment, she didn't know what two times two equaled, let alone how to teach it to someone else.

Echo went about her work as Gideon tried to come to grips with her unsettling situation.

"What sort of place is Watersweet?" she asked.

"A logging town. Not many of the jacks bring their wives to live here, but we do have some families. Mr. Lannigan sees to it their kids get schoolin'. He says if children are properly educated, they'll more likely get ahead in life."

"Mr. Lannigan?"

"Yes, ma'am. Tom Lannigan. He's foremen of Wakefield Timber."

Gideon sighed hopelessly. So many strange names and faces. "Well, I suppose it will be a few days before I'm able to take over my teaching duties."

"Yes, ma'am. I imagine so."

"Is there someone who could help until I've recuperated?" Gideon didn't want the pupils to suffer just because she was temporarily indisposed.

Echo's eyes steadfastly refused to meet Gideon's this time. "No, ma'am. Berniece, she's head of the school board, you know? Well, she's been teachin' the children lately, and she declares she don't want to do that anymore. She just wants to stay home and take care of her Hubert."

"Oh? Well, maybe something can be worked out," Gideon mused. "I wouldn't want to disappoint the children by having their studies interrupted."

"No, ma'am."

Gideon turned as the door to her bedroom opened. A man stepped inside. Gideon immediately recognized him as the giant who had been standing over her when she'd awakened in the doctor's office the day before.

Echo's face broke into a bright smile as she greeted the newcomer. "Hello, Mr. Lannigan."

"Morning, Echo."

"Miss Yardley's doing real fine," Echo assured him as she moved to pick up the breakfast tray she had set aside earlier. "I was just about to try and persuade her to eat a bite."

Tom Lannigan strode across the room, his boots scraping on the wooden floor.

Gideon watched him approach her bed, her eyes discreetly assessing the tall, blond man. She couldn't help but feel awed by such an impressive specimen of manhood. Large and uncommonly handsome, he carried his splendid steel-girded body with the authority of a man long accustomed to giving orders. When he reached her bedside, he looked down at her, and Gideon felt a shiver race down her spine as their eyes met and held for a moment.

Gazing into Tom Lannigan's heart-stopping blue eyes, Gideon felt sure that he must be the most attractive man she'd ever seen.

"Good morning." His voice was deep and resonant, the way she remembered it from the day before. "Are you feeling better this morning?"

"Yes, thank you." Her voice had a distinctly husky timbre that Tom found oddly disturbing. She was so small that she made a man want to protect her; he would have a hard time denying that. Exquisite was the word that came into his mind as he stared at Gideon Wakefield.

Her mass of coal black hair fanned out and

contrasted starkly against the snow-white pillows, and her warm brown eyes, lined with thick, black lashes that lifted shyly to meet his, caught Tom off guard.

The unsettling simplicity in her gaze brought him a momentary pang of guilt. But he reminded himself that no matter how good-looking this woman was, if she was Gideon Wakefield, she was as uncaring as they come. She didn't deserve his sympathy.

"I trust you're comfortable?" he asked.

"Yes, thank you, everyone has been very kind."

Tom had been awake most of the night. He'd never been deceitful, and he didn't like altering that now. Yet the possible opportunity to give Gideon Wakefield her well-deserved comeuppance was overpowering. If the whole town was convinced that Fedelia Yardley had survived the accident, then as far as Tom was concerned, she had. The children would have a teacher, and Tom would have control of Wakefield Timber for a while longer.

Of course, it was a hell of a thing to do to her fiancé, but Wellington-Kent had looked like a survivor. And Tom assuaged his conscience with the thought that this woman would regain her memory sooner or later. If she was Gideon Wakefield, she'd be reunited with her fiancé then, and his love for her should probably flourish all the more after her return from the jaws of death.

55

Tom couldn't say he was proud of what he was about to do, but he figured he could live with it.

Shoving any lingering reservations aside, he extended his hand to Gideon. "Tom Lannigan's the name. I was in the doctor's office yesterday."

Gideon's hand was completely devoured by his large one. "I remember."

The contact was brief and electrifying. Tom quickly stepped back from the bed. "Is there anything I can do for you?"

"No, I'm comfortable."

"Your memory still hasn't returned?"

"No."

"That's too bad."

Gideon summoned a brave smile. "I'm sure I'll have it back in no time at all."

"If there's anything I can do, tell Echo, and she'll let me know."

Gideon sighed, gazing at the ceiling wistfully. "It all seems so strange. Does anyone have any idea where I lived or where I taught or what my life was like before I agreed to come to Watersweet? Should my family be notified about the accident?" Gideon wasn't wearing a ring, so she assumed that she was unmarried.

"I suggest you talk to Andre Montague," Tom said, stepping around her question. "He might know. I leave most of the paperwork up to him."

Tom knew the answers. According to Fedelia Yardley's application for employment, she had lived in Philadelphia for the past few years, and she hadn't listed a husband or any immediate family.

"Andre Montague?"

"He was the one who pulled you out of the river yesterday."

"Oh, I shall indeed consult with Mr. Montague. First, I must thank him for saving my life. He was very brave."

"Diving into that icy water took some grit," Tom agreed.

"Mr. Lannigan, I was just telling Echo that we'll have to do something about my pupils," Gideon said, abruptly switching the subject.

Tom involuntarily tensed. "What about them?"

"Well, it will be a few days before I'm up and about. I would hate to think that school would be closed on my account."

"I wouldn't worry about it," Tom said, brushing the matter aside. "We'll make do until you're feeling better. You just rest up, and I'll be back in a few days when I can locate some living quarters for you."

"Thank you. That's so thoughtful of you."

The man's strapping good looks made Gideon's pulse race. She found her eyes skimming down the thick column of his neck, across the broadest set of shoulders she'd ever seen on any man, down the lean, tapered waistline,

lingering a moment too long at his belt line
. . . then on to his narrow hips and powerfully built legs.

Of course *he* would be married, she thought
disappointedly. Even though her memory
failed her, she was confident that a man like
Tom Lannigan could not be found on just any
corner. He could be any woman's ideal man.

Turning back to Echo, Tom said quietly. "If
she needs anything, drop by the office. If I'm
not there, Andre will take care of it."

"Yes, Mr. Lannigan."

Tom paused. "Has your husband been be-
having himself?"

Echo's gaze avoided meeting Tom's. "Yes,
sir. He's bein' real good."

"You sure?"

Gideon was surprised to hear the sudden
change in Tom's tone. It was sharper and more
insistent.

"I'm sure," Echo murmured softly.

Turning back to Gideon, Tom nodded
briefly. "I'll be dropping by to see if you need
anything."

A moment later the door closed behind him.

"My," Gideon sighed, "isn't he nice."

"Yes, ma'am. He's real nice," Echo agreed.

"I'm sure his wife has to keep *him* under
lock and key."

"Mr. Lannigan isn't married."

"No?"

58

"No, ma'am, but there's more than a few who'd like to have him."

Gideon winced as she settled her head carefully on the pillow. She could imagine the number of women who would like to have Tom Lannigan. She didn't find the thought all that unappealing herself.

She'd never met a man as good-looking or as overpoweringly male as Tom Lannigan.

Or at least she couldn't remember if she had.

5

"*B*y yimminy, vhere is dat voman!"

Sven Templeton paced back and forth in Tom's office late Saturday afternoon, furious that Gideon Wakefield still hadn't arrived. "Doesn't she know that Sven Templeton is a busy man! I can't spend half my life running to Wakefield Timber to see if she has finally gotten herself here. If dat young voman vants to sell her lumber company, then she darn vell better be gettin' here!" he roared.

Leaving Andre to handle the volatile little Swede, Tom kept his head down as he worked at his desk.

"I don't know where she is, Sven," Andre said evenly. "I agree that Miss Wakefield should have been here by now."

"Vell," Sven jammed his hat back on his head, "if she ever decides to shows up, tell her she has Sven Templeton in a veel pickle, by yimminy!"

Having made himself clear, Sven slammed out of the office in a heated departure.

"I do not blame him for being upset," Andre muttered as he moved back to his desk. "I wonder where Rutherford's granddaughter could be?"

Tom's look was noncommittal as he changed the subject. "Did you order the dynamite?"

Andre picked up a log book, and his gaze scanned the long, narrow columns. "Yes, fifty pounds, Monday."

"That should do it."

"I just do not understand it, Tom." Andre snapped the book closed and returned to the subject of Gideon Wakefield. "What do you suppose is keeping her? You would think that if she intended to sell Wakefield Timber, she would be here by now."

Shrugging, Tom rose and reached for his mackinaw. "I'm in no hurry to see Sven get the property. Are you?"

They both knew that Sven Templeton was an unscrupulous man who lived by the round forty rule: Cut your own forty acres and all the forties around it. Tom had been pushing for legislation to make that dishonest practice illegal, but it was slow in coming.

"I cannot think of anyone who is eager to see Sven get his hands on Wakefield Timber," Andre scratched his head thoughtfully, "but I still find it strange that Rutherford's granddaughter would fail to appear . . ." Andre paused, frowning. "Say, *mon ami,* you do not suppose that it might have been her on that train, instead of Burl Sutter's fiancée?"

Tom headed for the door. "Has Burl's fiancée arrived yet?"

"No." Andre chuckled. "And since they have never found a body, Burl is still a little uneasy, shall we say. I think he's afraid it might *not* have been her. He has finally admitted he was 'skunk drunk' and didn't know what he was doing the night he asked Miss Carlene Levana from East Saginaw to marry him."

Andre noticed that Tom was getting ready to leave. "Going somewhere?"

"I promised Miss Yardley I'd see her to her quarters."

Andre's brows lifted. "Is she well enough to be on her own?"

"Doc Medifer says she is."

Leaning back on his chair, Andre locked his hands behind his head, propped his feet upon his desk, and smiled appreciatively. "Now, there is a beautiful woman—*une vraie belle!*"

"If you say so."

The Frenchman's grin widened. "Ah, you have not noticed, my friend?"

"Can't say as I have." Tom rested his hand on the doorknob. "Don't forget to put a couple of icers on the new south tote road tonight."

"I have already seen to it." Though Andre was officially the ink slinger for Wakefield Timber, meaning he kept the time and production records for the camp, he also doubled as a camp scaler and Tom's right arm.

Even as they spoke, the requested sled was being harnessed to a team. Its square, strongly built wooden tank could hold up to a hundred gallons of water, allowing the teamsters to ice the sleigh road at night, making it easier for the work crews to slide the logs out of the forest the following day.

"I shouldn't be long." Tom adjusted his hat, wishing he didn't have to go out. Though the sun was shining, it was a raw, bitterly cold day.

"I am happy to offer my services and show Miss Yardley to her quarters," Andre offered, still grinning.

"There's no reason I can't."

"Where will you put her?"

"I had a couple of men fix up a small area this morning. It's not much, but it should do."

"Ah, *oui*? And where is that?"

Andre noticed Tom wouldn't meet his eyes now. "Does it matter?"

The question went unanswered as Berniece opened the door to the office and stormed in. "Oh, good. There you are," she said crisply, as she spotted Tom.

Tom shot Andre a trapped look. "Uh . . . Berniece. Sorry, I was just leaving—"

Berniece ignored Tom's attempt at a hasty departure. "I *hope* you're on your way to assist Miss Yardley in getting settled?"

"Yes, Berniece—"

"Good." Berniece briskly removed her gloves. "Then Miss Yardley will be able to assume her teaching duties immediately."

"If the doctor—"

"I've already spoken to the doctor," Berniece interrupted. "He informs me Miss Yardley should be in robust health by Monday morning." Tom eased a step backward as Berniece took two steps forward. "I feel I have done more than my share by consenting to teach this past week, thereby allowing Miss Yardley sufficient time to recuperate."

"Yes, Berniece," Tom repeated patiently.

"Consequently, I shall expect to be officially relieved of my teaching duties Monday morning."

"If Miss Yardley is prepared—"

"Of course, Miss Yardley is prepared! She's a teacher, isn't she?"

Tom shrugged.

"Then it's settled. I assume you have provided comfortable quarters for Miss Yardley?"

"I've done my best." Tom inwardly cringed. That wasn't exactly true. He should have been honest and said that he'd done the best his conscience would allow, under the circumstances.

"Good. Well, I must be running along. I want to make my Hubert a nice supper. Venison stew always brightens Hubey's day."

"Yes, ma'am."

Suddenly, Berniece was inches from Tom's

face again, wagging her finger at him warningly. "*Monday* morning, Tom Lannigan—not a moment later."

Tom drew back protectively. "Yes, Berniece. Monday morning."

Straightening, Berniece allowed herself a polite smile. "Thank you." She began pulling on her gloves as she walked to the door. "I feel sorry for our dear Miss Yardley, you know."

"Oh?" Tom had never known Berniece to feel pity toward anyone.

"After she spends a week in the classroom with those children, I suspect she'll develop a reverence for the barracuda."

Tom raised a brow expectantly. "The barracuda?"

"Yes." Berniece snapped the door open, and her eyes met his directly. "They eat their young."

Gideon pirouetted slowly in front of the mirror, her eyes fixed in horror on the front of her dress. The tiny rows of buttons on the unattractive gray flannel gown were about to pop.

"Mercy me," she murmured, appalled at the disturbing sight. Though the meals Echo had brought her were substantial, Gideon thought she hadn't overeaten.

But apparently everything she had swallowed had gone straight to her bust and hips, because she didn't have a thing that fit her now.

The two needlepoint valises containing her meager wardrobe were setting on the bed as a grim reminder that she had not only lost her memory, but her figure as well.

Her frown deepened as she sucked in, trying to create additional space inside the restricting waistband. After holding her breath for as long as she could, she expelled it in a whoosh, straining the hook to its full capacity.

Her eyes widened with alarm.

"I'm sure going to miss you," Echo confessed as she neatly folded the pile of discarded dresses and placed them back in the valises.

"Why should you miss me, Echo? I'll still be around." Gideon wasn't sure where her new quarters would be, but she was sure Tom Lannigan would see to it that she was comfortable. Sneaking one final glance at the mirror, Gideon edged away, determined to skip supper.

"Oh, I know I'll still be seeing you, but it won't be the same as gettin' to come here every day and take care of you." Echo's voice trailed off shyly.

Over the past few days, Gideon and the young girl had formed a close bond, and Gideon was beginning to believe that Echo had been starved for female friendship.

Echo had mentioned that Waite Burne was fifteen years her senior. From what Gideon had gathered, he was a bit possessive, a man who wanted his young wife to spend her time and energies on pleasing only him. Echo, being a gentle, simple girl, had probably been eager to oblige.

Yet Gideon suspected that the days Echo had spent with her had made the young girl realize how hungry she was for companionship with a woman close to her own age.

Gideon crossed the room, put her arm around Echo, and gave her a reassuring hug. "Don't worry. We'll see each other every day. Why, you're the only friend I have, Echo."

The girl was so slim that Gideon could feel her bony shoulders protruding from her slender body.

Echo smiled back at her shyly. "I surely hope so, ma'am."

"Now, haven't I warned you not to call me ma'am?" Gideon made a playful face at her. "We're friends, and friends call each other by their given names." Gideon sighed, her own given name still sounded a bit odd to her. "Please, call me Fedelia."

A timid, but proud smile was threatening to overcome Echo's usually serious features. "Yes, ma'am . . . Fedelia. I sure will."

"Good." Gideon pointed to the buttons on the front of her dress wryly. "Now, as my friend, dear Echo, promise me you won't bring me a morsel of supper."

Echo laughed out loud this time. "No, ma'am, I won't."

Gideon turned back to the mirror, thinking how the young woman had been a virtual godsend since the accident. Gideon had been confused and weepy at times, terrified at others, but Echo had been her strong and reassuring anchor over the past few days.

When Gideon would awaken in the middle of the night with one of her frequent nightmares, Echo had been there to draw her into her thin arms and assure her over and over again that her memory would return and that everything would be all right.

Luckily, Echo had made Gideon believe her words of encouragement, or Gideon didn't think she would have made it through the long days and nights of confusion.

Echo caught sight of Tom coming up the path and hurried to the window. "Mr. Lannigan's coming up the walk right now."

"Now?" Gideon turned away from the mirror. "He can't be! It's too early!"

Every time the handsome camp foreman had come to see her, Gideon had found herself growing more enamoured of him. Though he rarely spoke directly to her, on the occasions when he did, Gideon's pulse thumped as wildly as a trapped sparrow.

"He can't see me like this!" Glancing around the room, Gideon spied the two half-filled valises. "Quick, Echo, bring me another dress!"

Gideon knew from sorting through the valises that every garment she owned was just as unbecoming and drab as the one she was wearing. She could only hope all of them weren't as tight on her.

Echo rushed to retrieve a dress, and a moment later the gray flannel was hastily discarded in favor of a green muslin.

The new color brought out an unbecoming yellow tinge to her skin, but Gideon had little choice. She pinched her cheeks to add a bit of color before her fingers flew over the tiny buttons as Tom's knock sounded at the door.

Echo glanced to Gideon for permission to answer, and Gideon hurriedly nodded her consent.

Echo was about to open the door when her hand paused on the doorknob, her eyes anxiously surveying Gideon's newest attire. "Ma'am . . ."

"Fedelia," Gideon corrected automatically, "and we mustn't keep Mr. Lannigan waiting, Echo!" Her hands came up to fuss with her hair nervously. "Oh, dear, I do so want to make a good impression on him."

The man always seemed so distant. Gideon longed to have him show her even the tiniest sign that he recognized her as a member of the opposite sex.

"Yes, ma'am." Troubled, Echo obediently opened the door. "Afternoon, Mr. Lannigan."

A gust of cold air followed Tom into the warm room. "Good afternoon, ladies."

"Mr. Lannigan, how nice to see you." Gideon swept across the room, her hand extended graciously. "I'm afraid you've caught us dawdling."

Giving him what she hoped was her prettiest smile, she confessed, "I hope you won't be annoyed, but I'm not quite finished packing yet."

Tom took the hand she offered and bowed from the waist. "I'm in no hurry. Please take all the time you need." His deep, rich timbre sent her pulse flapping like a broken shutter in a high wind.

When he straightened, she was gratified to see that his eyes had suddenly fastened on her bust line.

Deciding this must be the advantage of blossoming nearly overnight, she soothed her wounded vanity with the satisfaction that at last she'd captured his attention.

"My, aren't we fortunate to have such a lovely day to make our move," she purred, allowing just the smallest hint of flirtation to seep into her voice.

Tom's gaze moved from her bosom momentarily, then involuntarily drifted back. "The weather could have been worse," he conceded quietly.

Assured that she now had his undivided attention, her smile became even lovelier. "I hope I'm not keeping you? I know a man like you must have more things to do than see me to my new quarters."

"No, I'm delighted to see you to your new quarters." His tone sounded wooden. He tried to smile, but she noticed it never quite reached his eyes.

"Well, if you'll excuse me, I'll only be a moment." She smiled again, tilting her head prettily.

Tom bowed politely. "I'll wait outside." His gaze momentarily skimmed back across the front of her dress before he reluctantly turned away. A moment later, he opened the door and stepped outside.

Leaning against the closed door, Gideon's eyes drifted shut as a long, wistful sigh escaped her. "Isn't he just about the most handsome man you've ever seen?" she murmured.

Just being in the same room with Tom Lannigan could turn her insides to a quivering mass.

Suddenly feeling as if she were very young again, Gideon clasped her fingers around her forearms and whirled around the room dreamily. Had she always reacted this way to a man? She hoped not. Tom Lannigan was not like any other man she'd ever met; Gideon was sure of it. "Do you think he noticed me, Echo?"

Echo nodded lamely.

"Really noticed me?"

Echo nodded again.

Gideon's feet paused, her face radiant with expectation. "Honestly?" To have a man like Tom Lannigan look at her—really look at her the way a man looks at a woman who's seriously piqued his interest—well, it would make the past few frustrating days all worthwhile, Gideon concluded happily.

Losing her memory had been unfortunate, but she wondered if it was possible that the accident had happened for a divine purpose.

Echo's gaze dropped hesitantly to the front of Gideon's dress. "Ma'am, would you like to change your dress again . . ."

Following the path Echo's eyes had taken, Gideon glanced down.

Her mouth dropped open, and her face flooded with color as she discovered the reason for Tom Lannigan's rapt attention.

Every button on her dress was gaping, revealing the transparent fabric of her chemise through the tiny openings. Groaning with embarrassment, Gideon's hands shot up to cover her crimson face.

"Oh, don't you be worrying, ma'am," Echo soothed faintly. "Mr. Lannigan—he won't say anything about this."

Gideon wasn't worried about what he would *say*. She trusted that Tom Lannigan was a gentleman. She felt sure he wouldn't deliberately point out what an idiot she had just made of herself.

It was what he must be *thinking* that horrified her!

Gideon prayed for a hole in the floor to open up and swallow her alive.

At this instant, Tom Lannigan must be outside rolling on the ground in amusement, she agonized.

And she had to walk out there and face him!

Half an hour later, Gideon reluctantly slipped out the front door. Taking a deep breath, she squared her shoulders and prepared to defend the ridiculous spectacle she'd just made of herself.

Tom was leaning against the trunk of a tree smoking when she came out. When he saw her, he straightened, dropped his cigar, and carefully ground it out with his heel before stepping forward to take the two valises from her hands.

"All ready?"

"Yes." Gideon could feel the blood rushing to her face, but mercifully they managed to avoid each other's gaze.

Moments later, she found herself trailing behind him, trying to keep up with his long-legged strides.

Apparently, there was no need to worry about having to explain the dress to him; the incident seemed to have totally escaped his mind. He seemed intent upon delivering her

74

to her destination with as little socializing as possible.

Gideon gradually became aware of her surroundings as she followed him down the planked sidewalk.

"Echo tells me that not all logging camps are alike," she began. "She mentioned something about haywire camps. What does that mean?"

Tom slowed down to let her walk beside him. "Echo was talking about the fly-by-night operations strung together with haywire. Some are larger and better managed. Watersweet is one of those."

Gideon detected the note of pride in his tone. "She said that this is the main logging town, but that there's a larger town five miles away."

"Shadow Pine," he said.

As they passed a small building, she read the sign aloud, "Mitts, Woolen Socks, Tobacco, and Hinkley's Bone Liniment for Man or Beast."

Tom nodded. "Everything a man needs."

"What about a woman's needs?" she asked without thinking. His gaze swung around to meet hers, and for an instant, the atmosphere felt so charged that Gideon forgot to breathe. Her footsteps faltered and she nearly tripped.

Tom dropped her valises and instinctively reached out to steady her. As he stood facing her with his fingers wrapped around her arms, he resented the intensity in her big brown eyes and the suggestive huskiness in her voice. From her, the casual remark sounded more like an invitation. "That's up to the woman, I suppose," he said curtly.

Gideon swallowed to stem the tide of longing that coursed through her under the heat of his gaze. She had only meant to ask if there was a store that carried women's clothing, but it seemed useless to explain that now. It was obvious he thought she was issuing some sort of insidious invitation.

She broke eye contact first to glance at the windows above the store. They looked like living quarters. "Am I staying here?" she asked.

"No," he answered abruptly, dropping his hands and taking a step away from her.

Has someone told her that this is where I live? He stared back at her, trying to assess whether she was being coy.

Her look revealed nothing.

Reaching for her valises, he reminded himself that he'd have to be cautious where she was concerned. She was either very innocent or very calculating. At any rate, he was determined to keep his distance.

He turned away and started across the street. Gideon followed without a word, mystified by his sudden mood change. She glanced at the buildings that lined the block and the spur line railroad running down the middle. On they walked past the camp office, a huge horse barn, the hay barn, the ice house, the blacksmith shop, the pig house, the chicken house, and the root cellar.

It was bitterly cold, and Gideon drew her cloak close around her. She assumed that the next building they came upon was a cook shack since the air surrounding it was filled with the mouth-watering aroma of apple pies baking in the oven.

Stepping off the sidewalk, Tom led her onto a small path that wound through the woods. The tangy, spicy aroma of pine filled the air as Gideon scrambled to keep up with him. Her shoes, like everything else, didn't seem to fit. They were one size too large and sank deeply into the heavy pine needles littering along the pathway.

Overhead, the trees soared to breathtaking heights, their branches outstretched to touch the blue of the majestic sky. Gideon glanced about in awe, fascinated with the sheer beauty surrounding her. At times, it seemed as if they were walking in circles, and she wondered where he was taking her. She'd hoped her quarters would have been more convenient, but she wouldn't complain.

The towering trees and Tom Lannigan's imposing height made her feel as if she were an insignificant speck dotting the forest floor as they wound through the stands of thick pine.

Her footsteps finally slowed as she tried to locate the steady, chopping sound of an ax.

Finally, she stopped altogether and tilted her chin upward. She shaded her eyes as she squinted into the bright sun up, up, up, up.

Tom slowed, aware that she had stopped to watch one of the highclimbers sitting some two hundred feet up in the top of a tree.

"There's a man up there!" she whispered in a voice filled with childlike wonder.

Shielding his eyes from the late afternoon sun, Tom watched as one of his men, Lane Garrettson, leaned back into his life rope and began an undercut with sure, swift strokes of his lightweight ax. While Gideon and Tom watched, Lane made his way around to the opposite side of the tree, beginning the back cut with his one-man crosscut.

Gideon stood transfixed, afraid to breathe for fear it would unseat the man. Prickles of apprehension crawled up her spine and her heart roared in her chest as she watched the young daredevil, his spurs dug tightly into the tree, go about his work.

The thought of hanging by a rope on the side of a tree that tall made her lightheaded. "How can he do that?" she murmured, moving closer to Tom, feeling safer when she was near him.

Her scent, a warm, spicy fragrance, tantalized him as she moved closer. He suddenly felt an unexplainable urge to draw her into his arms and make her feel protected. He increased his grip on the leather handles of her valises, and glanced away until the urge left him. "Do what?" he demanded, annoyed by his attraction to her.

Gideon peered up at him in disbelief. "Climb a tree that size, and . . . and start cutting it!"

"It's his job," Tom said casually, as the crown of the tree started to lean.

Gideon watched the man set his spurs deeper and wait. The jack suddenly let the saw drop as he shouted "Timberrrrrrr!"

"What's he doing now?" she whispered.

"He's waiting."

"For what?"

"For the damn tree to fall," he snapped.

"Doesn't he know how dangerous that is?"

"He knows. If the crown doesn't sever completely and split the trunk as it topples, his lifeline will pull him into the tree." What Tom omitted was that such an accident usually broke a man's back or killed him instantly.

"And he sits there knowing that?" Gideon didn't want to watch what was happening, but she was powerless to turn away.

Suddenly, the air was filled with an agonizing cracking and splintering as the top of the tree hurtled to the ground, propelling the young shanty boy outward in a violent thirty-degree arc.

Gideon's eyes clamped shut as her hands

flew up to stifle a scream. She was going to be sick. Why hadn't she looked away so she would have been spared the appalling spectacle of a man falling to his death!

Startled by her muffled scream, Tom whirled around to face her. "What's wrong?"

Gideon screamed out loud this time, and her terrified cry ricocheted throughout the pines.

For as far as a mile around, axes suddenly stilled, and men strained to identify the strange high-pitched squeal reverberating through the countryside.

Gideon was afraid to open her eyes. She could visualize the broken, bleeding body of the young man lying at the base of the tree, stone dead!

"Oh, he's dead, isn't he?" she moaned with her eyelids pressed closed.

Tom's brow furrowed as he glanced back up at the shanty boy. "Who's dead?"

Gideon's eyes flew open with amazement. A man had just plunged headlong to his death, and Tom Lannigan hadn't even noticed? "That—that man who was . . ." Her voice trailed off as she looked up to see the jack quickly disconnect his safety gear, climb to the flat top and stand, his arms spread wide with victory while he displayed a cocky grin to the crew working below him.

"Why . . . he didn't fall!" she gasped.

Tom began walking again. "He wasn't in any trouble," he said curtly.

"You mean that happens every time?"

"Every time."

A damn greenhorn, he thought disgustedly as he glanced back at her. She probably *was* Gideon Wakefield, the owner of this entire timber enterprise, a business she didn't know a thing about, a business she didn't care to learn about either, Tom thought.

Once again, anger fueled his strides. Gideon's legs were still threatening to fail her as she tramped along behind him. She couldn't imagine anyone in his right mind enduring such a frightening experience just to cut down a tree!

"How much farther is it?" she asked a few moments later, realizing that her question sounded more like a whine, but her feet were hurting from sloshing around inside a pair of oversized shoes. And she was cold. It must be twenty below zero, she thought miserably.

"Not much farther."

Not much farther, Gideon mimicked silently. His attitude was beginning to annoy her.

Why on earth would *she*, Fedelia Yardley, who apparently had held a perfectly good teaching position in Philadelphia and who purportedly had been of sound mind as recently as one short week ago, have given up a warm, secure, life-style to come to a remote

Michigan lumber camp filled with wild, bawdy, uncivilized men who barely spoke?

She blew her breath out in a frosty plume. She must have lost her mind.

6

They reached Gideon's new quarters just seconds before she was sure she'd drop in her tracks. Tom set the two bags on the ground and waited for her to catch up.

He listened to the heavy rustling in the thicket, aware that Miss High-and-Mighty Wakefield was having a hard time keeping up with him.

Reaching into his pocket for a smoke, he grinned as he relished the thought of how furious she was going to be once her memory returned, and it was discovered that she wasn't Fedelia Yardley after all. He'd wager Gideon Wakefield could pitch one hell of a fit if she wanted to, and Tom had no doubt that she'd want to, once she realized that she'd been tricked.

And how would she find out she was tricked? Tom figured that in due time he would be only too glad to inform her. After telling her what he thought of her plan to sell

83

the land to the unscrupulous Sven Templeton, he planned to walk out on her and leave her high and dry.

Gideon suddenly emerged from the thick undergrowth, muttering under her breath. Her hair was matted with briars, and the wind had stung her face a raspberry red. Tom could see that she'd lost all her former enthusiasm for the adventure. He straightened when she looked at him, replacing his grin with a sober expression. "I hope the walk hasn't been too tiring for you, ma'am."

"I'm fine!" she said curtly.

"You're sure?"

"Positive." Gideon had to force herself to remain pleasant, though she didn't dare attempt to smile. Her face was so cold that she was sure it would shatter into a million pieces if she tried to smile.

This has to be the most godforsaken place I've ever seen, she thought, as she ripped off her gloves and tried to blow warmth and feeling back into the tips of her stinging fingers.

"Well, there's a shorter route," Tom admitted.

"Oh?" *Then why in the blue blazes didn't we take it?* Gideon railed silently.

"I just thought you might enjoy the scenery," Tom explained.

He knew that if they'd taken the normal route, they could have walked around the back of Doc Medifer's house to get to their destination. But that would have been too easy on her. Much too easy, Tom reasoned. He planned to make everything as tough on Gideon Wakefield as possible. "Ever been in a logging camp, ma'am?"

"Never." Personally, Gideon didn't care if she ever saw one again once she managed to escape this one.

Tom smiled. "Is that a fact? Never?"

"Well . . . I can't be sure, but I'm reasonably certain I haven't."

She noticed his expression had become distant again.

"Well, I suppose most people don't know or don't much care where their lumber comes from, just as long as it keeps on coming. They want their bridges, their homes, their barns, their fences and their big, fine carriages. It doesn't matter to them that we're destroying the land to get it for them."

His remark sounded a bit radical to her; yet Tom Lannigan was, she supposed, a man who had strong opinions. Gideon suspected that she should be feeling guilty about the timber, but how one got it was not a burning issue on her mind.

"I guess not," she murmured.

"I imagine that timber would be the last thing you'd worry about." Tom seemed to dismiss the subject as he turned to admire the barracks nearby. "Well, here it is."

Gideon stared at the low, squat building

walled with massive logs and roofed with tar paper. "Here what is?"

"Here's your new home."

My new home, she mouthed silently. She wasn't sure what she had expected, but this wasn't it. Gideon stared at the ugly, windowless structure. She couldn't live where there weren't any windows, for heaven's sakes!

"Sorry I couldn't put you somewhere that would allow a little more privacy, but I guess you can always look at it this way"—his smile returned, and it was almost friendly—"you'll have a lot of close neighbors."

Gideon managed a wan smile, having not the faintest idea what he could be talking about.

Picking up her valises, Tom nudged the door open with his knee and motioned for her to enter first.

With a feeling of mounting trepidation, she obliged.

The room was long and narrow with rough board bunks, three tiers high, set around the walls. Each bunk was filled with straw and covered with a heavy woolen blanket. On every bed a grain sack served as a pillow, and by the thick lumps in them Gideon concluded that people probably stowed their personal belongings inside their pillows.

There was a huge horizontal stove, and above it, a haywire was stretched across the entire length of the room.

"Will I be sharing my quarters?" Gideon murmured as her eyes roamed the room curiously. She suspected the answer. She wouldn't be assigned a room this large just for herself. There had to be many other women living there.

"You will."

Gideon began to walk down the long rows of bunks, her eyes surveying the rough log walls chinked with mud and moss. "Echo told me that there are only a few women in this camp."

"That's right."

Gideon paused before turning around to face Tom. "But this room is huge."

"It has to be to hold a crew the size of mine."

She smiled lamely as his words began to sink in. "Your crew—you mean . . . *men* live here?"

He smiled. "Yes."

"I'm to live here . . . with your *men*?" she repeated, dumbfounded.

Tom shrugged. "Not all of them. Only a hundred and twenty-five. The rest are housed down the road a piece."

Speechless, Gideon began to trail helplessly behind him as he walked the length of the room, passing the long rows of bunks.

"As I said, I'm sorry I couldn't come up with anything better, but I'm afraid housing is in short supply around here."

They reached the end of the room, where

he paused and opened a small door on the right.

Drawing a sharp breath, Gideon viewed the tiny area that was barely big enough to hold a cot, a washstand, and a chamber pot. There was no window, no sunlight, no air. . . . Her hand came up to clutch her throat . . . especially no air.

"It isn't much," Tom conceded as she viewed the tiny cubicle with growing horror.

"Oh . . . well." Gideon tried to control the hysteria bubbling in her throat. *Does he really expect me to live here?*

She wasn't sure she could breathe, or that she'd even want to, in this rat hole! Her eyes harshly surveyed the large, black cat lying on the cot. She wasn't fond of animals. Cats, in particular, made her sneeze.

Tom absently brushed the cat off the bed, then set her valises on top of it. "You won't have to worry about the men bothering you."

Gideon stared numbly at the flour sack that had been provided for a pillow. "Why is that?" she asked lamely. Maybe Tom Lannigan had failed to notice that she was a woman, but surely a logging camp filled with crude, barely civilized men would figure it out soon enough.

"Because I'll tell them not to," he said simply.

And that's supposed to make me feel better? He's going to tell a hundred and twenty-five barbarians who haven't been with a woman in weeks not to bother me!

Gideon slumped weakly on the end of the cot as she reached up to remove her bonnet. *How will I ever live through this?* Her heart filled with despair. Surely, this was all a bad dream. "How far is the school?"

"About a five-minute walk from here." Tom crossed his arms as he leaned against the doorway. "The men are eating now. You might want to get settled before they get back," he suggested. "Later, you can go on over to the cook shack. Moose will see that you get something to eat."

"Oh . . . yes . . . thank you." *Moose! Dear God, am I to sleep with a hundred and twenty-five men and take my meals with a man called Moose?*

"If you need anything, you know where my office is," Tom offered.

Gideon nodded mutely.

Reaching into his breast pocket, he extracted a piece of paper and handed it to her. "Here are the rules. You'd better read them."

Unfolding the paper, Gideon read:

1. Teacher will fill lamps and clean chimneys in schoolhouse each day.
2. Teacher will bring a bucket of water and a scuffle of coal for the day's session.
3. Teacher will make pens carefully and whittle nibs to the individual taste of the pupils.

4. Men teachers may take one evening each week for courting purposes, or two evenings a week if they go to church regularly.

5. After ten hours in school, the teacher may spend the remaining time reading the Bible or other good books.

6. Women teachers who marry or engage in unseemly conduct will be dismissed.

7. Every teacher should lay aside from each pay a goodly sum of his earnings for his benefit during his declining years so that he will not become a burden on society.

8. Any teacher who smokes, uses liquor in any form, frequents pool or public halls, or gets shaved in a barber shop gives us good reason to suspect his worth, intention, integrity, and honesty.

9. The teacher who performs his labor faithfully and without fault for five years will be given an increase of twenty-five cents per week in his pay, providing the school board approves.

Gideon glanced up.

"Any questions?"

She shook her head silently.

"Berniece starts class at seven-thirty sharp. It seems to work out all right, so I suggest you do the same. See that you're there on time. The kids get rowdy if you aren't."

She nodded again.

"Oh, by the way. You have permission to

give thrashings—if you think you're big enough."

Gideon smiled faintly.

He left without further ado, closing the door behind him.

Once he was gone, she keeled over on the cot, stunned.

What had ever possessed her to come to Watersweet?

She suddenly sat up and sneezed violently. She plucked a black cat hair from the blanket and flung it to the floor before lying down again.

How soon does the next train leave? she wondered.

And even if there was a train, where would she go? Her own *name* sounded foreign to her, so how did she think she would know where to go, even if she could manage to escape this nightmare.

Tears rolled from the corners of her eyes. One of the first things she must do is talk to Andre about her relatives.

Surely, I have family. Everyone has family, don't they?

She swiped angrily at the tears that rolled down her cheeks. She hated this terrible, overpowering feeling of loneliness and desperation.

Of course I have family. And this man, Andre, will help me notify them that I've

*changed my mind about teaching and want to
return home.*

Her family would immediately comply with
her request, she thought consolingly, and she
would be out of this hellhole in a matter of
days.

She could stand anything for a few days, she
thought. She sneezed again.

Snuffling, she closed her eyes for a moment.
Everything would be all right. She had to believe that . . . she had to.

An hour later, a gut-wrenching, overpowering stench made Gideon sit straight up in bed
and fumble for a handkerchief to place over
her nose and mouth.

As the loud, raucous sound of men's voices
reached her, Gideon realized that she must
have fallen asleep. With a sinking heart, she
surmised that all one hundred and twenty-five
of her "close neighbors" were home.

Sliding from the cot, she kept the cloth
pressed to her mouth as she fumbled for the
doorknob. She burst out of the small room,
gasping for a breath of fresh air, only to find
none available.

Hearing the commotion, a hundred and
twenty-five pairs of male eyes swiveled in her
direction. Abruptly, the noise in the over-
heated, smoke-filled, steamy room came to a
halt.

Peering over the top of the handkerchief,

Gideon stared wide-eyed at the burly, rough-looking woodsmen who filled the room.

They stared back at her, open-mouthed.

As the silence closed in, Gideon's eyes traveled slowly around the room, trying to locate the source of the revolting odor. It didn't take long. The wire strung above the stove was heavy with wet socks, mitts, and shoepacs.

Not a word was uttered, as Gideon's gaze returned to the men.

They were so *big*. Gideon had never seen such massive and steel-muscled brawn assembled under one roof. She stood gaping, suddenly aware that some had already peeled down to their heavy woolen underwear, while others still wore their plaid wool shirts caked with grime and sweat, baggy woolen pants cut off midcalf, and leather boots that were run down at the heel and severely pigeon-toed.

Feeling slightly sick to her stomach, Gideon realized she had to say something—had to explain why she had violated the sanctity of their private quarters.

Allowing the handkerchief to drop slowly away from her mouth, she flashed the sea of giants a timid smile and said hesitantly, "Hello . . . uh . . . Mr. Lannigan put me here."

"Tom?" returned a hundred and twenty-five deep, baritone voices disbelievingly.

Andre Montague recovered first, rushing forward and hurriedly snapping his suspenders back upon his shoulders as the others clambered nosily to find their pants. "*Mon Dieu!* Miss Yardley! What are you doing here?"

Embarrassed, Gideon quickly averted her eyes as Andre and several of the other men hastily rebuttoned their trousers. "I . . . I believe I live here now."

"*Pardonnez-moi?*"

"I live here." Gideon gestured helplessly toward the small room that was to be her new home. "Really."

"*Tom* told you to live here? With us?"

Gideon nodded.

"Uh . . . men." Andre suddenly remembered his manners, as the others continued to stare. "I would like to introduce Miss Yardley, the new schoolmarm."

There was a polite chorus of "nice to meet ya, ma'am"s.

Art Medford was the first to edge forward, wiping his hand down his pants leg, then shyly extending it to her. "Welcome, ma'am. You'll have to excuse us—it's quite a shock to find a woman in our midst."

"I know. It came as quite a shock to me too," Gideon admitted, attempting a smile as she shook his beefy paw.

The others soon crowded around, offering their callused hands in a gesture of friendship, and a word of welcome.

Gideon took each hand, grateful that the men were willing to accept the unusual situation they all found themselves in.

Andre watched as the last of the introductions were made. He'd known that Tom had been acting strangely lately, but this topped it all. Housing the new schoolmarm with the logging crew? That was downright crazy. "I cannot imagine Tom putting you here with us," Andre exclaimed.

Gideon sighed. "Nor can I, but here I am."

"Well, I suppose if this is where Tom wants you. . . ." Andre's smile was sincere, but Gideon could see he was as puzzled by Tom Lannigan's choice of housing as she. "Have you had your supper, Mademoiselle?"

"No, but I'm not hungry. I'm so exhausted I think I'll just go to bed." Gideon glanced expectantly toward the men. "If that's okay?"

She wasn't sure if there was some procedure she would be expected to follow. She'd never lived with a hundred and twenty-five men. That much she was sure of.

"Yeah, sure. It's okay with us," consented at least a hundred deep male voices.

"Thank you, gentlemen." Gideon turned and walked back to Andre. "Oh, Mr. Montague?"

"*Oui*, mademoiselle." Andre smiled. "But please, *ma chérie*, call me Andre."

Various hoots and catcalls broke out, and Gideon blushed.

"Do not mind them," Andre apologized, shooting the men a look of warning. "They are imbeciles, but they mean no harm."

"Mr. Montague—Andre, Mr. Lannigan thought you might be able to shed some light on my past," Gideon prompted softly.

Andre's forehead knitted in a frown. "Tom said I could?"

"I'd like to talk to you sometime tomorrow, if that would be possible."

"Well, I do not know any more about you than Tom does, but I will be happy to tell you anything I know," Andre offered.

"Thank you. Well," Gideon smiled back at the sea of still bewildered faces, "I think I'll be turning in now."

"Good night, ma'am," the men chorused politely.

"Good night . . . and listen, I don't want to disturb your privacy. You just tell me if I get in your way," she urged. "I'll really try not to."

"Yes, ma'am."

"Now, let's see . . . breakfast is at four-thirty?"

"Yes, ma'am, four-thirty," they all agreed nicely.

Gideon nodded, then turned and closed her door.

"What the bloody bugger!" Jim Carten demanded as he sprang down from his bunk. "Has Lannigan lost his mind?" Fifty others joined him as they crowded around Andre the moment Gideon had closed her door. "*She* can't live here with us!"

"Be quiet!" Andre motioned for the men to lower their voices. "She will hear you!"

"Don't make no difference," Ray Sletzer said. "How are we gonna be expected to live with a woman in our midst! That's a hell of a predicament to put a man in!"

"Yeah, Andre, Lannigan can't expect us to live with a woman!" Alex McKinney blustered. "Why, we won't be able to cuss or even scratch our—well, hell, it just ain't fittin' for a woman to share our quarters!"

The door to Gideon's room opened, and the men fell silent as she poked her head out. "Is something wrong?" Her troubled gaze met a sea of polite smiles.

"No, ma'am." Ed Holman apologized. "We were just shootin' the breeze. Sorry if we disturbed you."

"Oh . . . well, I wasn't in bed yet." Gideon rushed her finger to her nose to block another sneeze. "By the way, do you mind if the cat sleeps out here? I'm afraid he makes me sneeze."

An assortment of I-told-you-so glances were exchanged, then someone spoke up. "No, ma'am. Just pitch him out here."

"Thank you—oh, and the smoke?" Gideon smiled apologetically as she fanned beneath her nose. The thick tobacco smoke was suffocating. "I hate to mention it, but would you mind smoking your pipes and cigars outdoors? I would appreciate it ever so much."

More than a few severely pained looks were exchanged this time.

"I am sure it can be avoided, mademoiselle," Andre promised.

"Thank you—and good night again." Gideon pushed the cat out and shut the door.

"Look at that! She ain't been here fifteen minutes, and we can't smoke in here anymore. You better do something, Montague!" Herb Jenson hissed. "And quick!"

"Shh! Calm down, Herb. I do not know what is going on, but I will get it straightened out with Tom first thing in the morning," Andre promised.

"Talk to him right now!" Shot Harrison demanded. "How are we expected to go to sleep with a looker like that in the next room?" He jerked his head in the direction of Gideon's closed door. "How does Lannigan think we're gonna sleep in the same room with someone like her and not be climbing the walls by mornin'?"

"I know Miss Yardley is very attractive—"

"It wouldn't make any difference if her looks would gag a maggot; she's a woman, and most of us ain't been around a woman in weeks," Alex seethed. "And it might be a hell of a lot longer afore we have the chance. You've got to do something!"

"I know, but we cannot disturb Tom tonight," Andre went on soothingly, as if he hadn't heard Alex's desperate recital. "It's past

98

nine now, and you know how Tom is when anyone disturbs his sleep."

"By bugger, I'll disturb him!" Jim declared. "We're going to settle this thing right now!"

"It can wait till morning." Andre held his ground stubbornly.

But Jim was not of a mind to wait. He turned and stormed out of the bunkhouse amid whispered calls of encouragement.

Ten minutes later, he returned, Tom Lannigan following in his wake.

The men crowded around Tom, all talking at the same time.

"What in the devil do you think you're doin'?"

"Is this your idea of a joke, Lannigan?"

"We can't even smoke inside anymore!"

"And the cat makes her sneeze!" Mort Sewell said incredulously.

Tom raised both hands in an effort to restore calm. "All right. One at a time."

Andre glanced at Gideon's closed door. "Perhaps we had take this outside?" he warned.

Tom turned on his heel, and the crew followed.

"Now, what's this all about?" he demanded once they were outside the bunkhouse. The men hunkered down in their shirt-sleeves against the harsh wind.

"We want to know what's going on here," Art challenged as he stepped forward.

"Concerning what?"

"Concerning that woman you've thrown at us!" Shot fumed.

"I assume you're referring to the new schoolteacher?"

"Yeah!" the jacks chorused heatedly. "We bloody well are!"

Tom met their angry glares calmly. "What about her?"

"What's the big idea of putting her in our bunkhouse?" Ray demanded.

"Because I have nowhere else to put her."

Andre glanced at his boss warily. "Perhaps you could arrange for her to live with Berniece, or Alice Waterman?"

"I thought about that, but it's impossible. Berniece lives with her husband in one room. Alice has her husband and three children in one room. I could hardly ask them to sacrifice what little privacy they have to take in the new schoolteacher."

"Then why don't you put her up with you!" Ray grumbled.

Tom returned Ray's scowl evenly. "She stays where she is."

A renewed chorus of complaints erupted as the men tried to digest the bad news that they were going to be stuck with Fedelia Yardley.

"There has to be somewhere else she can stay besides here," Jim reasoned.

"Well, you tell me where it is, Jim, and I'll arrange it."

But neither Jim nor anyone else seemed able to come up with an alternative. It seemed they were stuck with the woman.

Tom faced his crew again. "Any suggestions?"

The men murmured among themselves, but no one came up with a solution.

In a tone of authority that the men knew to respect, Tom said quietly, "Then I don't want to hear any more about it. The woman stays where she is. You are to treat her with respect, and keep your fly buttoned and your brain functioning above your belt buckle. If I hear of anyone stepping out of line, he'll answer to me. If anyone thinks he can't abide by that, then I want him to pack his gear and see me in my office first thing tomorrow morning."

The men quieted. No one was willing to lose his job over the dispute, no matter how annoying the arrangement.

"Any questions?"

There were disheartened grumbles, but no questions.

"By the way, while I have you all together, there is one other thing I might mention."

The men focused their attention on Tom.

"I understand some of you are having a hard time remembering the names of the neighboring crews." Tom's gaze pinpointed one or two in the crowd directly. His crew was cutting close to Shadow Pine's timberline, and rumor had it that trouble was brewing.

"Seems some of you have been referring to our good friends to the north as the 'Shadow Pine shits.' "

A few in the crowd glanced down sheepishly.

"Someone been complainin'?" Ed Holman challenged.

"The 'Shadow Pine shits' have, and I want you to knock it off before a brawl breaks out. You know the rules. If you're looking for trouble, you look for it on your own time. Do I make myself clear?"

"Yessir." The men's enthusiastic compliance shot frosty plumes in the cold night air.

"Good." Tom glanced at Andre, who'd said little during the exchange. "It's getting late. I think we'd better all turn in. Four-thirty rolls around early."

The crowd began to break up, and Andre fell into stride with Tom. "Are you insane, my friend?" Andre whispered.

"She stays where she is."

"*D'accord,* but I fear it will not work."

"It's up to you to see that it does."

"Having Miss Yardley in the bunkhouse is going to make it difficult for the men, Tom."

"I know it will be hard on them." Tom glanced at Andre and grinned. "In more ways than one."

"You enjoy this, no?" Andre accused.

"Why would I enjoy it?"

102

"I do not know." Andre's eyes narrowed. "That is what I am trying to figure out."

"Well, don't wear yourself out trying. The men can handle the situation, and unless I miss my guess, they'll only have to endure Miss Yardley's presence for a short time before she's on her way back to Philadelphia."

Andre's footsteps slowed as they approached the bunkhouse. "What makes you think so?"

Tom shrugged. "Call it a hunch."

Andre failed to follow Tom's logic of late. The boss was acting downright peculiar. "Do you know something I don't?" Andre asked.

"Only that I'm going to bed." Tom nodded curtly. "I suggest you do the same."

7

*G*ideon sat straight up in her cot. Someone was blowing a horn. The long, doleful wail filled the darkness, shattering the silence of the cold Michigan night. Groaning out loud, she threw her arms over her ears, wondering what moron was making so much noise in the middle of the night.

The hours had dragged by endlessly. She had tossed and turned on her cot for hours, listening to one hundred and twenty-five men snoring in various keys, discords, and harmonies. The constant whistling, wheezing, snorting concerto had left her ready to scream. Sometime after midnight she had gotten out of bed and rummaged through her valise for something to stuff under the crack of the door. But her effort had been in vain. The symphony had gone on and on and on.

And now someone was blowing a horn, for heaven's sake!

Slipping out of bed, Gideon cracked the

door to peek out. The men were just getting up. Some were pulling on their pants, while others still sat on the sides of the bunks, scratching the heavy stubble on their faces and yawning in a sleepy stupor.

Art Medford noticed Gideon's door ajar and cleared his throat to alert the other men. Andre glanced up and grinned when he saw her pair of curious eyes peering out expectantly.

Pulling his suspenders over his shoulders, he walked toward the door, smiling. *"Bonjour,* mademoiselle! Good morning!"

Easing the door open a fraction farther, Gideon asked grumpily, "What's all that racket?"

" 'Racket'?" Andre's face went blank for a moment. "Ah! You mean the chuck horn, *non*?"

Gideon tried to stifle an exhausted yawn. "The what horn?"

"The chuck horn! The cookee is blowing his tin Gabriel. It is time to get up and eat."

"Oh, dear Lord." Gideon slumped against the door frame wearily. It sounded more like Gabriel was trying to blow down the walls. "Is it morning?"

"Oui, ma chérie. I hope you slept well?"

Gideon turned a jaundiced eye on him. "Like a log."

"Then you must be hungry." Andre leaned closer to the doorway and winked. "I have yet to meet a woman who can dress in ten min-

106

utes, but you will try? Lannigan likes his crew to be on time."

"Oh . . . well, we wouldn't want to disappoint Lannigan, would we?" Gideon yawned again as she reached for the water pitcher on the stand beside her cot. "If you would be so kind as to bring me some fresh water?"

"Fresh water?" The smile on Andre's face faded momentarily.

"Yes . . . water," seeing that her request had taken him by surprise, she added, "so that I may wash."

"Wash?" His grin returned. "Now?"

"Of course . . . is there something wrong?"

"But it is Sunday. We do not wash on Sundays," he said.

"We don't?" Gideon glanced at the other men, who were all shaking their heads: they *never* washed on Sundays. "Well," Gideon was almost afraid to ask the next question, "just exactly when do *we* wash?"

"On Saturdays."

Gideon's eyes narrowed. "Only on Saturdays?"

"Every Saturday, *comme une horloge*," Andre bragged. "Lannigan likes his crew to be clean!"

Gideon reached for the water pitcher and handed it to him. "Then Lannigan is going to love me. I shall be washing every morning.

Would you please see that I have a pitcher of fresh water outside my door."

"Every morning!" Andre was clearly alarmed by such excessive bathing.

"If you don't hurry I shall never make it to breakfast on time." Gideon started to close her door, then suddenly turned back. "And tell that man to *stop* blowing that infernal horn!"

The door closed and Andre turned to meet a sea of amused eyes.

"Yeah, Andre. Tell that terrible ole man to stop blowing that horn!" Alex McKinney mocked in a high, feminine pitch.

The others broke into guffaws as Andre marched toward the front door.

"Don't laugh," he warned. "We are going to take turns getting Miss Yardley's water."

But the men were still snickering when he opened the door and marched bravely out into the subzero cold to get the requested water.

Gideon lit a candle and was brushing out her hair when he returned. Handing her the pitcher, he apologized for the chunks of ice floating on top.

Eyeing the water glumly, Gideon murmured a polite, "Thank you."

As she splashed herself with the freezing water, she could hear the men moving around in the other room. Trying to keep her teeth from chattering, she hurriedly slipped into her chemise and pulled the brown woolen dress over her head. She sat on the side of the cot and buckled her shoes, then quickly grabbed a handful of her hair and pinned it on top of her head. She heard the men beginning to file out of the building as she reached for her cloak and bonnet.

Andre was waiting for her when she emerged from her room a moment later, still tying the strings of her bonnet.

Extending his arm cordially, he smiled appreciatively. "You look lovely, *ma chérie.*"

"You're *much* too kind," Gideon grumbled softly as she took his arm. She knew that she probably looked like she'd dressed in a buffalo stampede.

It was snowing as they stepped outside. Large puffy flakes clung like white cotton to the bushes and tree limbs. Since it was still dark, Andre carried a coal oil lantern to light their path.

The air was so cold it stung Gideon's lungs. She snuggled deeper into her cloak as she recalled the long walk the day before. She couldn't imagine why the men who built this logging camp would have placed the bunkhouse so far from the cook shack.

Rounding the corner of the bunkhouse, Gideon saw Doc Medifer coming out of his house. The doctor glanced up to the sky, then turned his collar up as he started for the cook shack.

Gideon's footsteps slowed as she looked at

Andre in disbelief. "That was Doctor Medifer, wasn't it?"

Andre looked down at her and smiled. *"Oui."*

"His house is this close to the bunkhouse?"

"Only a few hundred feet. . . . Why?"

Eyes narrowing, she started walking again. What kind of games was Tom Lannigan playing with her? she wondered. He'd marched her around in the cold for two miles yesterday, and now she learned that Doc Medifer's house wasn't more than spitting distance from the bunkhouse!

The men were swarming through the doors of the cook shack. Gideon clutched Andre's arm tighter as she felt herself being jostled back and forth by men of all descriptions and nationalities. There were short men, fat men, tall men, handsome men, less-than-handsome men, grizzled veterans, men who smiled at her, and others who didn't.

Andre steadied her arm as Gideon stumbled into a large room with row upon row of tables covered with oilcloths.

Two big cookstoves had roaring fires going in them, and three burly-looking cooks were busy frying large skillets of potatoes.

Gideon's pulse quickened as she saw Tom enter the room with two other men. Glancing briefly in her direction, he barely nodded his recognition as he walked to the head of the nearest table and sat down.

110

Gideon was nearly knocked off her feet again as four energetic, hungry young men scrambled frantically for a seat.

Andre motioned for her to be seated, and she quickly positioned herself on one of the long benches.

She watched wide-eyed as one of the cooks stirred pancake batter in a fifty-pound lard can. Clouds of smoke billowed from the grill through an open flue in the roof.

Gideon had never seen so much food. Platters upon platters were piled high with potatoes, pancakes, sausages, and bowls of stewed prunes. There were pies and cakes and cookies and donuts, enough to feed a small army. Two wizened chore boys were moving up and down the rows of tables, pouring cups of green tea and coffee.

The clatter of dishes being passed back and forth filled the room as the men heaped monstrous portions upon their plates.

"Would you like some morning glories?" Andre said, offering her a platter of pancakes.

"No . . . thank you." Gideon passed the platter on, realizing that she had no appetite. She watched with horror as the men poured pitchers of bacon grease and heavy maple syrup over their stacks of hot cakes.

Suddenly, the room grew as quiet as a church.

Gideon glanced up expectantly, wondering what was wrong. Except for the creaking of a bench, or an occasional cough, or the clatter of steel utensils against tin plates, she could have heard a pin drop. The men were shoveling food into their mouths without conversation.

Leaning cautiously toward Andre, she kept a close eye on the men at her table, who went about eating as if they were being paid to do so. "What's wrong?"

"Wrong?" She noticed that even Andre was whispering now.

Tom gave her a stringent look from his place at the head of the table.

Deliberately ignoring him, Gideon leaned closer to Andre. "Why is everyone so quiet all of a sudden?"

"Talking is not allowed during meals," Andre murmured.

No one allowed to talk? That seemed strange to Gideon. The men had been chattering like magpies minutes before.

"For heaven's sake, why aren't they allowed to talk?" she blurted in a voice that ricocheted like a stray bullet throughout the silent room.

At least a hundred heads shot up, and the cook standing at the grill shot her a condescending look as she sheepishly fumbled for her fork to scoop up a small bite of potatoes.

She nibbled quietly for a moment, trying to think of a reason for such a silly rule.

Tom glanced down the long row of plates. It surprised him to see Andre sitting beside Gideon this morning. Ordinarily, the bookkeeper took his place of state at the head of the table just as the foreman and scaler did. Tom's features tightened as he watched Andre lean over to silently encourage Gideon to take another serving of potatoes.

She shook her head, but moments later Tom saw her lean over to whisper to Andre.

Andre should know better than to let her talk, Tom fumed. And he sure as hell shouldn't be sitting with her either. Tom forked another bite of hot cakes into his mouth. His irritation grew as he watched Andre place a second donut on Gideon's plate and lean over to laugh at something she'd whispered to him.

What in the hell did they have to talk about? Tom wondered.

"I think this is silly. Why can't we talk?" Gideon was asking.

"The cooks feel that it interferes with getting the men fed," Andre whispered back.

Gideon suddenly felt someone give her a swift kick beneath the table, and her eyes widened with disbelief.

"Someone kicked me!" she accused loudly.

"No talking at the table, schoolteacher!" Tom roared from the head of the table.

Gideon felt her face turn a thousand shades of red. She reached blindly for a donut and brought it up to her mouth obediently.

Why, the nerve of that man! Calling me down in front of all these men!

Andre took pity on her and chanced a brief

113

comment, "It is his job to see that the rules are obeyed." Quickly, he returned his attention to his breakfast.

Gideon sat through the remainder of the meal in stony silence. But she was learning the basics. Salt was called "gravel," ketchup was "red lead," pepper was "Mexican powder," pancakes were "morning glories," and sugar was called "sand." It wasn't much, but she figured if she ever got her appetite back, it would help.

She pointedly ignored Tom Lannigan as they left the cook shack twenty minutes later. Giving him her snootiest look, she hoped he got the message that she didn't appreciate the way he'd yelled at her like an unruly child. *"No talking at the table, schoolteacher!"* His humiliating treatment still rang in her head.

If he did understand her silent message, Tom gave no indication that it bothered him. He brushed past her without a word, as they left the building.

The snow was falling harder as Gideon took Andre's arm on their way toward the bunkhouse. "What is *wrong* with that man?" she asked petulantly.

"Lannigan?" Andre laughed. "He has a lot on his mind lately. The company is about to be sold, and he does not care for the new buyer."

"Is he concerned about his job?"

Andre threw his head back and hooted merrily. "Lannigan worried about a job? *Non, non,*

non! There are many other outfits that would wish to have him running their operations."

"Then what's upsetting him?"

"Tom would like to see Gideon Wakefield keep her grandfather's business and replant the trees we harvest. He has been concerned for years that the pines will run out and that there will be nothing left in these forests."

"Gideon Wakefield?" she repeated. Why did that name have a familiar ring to it?

"*Oui.* She is Rutherford Wakefield's grand-daughter. Rutherford died a few months ago and left his business to her. Tom has written many letters to Mademoiselle Wakefield, urging her to keep the business—at least, until he can get a program of replanting under-way."

"Sounds reasonable to me. Why won't she go along with it?"

"Who knows?" Andre shrugged. "All I know is she plans to sell Wakefield Timber to Sven Templeton."

"Would that be bad?"

Andre nodded. "Templeton is not a good man. He cares nothing for the land or the future. Mademoiselle Wakefield is due to arrive any day now, and Tom is quite unhappy."

Gideon turned to peer over her shoulder at Tom, who had paused to speak to one of his men. "I get the feeling he rather dislikes me."

"No, *ma chérie.*" Andre smiled down at her warmly. "Tom Lannigan may be hard to get to know, but once you know him, there isn't anything he wouldn't do for you."

Gideon found that hard to believe.

"Is there a particular woman in Mr. Lannigan's life?" she asked, deliberately keeping her voice casual.

"I don't think so."

That was hard for Gideon to believe. A man with his extraordinary good looks should have women flocking around him.

"Oh, there are many pretty girls who run after him, but besides Marcy Wetlock, I don't know of anyone Tom . . ." As if he suddenly realized that he was revealing more than he should, Andre clammed up.

"Marcy Wetlock?" Gideon probed innocently.

"*Ah, oui* . . . she is just a woman who lives in Shadow Pine. Say, the sky pilot will be here this morning. Perhaps you would like to attend his service, *non*?"

Gideon turned to peer over her shoulder again at Lannigan. Marcy Wetlock, huh?

Changing the subject, she asked what had been uppermost on her mind all morning. "Mr. Lannigan said you might be able to enlighten me about my background."

"You mentioned that last night, but I am afraid I don't know any more about you than Tom does," Andre admitted.

Disappointment flooded Gideon's face. "Nothing?"

116

"Your application says you lived in Philadelphia, that you're single, and that you have no close family. You're welcome to have a look at it," he offered. "Why don't you stop by after school tomorrow afternoon, and we will look it over together. Perhaps something will help prompt your memory."

"Thank you, I will do that . . ." Gideon hoped the application might contain a useful clue.

The "sky pilot," she discovered, was a traveling preacher. He arrived by sled around nine that morning and services began at nine-thirty. Not everyone came to hear the inspiring message read from the book of Acts, but those who did attend made the service a warm and enthusiastic one.

Gideon noticed that Tom Lannigan stepped into the back of the room just after the service started and remained until he was called away.

Lunch was another ordeal. The cookee stepped outside the cook shack about eleven-thirty and began blowing various trills and arpeggios on his tin horn. Immediately, the men stopped what they were doing and came running.

The tables were piled high this time with bowls of beef stew, slices of hot bread, bowls of rutabagas, the inevitable prunes, and more cakes, pies, and cookies. Gideon was sure she'd grow as large as the camp's prize horses if she ate half the portions that were offered.

The man sitting next to her informed her before the meal started that during the week the noon meal, called flaggins, was brought to the woods on a sleigh. But Sunday was their day of rest, so the men ate their meal in the cook shack.

With the storm of another meal over and the wreckage cleared away, the men returned to the bunkhouse to write letters to their wives and sweethearts, to sharpen their tools, or to mend their socks.

Gideon discovered that Sunday was also boil-up day. She watched with open mouth as the men dragged their clothes and blankets outside and dumped them into large vats of hot water in an effort to delouse their personal belongings.

Good-naturedly referring to themselves as crumb-chasers, the men went about picking lice and bedbugs out of their clothing.

The battle against the vermin was vigorously waged with tubs of boiling hot water mixed with laundry soap and Peerless tobacco. Soon Gideon found herself right in the middle of the melee, helping the crew scrub their sheets and blankets. At the end of the day, her hands were worn raw, but she felt a sense of accomplishment.

The men had been courteous and pleasant to her, and that evening a man they called deacon brought out his fiddle and sang funny little songs like "Six Whistles," "My Willie Oh!," "Tall Tales of Taylor," and Gideon's personal favorite, "Sixteen Men in a Pine-Slab Bunk." Everyone joined in on a chorus of

> "Beans are on the table,
> Daylight's in the swamp,
> Hey, you lazy shanty boys,
> Ain't you ever gettin' up?"

Then the deacon struck a chord for a hoedown, and Andre pulled Gideon into the circle of men who grabbed other men for partners. They stomped the pine boards of the bunkhouse until Gideon was sure the floor would cave in.

But she had a marvelous time!

Later that night, as she crawled wearily into her bed, she began to itch, imagining a great granddaddy of a bedbug cavorting around in her sheets.

An almost hysterical giggle escaped her as she squirmed and scratched aggressively. Sleeping with vermin! She was *quite* sure that she'd never had to worry about such things before.

Snuggling down between her clean sheets, she tried to clear her mind. She plopped her pillow over her face to drown out the noise in the next room, but tonight the men weren't bothering her as much. She knew some of the snorers personally now, and somehow that made their snoring easier to tolerate. Gideon was grateful for the new friends she'd made that day.

For some crazy reason, she wished Tom Lannigan had been one of them.

8

"Good morning, children. First of all, I'd like to say how very much I'm looking forward to having us learn together this year." Gideon walked to stand in front of her chair behind her desk, as she studied her class.

The children appeared to be pleasant enough. Scooter Wilson had placed a shiny red apple on her desk as he'd walked in this morning, and Tirza Reynolds had informed her that her mother had sent along a popcorn ball for the new teacher to enjoy after lunch.

Other than the fact that she didn't have the vaguest idea of what she was doing, Gideon was feeling slightly more confident today.

"Tirza Reynolds?"

A small, blond girl in the second row threw her hand into the air.

"What a lovely name, Tirza," Gideon complimented.

"Thank you, ma'am. It's Hebrew; it means cypress tree."

"How lovely. Class, I think it would be nice if each of you would stand to introduce yourself and tell me your age." Gideon smiled at her small flock encouragingly. There were nine in all, five boys and four girls.

A few grumbles broke out, but one by one the children got to their feet.

"My name's Modeen Menson, and my father owns the camp store." Modeen's tongue snaked out at one of the older boys before she sat back down.

"Uh . . . the name's Toby Miller. I'm eight years old."

"Pud Wilkerson. Fifteen."

"My name is Violet Ann Jump. I am eight years old, and my daddy says I'm the prettiest girl in camp." She tittered nervously before flopping back down on her seat.

"King Davis. Sixteen. And Violet Ann's old man is full of crap. Violet Ann's so ugly her pa has to tie a pork chop around her neck to get the dogs to play with her."

Gideon's eyes widened as Violet gave an indignant gasp.

A boy in the third row sprang to his feet. "Quinn Morrison, ma'am. I'll be eleven, Saturday. My pa's giving me a gun so's I can blow the heads off them sons-a-bitchin' jackrabbits."

Gideon quietly made a note in her journal: Work on children's language. Glancing up, she said, "Go on."

A shy, blue-eyed child moved out of her seat hesitantly. "My . . . my . . . name's . . . Ju-Ju-Juice Tett-tett . . . er . . . son. I'm sev-seven . . . ye-years ol-old, and . . . I-I . . . sta-stam-stammer a lit . . . a lit . . . a little bit," she confided.

The younger children burst into giggles, and Gideon quieted them with a sharp look. "Juice—that's a lovely name, too."

"Thank . . . thank . . . you. My moth-mother named m-me . . . af-after an or-or-ange." Juice grinned proudly, revealing the wide gap of her missing two front teeth.

"Tirza Reynolds, and I'm named after—"

"We know. A cypress tree," Pud Wilkerson finished in a bored tone.

"Scooter Wilson, ma'am. I'm nine years old. And no one fools with me," he gave the other boys a pointed look, "or they get the snot knocked clean outta 'em." He resumed his seat.

"Well," Gideon smiled back at the children lamely. Lord. "My name is Miss Yardley, and I think it's time we got down to work." Reaching for the spelling book, Gideon said a silent prayer that she could bluff her way through the first day. She realized she would have to study long into the night to prepare her lessons for the following day because she felt certain that she'd forgotten everything she'd ever known—about everything. "Can anyone tell me what page we're on?" she asked.

Feeling blindly for her chair, Gideon seated herself.

"Page fifteen!"

"Huh-uh. Page twenty!"

"Fifteen!"

"Liar, liar, pants on fire!"

"Shut up, pig face, we've already done fifteen. I think we're on page thirty-two. Ain't that right, Pud?"

Chaos broke out when Gideon's feet flew up into the air as the chair she was sitting in suddenly shattered into pieces, noisily sending her to the floor.

Stunned, she lay flat on her back, trying to focus her eyes on the ceiling. She could hear the children snickering, and her temper flared.

Someone had taken the screws out of the chair! Gideon could see them lying haphazardly about on the floor.

Gathering her fortitude, Gideon slowly pulled herself above the edge of her desk and leveled a stony look at the little hooligans. They'd see who laughed last.

"We will begin on page one."

That afternoon Andre strode into Tom's office and pitched a telegram onto his desk. "Take a look at that."

Picking up the scrap of yellow paper, Tom's eyes scanned the message. The wire was from

Talbot Wellington-Kent, inquiring about the whereabouts of his fiancée, Gideon Wakefield.

"What do you make of it?"

Tom handed the wire back to Andre. "Sounds like Mr. Wellington-Kent can't keep track of his fiancée."

"Come now, Tom! It says clearly that Gideon Wakefield left Philadelphia on a train headed for Watersweet on the first of this month. That could only mean one thing."

Tom calmly got up to pour himself a fresh cup of coffee. "Gideon Wakefield was the mystery woman on the train?" he prompted.

"Who else?" Andre's face grew troubled as he walked to his desk to pick up his cup. "It would certainly explain why she hasn't shown up to close the deal with Sven. *Mon Dieu*, if that's true, someone will have to inform Wellington-Kent that his fiancée was killed in that train derailment."

Tom moved back to his desk. "I think we'd better hold off on that for a while."

"Why?" Andre asked.

"Because we could be mistaken. We don't know that the dead woman was Gideon Wakefield, not for sure anyway. And we haven't found a body to identify. It seems cruel to inform a man that his fiancée is dead when we have no proof."

"Ah, yes, I suppose you're right," Andre murmured.

"Just hold off Sven for a while and send a

wire off this afternoon to Wellington-Kent telling him that we aren't certain where his fiancée is."

"Bon, d'accord." Andre whistled sympathetically under his breath as he stirred his coffee. "This will be very bad news to the man. His fiancée is missing, and we can't help him."

Tom quickly shoved aside a brief pang of guilt. "Just tell him what we know for sure. The train derailed."

"Do you suppose we ought to tell him about the woman that got swept downstream? She had to be Mademoiselle Wakefield."

Tom sat down behind his desk and lowered his gaze to the journal sheet. "Burl Sutter's woman still hasn't shown up yet. Who knows? Maybe Miss Wakefield decided she didn't want to get married, and she just skipped out on Wellington-Kent. It's happened before. She could be anywhere in the United States right now for all we know. Or," Tom snapped the journal closed, "she could have been on that train."

Andre shook his head. "I believe she was on the train."

"Well, that's your guess, but I don't think we should be sending out news we can't substantiate." Tom stood up and reached for his coat. "There's trouble at the rollway. I'll be up there the rest of the day."

Andre waved him off absently. "I wonder what will happen now? With Rutherford's only heir missing, the business could be tied up in the courts for years."

"I suppose it could." Tom pulled his gloves on. "They're having a problem at the skidway too. Can you handle it for me?"

"Oui, oui."

Gideon was just putting her cloak on late that afternoon when she looked up to find Echo standing in the doorway. Overjoyed to see a friendly face, Gideon beckoned her inside. "Hi!"

Smiling shyly, Echo walked to the front of the schoolroom. "I was on my way home, and I thought we might walk together."

Gideon sighed. "You don't know how glad I am to see you."

The two women embraced warmly. Gideon draped her arm around Echo as they walked down the row of desks. "You can't imagine the day I've had!"

"Was it bad?"

Echo waited while Gideon banked the fire and wrapped a heavy wool scarf around her head. "Half the children in class should be in jail," she confided.

Echo flashed an amused grin. "It's been a real chore to keep a teacher," she confessed.

The two stepped outside, and Gideon drew her cloak around herself protectively as she surveyed the leaden sky. "It looks like snow again."

"It always snows up here." Echo made the remark disparagingly as if the long winter bothered her.

"Don't you like snow?" Gideon asked as they began walking.

"No, I look forward to spring," she confessed. "I love to see the tiny flowers sprouting up through the tender shoots of green grass, and I love to listen to the birds singing so sweetly in the mornings."

Gideon became concerned that Echo's coat was not warm enough. She could hear the young girl's teeth chattering as the strong wind buffeted her frail body through the threadbare material. Gideon's cloak was thick and warm, and she felt guilty being so toasty warm when Echo was so cold.

"Where have you been this afternoon, Echo?"

"To Menson's store."

"On such a bad day?"

Echo smiled. "I needed to get out. Sometimes I get so lonely."

"Echo, I have a coat I've outgrown." Of course, I've outgrown everything else in the two valises, Gideon thought wistfully, but Echo seemed in most need of the coat. "The color would look lovely on you. Since I can no longer wear it, would you like to have it?"

Echo's head dipped shyly. "That's very kind of you, ma'am, but I don't think I should . . .

128

I appreciate you offering though," she was quick to add.

Gideon was surprised by her quick refusal, but she recognized pride when she saw it, and she knew that the coat Echo was wearing could not adequately protect her from the long Michigan winters. "You really are welcome to have it, Echo. I'd like to have some new clothes, but I can't very well justify them, if I keep the ones I have. You'd be doing me a favor if you'd accept the coat."

"I surely do thank you for offering," Echo said hesitantly. "I'm sure your coat's very pretty, I—"

"Your husband wouldn't mind, would he?" Gideon wondered if that could be the cause for the girl's hesitancy.

Echo shrugged. "Waite is gone a lot. I don't think he'd care."

"Good. Then it's settled."

Echo chuckled softly. "You surely are a stubborn woman, Miss Yardley."

"That I am. You'll help me out then. You'll take the coat?"

Echo nodded. "You aren't an easy person to refuse. And I thank you."

"I thank you." Gideon giggled as she squeezed her friend's elbow. "You haven't seen it yet."

The two friends began to talk about other things as they made their way carefully along the icy roads. They were forced to step aside several times as horses pulling sleighs laden with monstrous logs edged by them.

Occasionally, one of Gideon's bunkhouse "neighbors" would call a friendly greeting, and Gideon would smile and wave. From the deep woods, they could hear the familiar sounds of crosscuts, the splintering of trees as they began to fall, and the faint cries of "Timberrrr" as the giant widow makers came crashing to the ground.

When the two women arrived at Gideon's quarters, their footsteps rang across the boards of the huge empty building. "Don't you get scared staying here with all those men?"

"At first, I was scared to death, but not anymore." Gideon slipped the plain coat over Echo's shoulders. "I just wish I had a place with windows and light and. . . . Oh well, it's useless to wish for such things. No one has a place to himself in this camp."

"Mr. Lannigan does," Echo replied, running her hands over the thick gray wool with awe.

"He does?" Gideon's brows lifted. "Where?"

"Over Menson's store," Echo answered as she hunched her shoulders under the unaccustomed weight of the coat.

"How many rooms does he have?" Gideon asked, glancing around what she thought of as her cell.

"I don't know. Probably a couple, I guess."

Echo turned in a slow pirouette. "Thanks." She grinned. "I like the coat."

"Then you must keep it." Gideon smiled warmly.

"Well, I'd best be getting home. Gotta start Waite's supper." Echo's eyes grew sad. It was obvious to Gideon that the girl was reluctant to leave her new friend.

"I'll walk part of the way with you."

Echo's eyes lit up. "I'd like that."

The two women said their good-byes at the fork in the road, and Gideon continued on until the road forked a second time. It was getting late. Darkness would be falling soon. Pines many generations old soared straight and tall overhead as she walked along the road.

Up ahead, a giant bluff came into view, and she could see great piles of logs stacked horizontally upon each other. She began to wonder if she might be lost. Andre had said that when she reached the fork, she should take the road on the right, for it would lead her straight to the bunkhouse . . . or had he said to take the one to the left?

Gideon was confused, but she knew that she was in no immediate danger, since she could see a crew of jacks working on the pile of logs.

Wrapping her scarf more tightly under her chin, she walked to the top of the bluff. Up there, the wind sent a bone-rattling chill through her. Leaning over a wooden railing, she peered cautiously down the steep incline some five hundred feet below. The men working above her were systematically feeding the logs into a wooden flume to land below on the banks of Lake Huron.

She could see several men, positioned to the side of the wooden shoot, throwing shovels of sand on hot spots to prevent fire breaking out from the friction created by the logs zooming down the flume, one right after another. She watched for a long time until she heard a familiar voice saying, "You're going to freeze your butt off up here."

She turned to find Tom Lannigan standing behind her, cupping his hands as he lit a smoke.

A different sort of chill raced up her spine as she turned to face him. He towered over her petite frame and took her breath away, just like the trees he harvested did.

"What are they doing with the logs?" she asked, turning back to watch another one sail down the flume.

Taking a long draw, Tom stepped closer, to stand beside her at the railing. The fabric of his coat sleeve brushed hers, and she found the unexpected contact made her heart beat faster.

"This is the rollway or the banking ground. The logs will stay here until spring breakout. Those men on top of the piles handling the cant hooks are top loaders."

Gideon was fascinated by the scene taking place below her. The men, working high atop the decked logs at the base of the flume, would place a six-foot pole with a loose dangling hook on its end against a log and bear down on the handle to give it a pull, and the log would cant over. Like everything else she'd seen in this logging camp, the job looked dangerous.

"Those men must be extremely sure-footed."

"A good cant-hook man has to be," Tom conceded in a voice that was almost cordial for a change.

"Then what happens to the logs?"

"With the first sign of spring thaw, the logs will be sent downstream to the booming grounds. There, they'll be sorted according to company marks, gathered together into rafts with rope and hardwood pins, then towed to the sawmills."

It was almost peaceful standing on top of the bluff, but Tom could almost hear the deafening roar as the decked logs spilled out into the boiling jets of water in the spring.

The riverhogs would be ready with piked poles and peaveys to keep the spinning, twisting logs floating freely downstream. Men would ride the logs down the lake to the mills, where they would eventually be processed into lumber.

Any small error in judgment during a log jam could prove fatal for the men, bringing tons of mighty timbers down to crush their bodies into pulp.

"Those marks on the end of the logs? What are they?" Gideon could see the initials W. T. encased in a tight circle on the bottom of each log.

"They're the company marks. The sorters at the booming grounds will pull them into individual pens as they come through."

Tom flipped his smoke over the railing to the water below, and Gideon watched as the wind caught it, sending a shower of a tiny red sparks into infinity. "You'd better be on your way. It gets dark early," he said quietly.

Turning, Gideon walked beside him for a while. "I'm not sure I know how to get back to the bunkhouse," she confessed. "Andre said to take the second fork to the right. I did, but it brought me here."

"You should have taken the left," he said bluntly. Not, "I'm sorry, Andre must have misinformed you," or "Oh, that's a shame, Miss Yardley, let me escort you back to camp." No, the best Tom Lannigan could muster was a clipped "You should have taken the left."

Gideon wasn't sure why she would even want him to walk her back, but she did. So much so that she found herself sighing audibly when he finally said, "I'll be tied up another few minutes, but if you want to hang around, you can walk with me."

"Thank you. I'll hang around."

The first flakes of snow began falling as Gideon huddled deeper into her cloak. She watched as Tom spoke with a couple of his crew members. His tall, rugged demeanor made her stomach flutter as she thought about being able to spend a few moments alone with him. Though he would consider the walk as nothing more than a duty, she would find it a bit more stimulating.

A few minutes later, he came striding toward her. "It's a twenty-minute walk back to camp. I could arrange for you to ride with one of the teamsters."

"I don't mind the walk." Actually, she was numb to the bone, but she was willing to endure another twenty minutes of the cold if it meant she could spend it in his company.

They fell into step, and Gideon wasn't surprised that he had very little to say. She racked her brain for something intelligent to chat with him about, but she was painfully aware they had little in common. He cut trees and she taught school, though she hoped that he was better at his job than she was hers.

She had to take two steps to his one, so he was forced to slow his pace when he noticed that she was having difficulty keeping up.

"Are you cold?" he asked.

"Just . . . a little."

She was shocked to watch him suddenly peel out of his heavy jacket and drape it around her shoulders.

"I can't take your coat!" she protested as the heavenly warmth from his body enveloped her. The feeling was quite intimate, as she drew the coat closer around her.

"I'm used to the cold."

His scent lingered, and she found it intoxicating. He didn't smell the way the other men did. He smelled of woods and pine and, unless she missed her guess, soap. He must wash more often than Saturdays, she surmised.

Gideon found herself shamelessly fantasizing about big Tom Lannigan as they walked along in the falling snow. She had heard talk in the bunkhouse. As foreman of Wakefield Timber, Tom Lannigan had to be able to whip any man in his camp if the need arose. And apparently it had, many times.

His strength was respected among the men, and Gideon had concluded from what she'd overheard that Tom never picked a fight unless he had a just cause and that he was never bested in a fair battle.

She glanced at him from the corner of her eye. The fabric of his woolen shirt couldn't begin to hide the tight ridge of muscles in his brawny arms. She wondered what it would be like if he took her into his arms and held her tightly against his chest, which was so broad his shirt strained to confine it. His strength would be frightening, for she knew he could probably snap her in two with his bare hands,

136

yet Gideon would bet that when Tom Lannigan wanted to, he could be as gentle as a lamb.

She giggled when she thought of how she'd just mentally compared this tall, powerful giant to a lamb. He could probably just as easily turn into a hungry, lusty, insatiable animal. . . .

"Did you say something?"

Gideon shuddered when she heard his question. Her face flooded with guilt as she realized he'd caught her fantasizing. "Beg your pardon?"

"I thought I heard you say something."

"Oh . . . uh, no."

"How did your first day at school go?"

"Oh." She drew a deep breath of cold air because she suddenly felt extremely warm. "It went okay."

"The children give you any trouble?" She noticed his tone was almost guarded.

She glanced up and smiled. "None that I couldn't handle." Scooter Wilson had turned all the girls' coats inside out after recess, and it had taken Gideon forever to get them back in order. In the meantime, Toby Miller had thrown a pile of horse dung into the stove, and the ensuing stench had nearly caused her to cave in and dismiss class early. But she'd grimly refused to knuckle under to their pranks.

She'd continued the history lesson with a handkerchief pressed over her mouth, then calmly announced at the end of the day that she was assigning the boys the unpalatable task of memorizing the prologue to *Romeo and Juliet,* which they were to recite orally before class the following morning. King Davis had let out a string of cuss words that made the hair on her arms stand straight up, but she'd held her ground.

"Good. Let's hope it stays that way." Tom's ensuing chuckle sounded almost sinister to her.

Gideon glanced up at him. "Did I say something funny?"

His face sobered instantly. "Oh, no, ma'am. Just clearing my throat."

"You don't have to keep calling me, ma'am," she said. She noticed he never called her by her first name. "My name is Fedelia."

A shout from the side of the road diverted their attention, and they paused as three of Tom's crew came running out of the woods. One of the men was carrying another man over his shoulder, and blood was streaming from the injured man's leg, leaving a bright red trail in the white snow.

"We need help here!" one of the men shouted.

Tom broke into a run, and Gideon was close behind.

Hite Mason and Sherman Toddman had Frank Kellier on the ground when Tom and Gideon reached them. Gideon quickly averted her gaze when she saw the deep, bloody gash in the man's leg. The wound was so deep, it seemed certain that the man would lose the limb. The sight of blood made Gideon feel faint. The pounding inside her head grew louder as she grew lightheaded.

Tom had dropped to his knees, trying to stem the flow of blood. Frank was writhing on the ground, his face contorted with pain.

"What happened, Frank?"

"Damn ax bit into me. . . ." Mercifully, Frank passed out before he could finish telling his story.

"I've got to have some kind of a tourniquet. . . ." Tom started to unbutton his shirt, but Gideon was already reaching under her skirt to tear a strip from her petticoat. An instant later, she handed it to him.

Tom worked frantically to stop the flow of blood, but it was gushing out of Frank into red pools.

"God, Tom, he's gonna bleed to death," Hite Mason warned, as he peeled off his coat and tried to cushion the injured limb.

Leaning back on his haunches, Tom drew a skinning knife from the leather sheath fastened to his belt. "The leg can't be saved. It's going to have to come off. I'll need someone to hold him down."

Hite, growing paler by the moment, turned away sickly.

"Sherman?" Tom barked.

"I can't do it, Tom. I'll puke for sure."

Tom suddenly felt a supportive hand touch his shoulder. "I'll do it," Gideon said softly.

Tom glanced up. Her face was as white as the strip of petticoat she'd handed him, and yet he saw a spark of determination in her eyes. "Are you sure? It won't be pleasant."

Gideon nodded, swallowing back the rising bile in her throat. "Just tell me what I should do."

With Tom's brief instructions, Gideon held down the powerful two-hundred-and-ten-pound man as Tom cut off his leg. Drifting in and out of consciousness, Frank screamed for mercy each time the knife sawed back and forth through the bone.

His agonizing cries shattered the quiet hillsides, as tears began to trickle down Gideon's face. She willed herself not to cry or to faint. Occasionally, she leaned over and gently cradled Frank's face against her breast, crooning softly to him as his tears soaked the front of her cloak. He was so young—maybe twenty or twenty-one—and so afraid of losing a leg. The physical pain was excruciating, but the agony in his heart was worse.

"My God, my leg . . . don't cut off my leg, Tom," Frank begged as his cries echoed across the frozen countryside.

"I have to, Frank. Otherwise you'll bleed to death."

"Let me die then. Just let me die. I don't want to lose my leg," he pleaded.

When it was over, Frank lay very pale and still. The lower part of his leg, his boot still on his severed foot, lay in Hite Mason's bloody coat.

The bleeding had slowed, and Tom hurriedly wrapped another strip of Gideon's petticoat tightly around the wound.

"Frank, we're going to have to get you to Doc Medifer," Tom said as he rolled the severed limb into the jacket and set it aside. "He'll have to cauterize the wound."

Snowflakes clung to Frank's wet lashes as he stared vacantly up at the growing twilight.

"Can you hear me, Frank?"

Frank barely nodded.

"Hite, see if you can flag down some help," Tom said.

Ten minutes later, four of Frank's fellow workmen came running up the hillside. Jorge Cypren lifted Frank in his arms as gently as he would a baby, and carried him to the waiting sleigh.

Turning to Gideon, Tom replaced his coat around her shoulders. It had been cast aside during the crisis. She was near frozen, but he realized she hadn't complained once.

"Are you all right?"

She nodded numbly. "I just feel so terribly sorry for him."

"He's alive," Tom said gruffly.

Gideon looked up at him, her face still wet with tears. "And that's enough?"

Tom stood beside her, watching the sleigh carrying Frank slowly fade out of sight. "I suppose if a man has no other choice, it has to be," he acknowledged softly.

9

Gideon's life had settled down after the tragic afternoon when Frank Kellier had lost his leg. She had visited Frank often during the bleak, dark days of his convalescence, since the loss of the limb had left Frank in a deep depression. Every day for over a week Gideon had stopped by Doc Medifer's house on her way home from work to read to him from the works of Charles Dickens, but Frank had failed to respond. It would take a long time for both his wound and his heart to heal.

The winter winds whistled around the eaves of the tiny schoolhouse, while thick layers of snow fell with monotonous regularity.

The cramped quarters of the schoolroom wore on the dispositions of both the students and Gideon. With each passing day she knew that something needed to be done about the learning conditions. A new, larger schoolroom desperately needed to be built.

Teaching was the greatest challenge she'd

ever faced. The coal-oil lamp sitting beside her cot burned long into the night, as she struggled to prepare the lessons of the following day. Over and over the question came back to haunt her. *Why* would she have chosen to teach, when she apparently had no talent for it? The most basic arithmetic problem had her pacing the floor and wringing her hands in frustration.

It hadn't taken long for Gideon to reach her first firm decision. Having children of her own was out of the question. She seemed to vaguely recall someone saying that children were a blessing sent from above. However, if the children of Watersweet were an example of parental bliss, Gideon would happily forgo that hallowed sanctification and buy a goat instead. She figured she could always sell the goat if it got out of hand, but she didn't have the same option with children—though, Lord knows, at times she was sorely tempted.

And yet her days weren't all bad. There were times when Gideon found herself almost happy. She had formed a satisfying and close relationship with Echo, and the men couldn't have treated her with more respect.

Whatever Tom Lannigan had said to them about leaving her alone had worked; they implicitly heeded his advice.

Gideon could recall the nights when she'd listened to the men talk, while she stayed in her room trying to study.

Every night some sat around playing cards, while others were already snoring away in their bunks. A number of them would lie in bed reading Western novels and outdated pink copies of the *Police Gazette* as the rancid odor of drying socks, melting shoe grease, and pitch pine filled the air.

A few of the men gathered around the deacon's seat, listening to some of the old-timers spin their tall tales about Ho-dogs, Paul Bunyan, Johnny Inkslinger, and snowsnakes. From a far corner someone would strum a guitar and softly whistle "The Red Light Saloon."

Men were a funny lot, she'd decided. They liked to think they were the stronger sex, but Gideon knew otherwise. Though their brawn rather than their brains made them seem indomitable, they had a simple honesty and concern for their fellow workers that she found admirable. She knew that the men would fight at the drop of a hat, going directly for physical satisfaction, using fists, boot caulks, and sometimes teeth to settle a dispute, but she'd also seen a gentler side to them.

To those who treated him fairly, the shanty boy, as the timber worker was called, was a square dealer and a true friend. He might have a rough exterior, but he also had a heart of gold. Gideon would find herself smiling as she listened to a man brag about his record cuts in the woods, the amount of whiskey he could drink, the fights he'd fought, and the women he'd loved. Yet she knew this rough bear of a man could have his heart touched by a friend's anguish, the love of a good woman, or the touch of a small child's hand.

But with every rule of thumb, there was an exception, and Gideon happened to run into one on a late Saturday afternoon.

She stopped into Menson's store to buy material for a hat. The idea had suddenly occurred to her that afternoon. She had no idea if she could construct one, but the idea intrigued her.

The camp store was bustling with activity. Christmas was only a few days away, and Henry had his hands full waiting on customers. Gideon browsed through the piece goods trying to decide what she wanted to buy. The ribbons and lace were eye-catching. She thought about purchasing one or the other for Echo, but she knew her friend had nothing decent to sew them on.

Three jacks suddenly burst into the store, talking loudly and shoving each other like small, rowdy boys. The odor of their dirty, unwashed bodies cast a pall over the ladies present.

Henry glanced up from behind the counter and seemed unhappy to see them. It was obvious that the men had been drinking, a vice that was strictly prohibited in camp during cutting season. Although a few of the crew piled into wagons and made the trip to

Shadow Pine on Saturday nights to carouse, they knew that they had to be stone sober by the time four-thirty Monday morning rolled around.

The bell over the door tinkled again, and Gideon's pulse leaped as it always did when she saw Tom and Andre enter the store. Since the accident involving Frank, Tom hadn't been quite as reserved toward her, but she sensed that he was still going out of his way to avoid her.

Tom walked to the counter to make his purchase, while Andre spotted her and walked over.

"*Bonjour,* Mademoiselle!" he said warmly.

"Hello!" Gideon wished she could find the sight of the tall, dark Frenchman as stimulating as the sight of his reticent companion. Andre was good-looking enough to attract any woman he chose. Not only was he handsome, but he was polite as well, and Gideon knew that most women would give their eyeteeth to have him show the smallest amount of interest in them, but it was Tom Lannigan's interest and fair good looks that made her heart race.

He was just a bit taller, a bit more handsome, his eyes a little bluer, his lashes a little longer, his hair a little blonder, and his close-mouthed, knowing smile more intriguing than any other man.

And in the midst of such superb masculine

specimens on which to base her opinion, that was saying something.

As usual, Tom seemed to glance at her with little more interest than if she'd been the potato barrel.

But Tom did notice her. And it annoyed him that he found her attractive, and worse, that he found the interest he saw in her eyes so unsettling. He didn't want to like her, and he didn't want to want her. He found his best defense was simply to ignore her as much as possible, but Andre didn't make that easy for him.

"Are you going to the sleigh ride tonight, *ma chérie*?"

Gideon snapped out of her daydreams, returning her attention to Andre. "Tonight?"

"*Oui,* it's an annual event this time of the year. We meet after supper in front of the bunkhouse. A few of the men have sweethearts in Shadow Pine, and they join us. There are ten—maybe fifteen—sleighfuls, and we stop along the way to cut the town Christmas tree." Andre snapped his heels together and bowed politely. "You will find the evening quite enjoyable, mademoiselle, and I would be most honored if you would permit me to escort you."

Gideon glanced wistfully at Tom as he placed his order and paid for it. "It sounds like fun, Andre, but I won't be able to go." There was a geography test first thing Monday morning, and she knew she would have to spend the entire weekend preparing for it.

"Oh? *Pourquoi pas?* You do not like sleigh rides?"

"Oh no, a sleigh ride sounds wonderful, but I have work I must do." Gideon's eyes drifted back to Tom. If by some miracle he had been the one to ask her to go, would she have cast her responsibilities aside to go? she asked herself. Most likely.

"Can the work not be postponed?" Andre's smile had turned boyishly coaxing. "The holidays come but once a year, *ma chérie.*"

Gideon sighed. "I know, and I would love to go, Andre, but I really mustn't."

"Such a shame," Gideon could hear a note of teasing creep into Andre's voice, "for one so lovely to be stuck in a small, stuffy room with only the smell of drying shoepacs to keep her company, while others are skimming across the countryside, having a wonderful time! Are you sure your work cannot be postponed for only a few hours?"

Gideon was about to refuse again, when her attention was diverted by the three men who had entered the store earlier. Their playful remarks were beginning to contain some offensive language.

Tom finished paying Henry and sent the three men a harsh glance, discreetly reminding them of the women's presence.

The jacks quieted momentarily, but a few

minutes later one shouted a ribald joke to the other, and the three burst into snickers.

Tom quietly stepped over to confront one of the men. "Waite, you and Ben and Jess take it outside," he said quietly.

"Oh hell, Tom, we was jus' havin' some fun," the drunkest of the three scoffed.

"Have your fun somewhere else. There are ladies present."

"Ladies?" Waite Burne glanced around until his drunken gaze found Gideon. His mouth spread into a jolly grin. "Well, you're right, there shore is. Lookee here, Ben, there's a right purty woman among us!"

"Waite," Tom kept his voice low, but firm, "you know the rules. No drinking in camp. You and your friends see me in my office when you sober up."

"We're jus' havin' us a little Christmas nip," Waite whined. "You can't really consider that drinkin', Tom."

"Move on, Waite."

"All right . . . I'm goin'. I just want to wish this purdy woman a Merry Christmas first." Waite edged past Tom. "Hello there, honeybunch." His bleary-eyed gaze skimmed over Gideon, as he swayed unsteadily. His voice lowered to a conspiratorial whisper, "If you've been a good little girl, ole Waite'll give you a little sugar in your Christmas stocking."

Tom stepped back into Waite's path. "Leave," he warned with a note of finality.

An uneasy silence fell upon the room as the two men faced each other. They were both large, both formidable examples of manhood.

"Ah, I don't mean no harm," Waite sniveled.

"Just leave, Waite," Tom repeated again.

Sensing the trouble Waite could get himself into, Ben and Jess eased forward. "Com'on, let's git on over to Shadow Pine, Waite. We don't want no trouble here."

Waite's eyes moved to Gideon, then slowly back to Tom's. "Shore, Ben, Big Say knows I'm just liquored up—don't mean no harm." Waite winked at Gideon as he began to move toward the doorway. "Merry Christmas, ma'am, and a fine New Year to you."

Gideon turned away.

A moment later the door rattled shut. Tom turned and, without a word, followed on the heels of the three men.

"I am sorry you had to witness that," Andre apologized, as the shoppers began to browse again.

"Is that Waite Burne?" Gideon asked, appalled by the thought that the unkempt man could be Echo's husband.

Andre nodded as he watched out the window as Tom cornered the three men and began talking to them. "Yes, that is Waite."

"Does he get like that often?" Gideon asked, concern for Echo etched in her frown.

Andre shrugged. "Old Waite would not hurt a fly. When he is sober, he can outwork any

151

man in Watersweet, but when he drinks, he is a crazy man. He is always very sorry afterward, but I swear I do not know how Echo puts up with him."

Dismissing the subject, Andre returned to their earlier conversation. "You're sure you won't change your mind about the sleigh ride?"

"Thank you, Andre, but I'd really better not."

He shrugged good-naturedly. "It will be fun."

"I'm sure it will. Maybe another time." Picking up a bottle of lemon berbennia toilet water, Gideon quickly made her purchases and left the store.

When she stepped outside, there was no sign of Tom or the other three men. She tried to shrug off the feeling of disappointment that suddenly cast a shadow over her day. She realized that she'd been hoping that Tom might have had business near the bunkhouse, so they could walk together.

But, of course, that was silly. Tom Lannigan would never wait around to walk her home, Gideon realized.

Wrapping her scarf tighter under her chin, she started to cross the street as the loggers began bringing their horses into camp. Her mind was still on Tom, and she glanced up just in time to see eight or nine of the horses unexpectedly come galloping in her direction.

Stunned, she froze helplessly as the horses came thundering down on her in a mutual quest to reach the watering trough first. She would have been trampled to the ground if a pair of strong arms had not snaked out to snatch her quickly out of harm's way.

She felt her feet touch the ground again and her startled eyes met a pair of deep blue ones.

"You'd better start watching where you're going, teacher." Tipping his hat politely, Tom walked on.

Gideon lost her temper. The man was insufferable! Jerking her bonnet off, she childishly stuck her tongue out at his retreating back.

Whirling, she marched back to the bunkhouse, happy to have that out of her system.

The creaking of leather harness, and the melodious jingle of sleigh bells brought an envious smile to Gideon's face as she stepped out of the cook shack later that evening.

Row upon row of horse-drawn sleighs were waiting in a line to be boarded. In a jovial mood as they piled aboard the sleighs, the wild woodsmen broke out into hearty choruses of "Jingle Bells."

French-Canadians, wearing their colorful headgear and bright scarves, hoisted giggling women into the sleighs. Blond Finn giants already had their women snuggled down tightly beneath furry lap robes, waiting for the festivi-

ties to begin, while men from "down below"—
southern Michigan, piled into the sleds, prepared to put aside their good-natured rivalry
to have a good time.

Gideon could hear the friendly ribbing as
men shouted back and forth to one another.
The French-Canadians were dubbed "frogs,"
the men from across the pond were called
"greenhorns" and "hunkies," and the Saginaw
toughs were "the valley boys." Gideon had
stopped trying to keep them all straight long
ago.

Lars Rurik, a big congenial Swede, spotted
her. Gideon grinned and started backing up as
Lars stood up in his sleigh and shouted at her
to climb aboard.

Waving back at him, she called, "I can't. I
have work to do!"

Lars waded through the maze of bodies and
bound out of the sleigh, shouting, "No one
works the night Lars cuts the Christmas tree!"

Before Gideon could stop him, the big burly
woodsman descended upon her. Amid her
shrieking protests, he swooped her up in his
Herculean arms and carried her to the waiting
sleigh.

"Lars, put me down!" Gideon demanded
laughingly, though by now she was longing to
join the merriment.

"Vork later, voman. Tonight ve have fun!"
Lars boomed.

Bells jingled merrily and laughter filled the

air as the sleighs began pulling out of camp. Gideon quickly made up her mind that the test could wait.

For once, it wasn't snowing. Overhead, a full moon lit the snowy countryside as brightly as day while the sleds raced through the center of town.

Tom was just coming out of his office when the first of the sleds came sailing by. Andre appeared and paused beside Tom as the two men watched the crew's lighthearted shenanigans.

All of the men threw up their hands as they passed, amid friendly shouts of "Hey, Big Push!" and "Hop a sleigh, Main Say! There's a seat for you, Montague!"

Tom and Andre smiled back at the crew, waving the friendly invitations aside.

"You might as well go, Andre. We're through for tonight," Tom remarked.

"I think I will go to the bunkhouse and pay a visit to Miss Yardley."

The sleigh carrying Gideon swept by, and the smile on Andre's face suddenly dimmed as he saw her stand up and wave merrily at him.

Pulling a smoke out of his pocket, Tom watched as the sleigh raced around the corner amid a loud, cheery chorus of "Deck the Halls." "I thought you said she wasn't going."

"She wasn't," Andre murmured. "She must have changed her mind."

Lars noticed the glow that had suddenly lit

Gideon's face when the sled had whisked by Tom Lannigan, and he shouted for the driver to turn around.

Tom and Andre were still standing on the planked walk when two sleighs came barreling back around the corner. When they reached the two men, three jacks leaped out of the lead sleigh, and Tom began grinning.

"Don't even think it," he warned, but his words fell on deaf ears.

The three men picked up the two hundred twenty-five pound man as if he were a sack of flour and pitched him headlong into the sleigh, landing him facedown in Gideon Wakefield's lap.

He twisted his body over to stare up into a pair of familiar laughing brown eyes and heard Gideon shout, "Merry Christmas, Big Push!"

The sound of bells filled the air again as the sleighs raced along the icy roads to catch the others. Andre had been manhandled into the second sleigh, and Gideon saw that a woman from Shadow Pine had latched onto him.

The madcap ride took them over hills and hollows, through tall stands of pine and across frozen ponds.

Gideon laughed until her sides hurt. The lumberjacks played as hard as they worked, and she began to see a new and encouraging side to Tom Lannigan. He stood in the middle

156

of the sleigh exchanging friendly banter tit for tat with his crew. His deep baritone boomed out the old, traditional carols as heartily as anyone's.

The harrowing ride went on for over an hour before the sleighs finally pulled into a large field covered with fir trees. Everyone piled out, and the search for the perfect tree was on.

It was announced that the head cook, Moose Bentson, would award a Christmas goose to the one who found the town tree.

Gideon found herself running laughingly beside Tom as they scoured the hillside for the perfect tree. It must be large, at least twenty feet tall, with perfectly shaped boughs.

Gideon squealed when she found it first. Motioning for Tom excitedly, she watched with bated breath as he examined the tree. It stood way over twenty feet high, and the branches were arched in perfect symmetry. What a lovely sight it would be, standing in the center of town, dressed in tinsel and shiny ribbons and bows!

Tom stood, brushing the snow off his pant legs as he smiled admiringly at her. "Looks like the pretty lady from Philadelphia wins the goose."

Gideon grinned back at him with her heart in her eyes. Who wanted a goose? The greatest prize of all was to hear him say that he thought she was pretty!

The tree was chopped down, and it took seven men to carry it back to the sleigh. The occupants of the sled had to crowd in with the others, but Gideon didn't mind. She was wedged so tightly against Tom that he was forced to put his arm around her on the ride home. Sighing with contentment, she snuggled against his broad chest, surrounded by his warmth.

Once they reached camp, the tree was hauled out and placed in the center of town. Hot mugs of cider began circulating, and carols broke out again. Gideon knew she had shamelessly trailed Tom all evening, but until he said something to discourage her, she didn't plan to stop. Wherever he went, she wasn't far behind, and should she stray momentarily, he seemed to pop up nearby.

"Cookie, ma'am?" Tom offered. Gideon turned from speaking to Berniece, and smiled. The cookies in camp were cut the size of stove lids.

She curtsied politely. "Thank you." She selected a nice, tasty-looking one and bit into it.

"Only one?" he asked, surprised.

She nodded. One was the equivalent of four. "May I get you a cup of cider?" she asked him.

"Thank you. You'll join me?" he invited.

Gideon's pulse hammered in her throat. Yes, she would gladly join Tom Lannigan. She went in search of the cider before he could change his mind. Her stomach was still jumpy as she

158

hurried back with the two steaming cups a few moments later. As she turned the corner she saw that one of the women from Shadow Pine had Tom cornered. The little strawberry blond was uncommonly pretty, with sparkling emerald-green eyes and breasts that could provide adequate shade for a small boy. Gideon's heart sank when she saw the way Tom was looking at her, as if they were more than casual acquaintances.

Jealousy welled up in Gideon's throat. A painful knot formed in the pit of her stomach as she watched the woman rise on her tiptoes to place a brief kiss on Tom's lips. The kiss might have been casual, but the look in the woman's eyes was not. Gideon's hands began to tremble, sending the cider spilling over the sides of the cups.

Tom glanced up. When he saw Gideon, he murmured something quietly to the woman. A moment later, the woman merged back into the milling crowd.

Summoning up her brightest smile, Gideon walked over and handed one of the cups of cider to him.

"Thanks, that smells good." Tom took the cup, and they walked over to sit on the wooden sidewalk.

Gideon longed to ask him who the woman was, but she knew she had no right. Deep inside, she knew it was Marcy Wetlock, the woman Andre had said Tom visited in Shadow Pine occasionally.

"Berniece stopped by the office this afternoon. She thinks it would be nice if the children had a Christmas program," Tom remarked.

"Then let Berniece come and organize one," Gideon returned nicely.

Tom smothered a grin as he drew back in mock surprise. "But that's your job."

"Tell me, Mr. Lannigan, did the shepherds watching their flocks in the fields use crude and offensive language with one another? Did they fight with their fists, spit tobacco on their sheep, try to brain each other senseless with their staffs, and repeatedly refer to the Virgin Mary as a common trollop? You see, I, too, thought a Christmas program would be nice. I've even had the children busy working on it, but you've just heard the results of such wishful thinking. The little heathens did all those things I just described, and more."

"Well, maybe it's a little late to worry about a Christmas program," Tom admitted.

They sat in easy silence until a burst of merriment broke out in the crowd.

Lars Rurick, Angus Brutsmeyer, Ray Sletzer, Mort Sewell, and Jim Carten came bounding in the direction of Tom and Gideon. They had devilish grins on their faces, and it was plain to see that were up to trouble.

"Oh, hell. Here we go again," Tom muttered as he spotted the clumps of mistletoe clasped in their hands.

Gideon started grinning as the men made a beeline for her. Scooping her off her feet, she was kissed so many times in the next few minutes that she began to lose track.

Everyone soon joined in the melee, and chaos reigned. Gideon tried to keep track of how many women Tom kissed, and how long the kisses lasted, but it was nearly impossible. The handsome foreman of Wakefield Timber had no trouble attracting the opposite sex. But she noticed that he generally made the embraces brief and casual, in keeping with the lighthearted holiday spirit.

It was only when Gideon saw Marcy Wetlock heading in Tom's direction, that she broke from Ed Holman's clasp, snatched his clump of mistletoe, and ran.

"Hey, woman! Bring that mistletoe back here! You've disarmed me!" Ed bellowed.

Sauntering casually past Marcy, Gideon broke into another run as she headed straight for Tom. By the time she reached him she was breathless, but she had her mind set on what she was going to do.

Tom was momentarily startled as Gideon rushed up and came to a sudden halt in front of him. Taking a cautious step backward, he grew uneasy as he saw the look of determination glinting in her eyes. "Now, look . . ."

"Merry Christmas!" Before she lost her

Lori Copeland

nerve, Gideon bounded onto the wooden sidewalk to give herself an advantage in height.
She thrust the mistletoe above his head, took a
deep breath, and threw her arms around his
neck. Shamelessly, she covered his mouth
with hers.

Staggering backward, he caught her to him
and she pressed even closer.

It was a reckless, indiscreet thing to do, and
Gideon was certain that sometime later she
would wish she had tried to control her im-
pulse. He would think that besides her memory, she had lost her mind as well—and perhaps she had.

Tom Lannigan had never encouraged any
sort of personal attraction between them—
quite to the contrary—but her selfish needs
drove her. She was tumbling hopelessly,
wildly, madly in love with this handsome,
brawny woodsman, and at that instant she
didn't care!

Her heart sang as she felt his arms hesitantly
begin to accept her as she poured her whole
heart into the kiss. She was powerless to help
herself. He was everything she wanted, even
though it seemed that she was the last thing he
needed.

For one heart-stopping moment, she
thought he wasn't going to respond. Dropping
the mistletoe, she brought her hands down to
clutch the lapels of his jacket and moved
closer against the width of his chest, her

mouth hungrily seeking his, as his arms gradually drew her closer.

Stunned, he broke the kiss momentarily, and their eyes met. The world around them suddenly disappeared as they gazed with new awareness into each other's eyes.

"Just kiss me, Tom Lannigan," she coaxed breathlessly. "It won't do any good to try to talk yourself out of it."

An impertinent grin spread across his handsome features. "Who said I'd even try?"

And then the miracle occurred. Happiness bubbled within her as she was suddenly lifted in the cradle of his muscular arms and kissed like she'd never been kissed before. Her body felt as if it detached and soared heavenward, as his mouth hungrily devoured hers. She could feel her body trembling as he pulled her closer, making her suddenly aware of the swift effect she was having on him as she returned his kiss with reckless abandon.

If it had been left up to Gideon, the kiss would have gone on forever. She loved the way he tasted—cold and sweet. She loved the way the rough fabric of his coat felt against her cheek, the smell of soap and fresh pine. She felt giddy and lightheaded and wonderful, as the kiss deepened.

But the ring of laughter intruded on their heated embrace. Tom started, glancing up to find half his crew watching the spectacle with growing amusement.

Clearing his throat sheepishly, he casually lowered Gideon to her feet, but his hands remained possessively around her waist.

The crowd broke into a round of applause, causing Gideon's face to flush a rosy red, but the men rapidly dispersed with Tom's none-too-subtle suggestions.

With growing horror, Fiona Miller and Berniece watched the disgraceful antics taking place between the new schoolteacher and the camp foreman. Their eyes wide with astonishment, they peered from behind the water barrel. The women knew that they shouldn't let such impropriety go uncensored, but Miss Yardley had them stumped. It would be impossible to find a new teacher until spring.

"The rules clearly state that the teacher is not to be carousing with the men in camp," Fiona hissed, in her most self-righteous tone.

"Don't hiss at me, Fiona!" Berniece snapped. "If you don't want Miss Yardley's job, I say we turn our heads and let her break all the rules she wants."

Fiona and Berniece listened to the good-natured ribbing the men were throwing at Tom.

"It *would* be terrible to be forced back to that horrible schoolroom," Fiona mused.

"With those nine hideous children," Berniece added for insurance.

They could plainly see that Tom Lannigan

still had his arms around Gideon's waist. Such a disgrace! They really should do something.

"Well, I never!" Fiona muttered as Gideon reached up to wind her arms around Tom's neck for one final, forbidden kiss.

"Well, Fiona, maybe you should put the bug in Jack's ear when you get home," Berniece said, deliberately turning her back on the sordid scene.

She wasn't about to confront the issue and run the chance of being imprisoned in that drafty, deplorable schoolhouse with those uncivilized yahoos again.

10

Gideon glanced up from her desk Tuesday afternoon to find King Davis standing in the doorway. School was over for the day, so she was surprised to see him there.

"Yes, King?"

"Mr. Lannigan says for you to git your butt over to his office."

"Are those Mr. Lannigan's exact words, King?" Her tone held its usual note of condemnation for the boy's crude vocabulary.

"Close enough."

With a sigh Gideon closed her grade book, realizing that her message had lost something in the translation. "Thank you, King." King disappeared as Gideon stood and went to bank the fire.

The message was encouraging. Gideon felt her hopes rising as she reached for her cloak. Tom wanted to see her! Had the kiss they'd shared three nights ago finally broken the ice between them? Was it possible the stubborn

Mr. Lannigan was finally ready to admit that an undeniable attraction did exist between them? Gideon couldn't see how he could ignore it much longer. She had recognized it from the first: Tom Lannigan was destined to be hers.

The shadows were beginning to lengthen as Gideon left the schoolhouse. A pale sun sank in the west, its appearance the first in many long days.

The ridges of deep snow cracked beneath Gideon's feet as she hurried along the sled path. Thoughts of being with the handsome foreman made the bone-chilling walk much easier to tolerate today.

Her mind wanted to play little games, imagining the purpose of Tom's summons. Perhaps he would invite her to take supper with him, she thought with excitement. She recalled that his room was above Menson's General Store, but she realized that she really knew so little about the man she loved.

She longed to know so much more—the way he looked when he was sleeping, what sort of pie he favored. Did he like cream and sugar in his coffee, or did he drink it strong and black? Did he have brothers and sisters? Did he get his strong, aristocratic features from his mother, or did his fair, stunning good looks come from his father? What made him laugh? What touched his heart?

Though she knew it would be improper for

her to visit him in his room, she was tempted to overlook the impropriety.

She felt safe, safe and warm and incredibly happy whenever she was near him. She wondered if somewhere in the dark, mysterious part of her life there had been a man who had made her feel this contented, this at peace with herself. She didn't think so. Feelings this strong could come but once in a woman's life. She didn't need her memory to remind her of that.

Climbing the steps to the lumber office, she paused a moment to take stock of herself. She was glad that she'd worn the blue wool today. Now that she had lost a few pounds, the dress fit perfectly. The swells and tucks were all in the proper places again.

Taking a deep breath, she turned the doorknob and walked in. She was relieved to see that Tom was the only one in the office this afternoon. She welcomed the few moments alone with him.

"King said you wanted to see me?"

Tom glanced up as a rush of cold air preceded her. His gaze ran over her with lazy proficiency as her heart rose to her throat.

"Have a seat. I'll be with you in a minute."

Disappointed that his greeting was not a little more cordial, she quietly removed her mittens and bonnet and walked over to stand beside the stove. Trying to keep her eyes off him, she waited patiently as he finished what he was doing and finally pushed back from his desk.

Reaching inside the top drawer, he took out a small pouch. "I trust your day was productive?"

She smiled, making it one of her prettiest. "Yes, we're about to study the continents." She frowned. "I never realized that there were so many—five!"

"Five? I believe that there are seven."

Her smile faded. "Seven? Honestly?" *That darn King Davis had lied to her again.*

"I know you must be wondering why I asked you to stop by." He stood, and she was reminded again of how tall he was. Her head barely came to his shoulders.

Summoning her sunniest expression, she said, "Not really . . . I was glad to have the opportunity to stop by—"

"This isn't a social visit, Miss Yardley."

She realized how transparent she must seem and quickly tried to cover her eagerness to be with him. "Oh . . . no, of course it isn't . . . well, exactly why did you send for me, Mr. Lannigan?"

Tom handed her the pouch he'd taken from the drawer earlier. "It's payday."

Gideon took the pouch and opened it, dumping the contents into the palm of her hand. Viewing the paltry sum with growing horror, she heard him trying to explain. "I know it seems small, but let me remind you that you'll receive a twenty-five-cent raise in five years if you perform your job faithfully and without fault, provided the school board approves."

Her gaze lifted slowly to meet his. Amusement flickered in the eyes that met hers. "Something to aim for, isn't it?"

Speechless, she nodded.

"That will be all, Miss Yardley." Turning back to his work, he dismissed her. "Better run along; it'll be dark in a few minutes."

The few coins in her hand were discouraging enough, but the realization that his summons had not been of a personal nature was even more crushing. Dropping the coins into her purse, she squared her shoulders and turned to leave.

"Don't spend all of that in one place," he murmured absently, then he flinched as he heard the door bang solidly shut behind her.

Christmas came and went. On New Year's Eve an ice storm hit the logging camp, rendering the crew idle for two days. Gideon could see that the men had developed a severe case of cabin fever. Shouting matches broke out in the bunkhouse, and tempers flared quickly.

To pass the time, she bought some fabric at Menson's, and in the evenings she worked in her little room, fashioning herself a hat.

As she sewed the finishing laces and bows, she sat back on her cot and admired her talent.

She couldn't imagine how she'd thought of it. The idea had just sort of sprung into her mind during a spelling bee one long afternoon. One minute she was doodling in the margin of her speller, and the next moment she was sketching a hat. A large, elaborate design of lace and silk and ostrich feathers.

Of course, Menson's didn't carry ostrich feathers and silk, and certainly not the intricate lace that she had drawn—just some yard goods and buttons and such—but she'd substituted where she could. She'd been lucky enough to find some crow feathers in the forest.

I really have a knack for this sort of thing. I wonder where I got this talent? Perhaps I inherited it.

Holding the creation out before her, she sighed.

Lovely, simply lovely.

The middle of January turned bitterly cold, and the children seemed more unbearable with each passing day. And it snowed, and snowed, and snowed.

The door to the schoolhouse slammed shut Tuesday afternoon, and Scooter Wilson made a beeline for the outhouse. Gideon could hear his feet thundering purposefully down the ice-covered path as he hurriedly unbuttoned the front of his pants.

Four of the children had complained of having bellyaches after eating their lunch. King Davis had passed out green apples all morning, and Gideon was beginning to wonder if he wasn't playing one of his unamusing pranks again. She had wisely refused the apples, saying that she didn't feel well herself. She had learned that she could trust King just about as far as she could throw him.

Tirza Reynolds's hand shot up in the air and wagged frantically.

"Yes, Tirza?"

"It's hit me again!"

"Scooter, Quinn, and King are all using the—"

"I can't wait!" Tirza's pained expression convinced Gideon that she would have to make an exception this time. Ordinarily, only one child was allowed out of the room at a time.

"All right, Tirza. You may be excused—"

Tirza shot out of her seat and bolted for the door, trying to run with her legs crossed.

Cautioning the class to settle down, Gideon went on with the lesson.

Five minutes later, the door opened again, and Quinn stuck his head in.

"Guess who has her tongue stuck to the pump handle?"

Gideon glanced up expectantly. "Who?"

"The ole cypress tree. You'd better come and see to her. She's screaming her fool head off."

Gideon laid her book aside and stood up. "Thank you, Quinn. You may take your seat."

Quinn took his seat as Scooter burst through the doorway and scrambled back to his desk.

Slipping into her cloak as she walked to the back of the room, Gideon called over her shoulder, "I shall expect your best behavior while I'm gone."

The newest crisis failed to disturb Gideon, and neither did the persistent hammering that had suddenly started up at the front door. The children's incessantly bad behavior had tried her patience hourly, but she had learned that it was far better to try to outwit them than give in to them.

An eraser came whizzing by Gideon's head and smacked the door, causing a fine sheen of chalk dust to powder her face.

Ignoring the deliberate provocation, Gideon calmly reached for the door handle and gave it a pull. The door refused to budge.

She tugged harder, and the children began to snicker. Undoubtedly, one of the boys had tricked Tirza into touching her tongue to the frozen handle of the well pump, and Quinn had then been sent to inform Miss Yardley of Tirza's plight, while King nailed the door shut.

Gideon tried to control the knot of hysteria crowding her throat. It was going to be a long afternoon. Nailed shut in a tiny room with no ventilation, no windows, and with seven children, four of whom were suffering from a roaring case of diarrhea, was not going to be pleasant. Not in the least.

Taking a deep breath, Gideon whirled and began dragging the slop jar to the far corner of the room as she calmly instructed, "Please open your poetry books."

Pained groans filled the room.

"We shall read from the works of Robert Burns loud enough for both Tirza and King to enjoy while we wait."

"Oh no! Do we have to read that 'My love is like a red, red rose' again?" Toby demanded hostilely.

Juice Tetterson's hand suddenly flew up. "I-I . . . ha-have . . . to . . . thunder . . . Miss . . . Yard-Yardley!"

Motioning her permission for the child to leave her seat to use the slop jar, Gideon summoned a brave smile. "Yes, we might even have time for Elizabeth Barrett Browning's sonnets." Gideon gazed off pointedly. "How do I love thee?" she quoted. "Let me count the ways . . ." She snapped back, realizing that there were none, as she grimly ripped the lid from the pot and braced herself for the siege.

Tom came into the office late that afternoon, stomping the snow off his boots and heading straight for the stove to thaw out. He noticed Andre was deeply engrossed in a letter he was reading.

"What has you so preoccupied?"

A frown began to form on Andre's features as he read on. "We just received a letter from Monsieur Talbot Wellington-Kent."

Tom shrugged out of his coat and hung it on the peg. "Oh?"

"Yes, he's concerned about his fiancée, Tom. It's been weeks, and he hasn't heard from Miss Wakefield. He wants to know more about the train accident. I think he may be suspecting the worst—we have to tell the poor man something."

Reaching for his coffee cup, Tom walked back to the stove, parroting his usual answer when the subject of Gideon Wakefield was brought up. "Tell him everything we know."

"I have, but you can see why he's upset. Miss Wakefield hasn't contacted him since she left Philadelphia. Talbot says here that her engagement ring alone was worth over ten thousand dollars." Andre slid the letter back inside its envelope thoughtfully. "I sympathize with the poor man—he has a right to know what we suspect."

Tom walked over to the window to stare out at the falling snow. Engagement ring? Gideon wasn't wearing a ring, nor had she been the day Andre fished her out of the water. Tom would have noticed a stone of that value. Was it possible that the woman in their midst *was* Fedelia Yardley? For a moment, a spurt of hope flooded him, but it quickly faded. No, he would bet his life that she was a Rutherford. He didn't know where Talbot's ring was— maybe Gideon had lost it in the accident or maybe she hadn't been wearing it that day.

His conscience nagged him constantly to get to the bottom of it, to discover who she was, once and for all. He was even beginning to wonder if Gideon was the selfish, conniving woman that he had assumed she was.

It had taken him awhile to admit she didn't appear to be. Losing her memory would not alter her inherent personality. He had watched her struggle to perform a job she suspected she wasn't trained to do without a word of complaint. Her predecessors had been in his office every hour on the hour demanding to be replaced, but Gideon, facing an overwhelming task, was quietly gritting her way through it.

She had adjusted to living in the midst of one hundred and twenty-five rough, barely civilized woodsmen, and only rarely did she show signs of losing her sunny disposition. Her aristocratic behavior and refined breeding were making gentlemen out of the burly lumberjacks, an enviable accomplishment for anyone.

The crew had even ceased their constant harping about her not allowing them to smoke in the bunkhouse. They had good-naturedly bowed to her wishes and taken their pipes and tobacco outdoors, along with their prized bunkhouse cat.

And the afternoon when she had helped him take Frank Kellier's leg off had left him feeling deeply ashamed for what he was doing to her. She had worked beside him, her face pale and her hands shaking, but she had been determined to see it through, even when grown men had threatened that they'd lose their dinners if they had to help.

Tom had watched her sit by Frank's side like a mother hen, sharing her strength until he could find his own again.

And the way she was standing her ground with the Watersweet hellions—Tom had to hand it to her on that one. Everyone knew that took grit and determination.

He moved back to his desk and sat down, trying to get his thoughts off the young woman who had come unexpectedly into his life a little over six weeks ago. Staring blankly at the mound of papers before him, he admitted to himself that she was falling in love with him.

The concession left a bitter taste in his mouth. Under other circumstances, Tom knew that he would welcome her attentions, now that he knew her.

She was so beautiful that he was left aching with raw need every time he looked at her. The cloud of dark hair, the arched brows, the long black lashes, the sensuous mouth, the ivory skin—she was a woman designed for a man's pleasure. And yet Gideon Wakefield possessed more than superficial beauty. She had an inner strength he found compelling.

Her sunny outlook, her ability to accept whatever came her way without complaint, her kindness to offer a helping hand to anyone who needed it—those were the qualities he was discovering in her. He should have known that she would be a special kind of woman, especially if she had Rutherford Wakefield's blood running in her veins.

Tom tried to recall what Rutherford had said about his young granddaughter living in Philadelphia, but he could remember nothing. Though Rutherford had been a good, kind-hearted man, he had been reserved, not one to share his personal life with others.

What would Gideon think now of Tom's dream to replant the trees? Somehow, Tom knew that she was seeing what man was doing to the land, and he'd bet that she shared his concern about the future.

Tom was beginning to dread the day that Gideon regained her memory. What would she think of him then?

Now she was openly falling in love with him. Her eventual discovery that he had suspected her identity but done nothing to confirm it would surely alienate her. Tom had tried to discourage her attention at first, but he couldn't deny that he recognized love shining brightly through her eyes when she looked at him. And he couldn't deny that it gave him a certain sense of pride to see it there.

Rubbing his hand over the back of his neck wearily, Tom tried to concentrate on his work, but his mind kept drifting to the dark-eyed temptress.

She had a way of popping into his office on her way home from school. At first it had annoyed him, but as time wore on Tom found himself looking forward to seeing her.

Her impromptu visits were usually short and served no practical purpose. He usually ended up walking her back to the bunkhouse as they talked about the day's events. But he had carefully avoided touching her again.

The kiss they'd shared the night of the sleigh ride had left him restless and wanting liberties that he knew he had no right to take. Her small body had felt good pressed against his— too good. Sleep had been long in coming that night as he'd lain in the dark and thought about how she would feel lying naked in his arms . . . in his bed . . . as his woman. What would her hair feel like if he could loosen the pins and bury his hands in the shiny, sweet-smelling mass? He dreamed of this, yet at the same time he realized that Gideon was in love with another man—now forgotten, but surely when her memory returned . . . ?

It was a mess, one hell of a mess, and he could see no way to correct it. Once she regained her memory, she would leave Watersweet and return to Philadelphia to marry Talbot Wellington-Kent.

Tom knew he didn't want that to happen—at least, not yet—so he would go on ignoring his conscience. If he told her that he suspected she was Gideon Wakefield, she would leave immediately, despising him for his part in the charade.

If he waited until her memory returned, she would leave, despising him even more for setting her up the way he had. . . . He was clearly caught in a trap of his own making.

"Do you mind?"

Tom glanced up blankly. Andre was looking at him as if he expected an answer. "Do I what?"

"Do you mind if I ask her to go?"

"Who?"

"Fedelia—where's your mind, Lannigan?"

Snapping back to the present, Tom pitched the work sheet on the desk irritably. "On my work, where yours should be."

"My, my," Andre said with a curious look. "We're a little touchy, aren't we?"

Tom, realizing that his thoughts of Gideon Wakefield had put him in a defensive mood, relented, "Sorry. What was it you asked?"

"I asked if you thought it would be improper for me to ask Miss Yardley to go for a walk with me Sunday afternoon."

"Yes, it would be improper." Tom got up to get another cup of coffee.

Andre twirled his pencil up between his fingers thoughtfully, ignoring Tom's puzzling attitude. The man claimed to have no interest in the new schoolmarm, but his actions of late would indicate otherwise. "Why?"

"Why? Because her contract states that she isn't to socialize with men."

"My friend, are you serious? She has the run of the town, and you know it. Besides, I do not believe that you have been overly concerned about her following the rules. I seem to recall the Christmas sleigh ride and the many times you've walked her home lately."

"I haven't walked her home," Tom dismissed curtly. "We just happened to be going in the same direction at the same time."

"*Ah, oui.* Every afternoon at five you just happen to be going to the bunkhouse—not that you live there, or have any particular business in that direction—but *every* afternoon . . . around five?"

Tom met his gaze stringently. "So what?"

Andre shrugged. "Nothing. It just seems strange."

Tom returned to his desk, and the two men worked in silence for a moment.

"Are you telling me to stay away from Miss Yardley?" Andre inquired at last.

"No."

"Then what are you saying?"

"I'm saying it isn't any of my business what she does. If you want to ask her to go for a walk with you, do it and stop bothering me about it."

"I think you are saying you're interested in her and for me to back off. Isn't that it?" Andre asked.

"If that's what I was trying to say, I would say it."

"Are you sure?"

Tom glanced up. "Montague, how would you like to be head chickadee from now on?"

Andre grinned back at him. "Now the man threatens to have me shoveling horse droppings off the roads. Could this not possibly lead me to conclude that our lovely Miss Yardley has done what no other woman has been able to accomplish in thirty some-odd years? Has the new schoolmarm captured big Tom Lannigan's heart?"

Before Tom could dispel the foolish notion, the door opened, and a rosy-cheeked Gideon walked in. The wind had stung her face a bright red, and snow lay heavily on the collar of her mantle.

"Does it ever stop snowing around here?" she asked as she reached to brush the snow from the new hat she'd made. After making sure that her creation was intact, she proceeded to blow feeling back into her numb fingers.

Tom went back to his work as Andre got to his feet. "Hello, *ma chérie*! Let me get you a cup of coffee to ward off the chill."

"No, thank you, Andre. I don't think I care for one." Gideon glanced at Tom hopefully, but he refused to look her way. Recognizing that he was in another one of his aloof moods, Gideon ambled over to his desk and positioned herself on the corner. Laying her hand over his, she greeted him softly, "Hello."

Reaching out to prevent a bundle of papers from spilling to the floor, Tom ignored her.

"Are you busy?"

"Yes."

She sighed as she began to swing her feet absently. Tom frowned sourly at the disruption. He noticed the god-awful hat she was wearing and his frown deepened. The frivolous thing reminded him that Gideon Wakefield had been all too eager to sell Wakefield Timber downriver so that she could open another stupid hat store!

Are those crow feathers drooping from the third tier of that monstrosity sitting on top of her head?

Tom's jaw dropped as he did a double take.

"You like it?" she asked sweetly. "I made it myself!" *He can't keep his eyes off my hat. I just knew he'd be impressed. Everyone has been staring. Why, I'm the envy of Watersweet.*

"What a day I've had," she began. "Tirza Reynolds, Scooter Wilson, King Davis, Quinn Morrison, and Juice Tetterson all had frightful diarrhea, and wouldn't you know it, Tirza stuck her tongue to the frozen well handle, and then King Davis nailed the front door shut from the outside."

Andre whistled sympathetically under his breath as Tom glanced up again.

Gideon nodded succinctly. "It was horrid."

Both Tom and Andre didn't even want to imagine it.

"But time for school to be dismissed finally rolled around. King knew he couldn't leave us nailed in the schoolhouse forever, so a little before four he finally removed the nails. Tirza had managed to get her tongue unstuck from the pump handle sometime during the afternoon and had gone home early, bawling. I must stop by later and explain to her mother what happened."

Gideon paused, taking a deep breath. "So, needless to say, I'm glad to see this day end." She glanced at Tom and smiled. "I thought if you had business near the bunkhouse, we could walk there together."

Andre shot Tom a knowing grin.

Tom ignored him. "I'll be tied up here at least another hour."

"Oh," Gideon's mouth formed a mock pout. "You work too hard. Can't you finish whatever it is in the morning? I have something very important I would like to talk to you about."

"No."

"Yes, he can."

Gideon and Tom glanced at Andre, who by

now was walking over to Tom's desk, grinning. "Whatever it is, Tom, I will finish it for you. I have not a thing to do but polish up on my chickadee skills." Andre's grin widened.

Tom shot him a warning look. "No, thanks."

"No, I'll take care of whatever it is," Andre urged. "You heard Miss Yardley. You work too hard, and she has something very important that she wants to discuss with you."

Gideon smiled at Tom persuasively. "Come on, grump."

Andre reached for Tom's jacket and shoved it into his hands over his protests. "Have a nice time, boss."

Gideon was bubbling happily as they stepped outside the office. A heavy, wet snow was falling from a gray, overcast sky. It would be dark soon.

"Let's go ice skating!" she burst out recklessly.

Tom's footsteps paused, and he looked at her as if she had lost her mind. "Ice skating!"

"Yes! We can both use the distraction." Grabbing his hand, she pulled him along the planked sidewalk. "I saw some skates at Menson's store, and I just couldn't resist buying us each a pair."

"You could afford skates *and* a new hat this month?"

"Well," she sent him a sly smile, "Mr. Menson put your pair on your bill. He knows your size and everything."

"I'm sure he does," he said wryly.

"And my hat is a real bargain since I made it myself, you know."

He looked at the hat again and frowned.

Her cheery voice continued, "I saw this perfectly lovely pond as I was walking to your office—"

"Suppose I don't know how to skate?"

"I'll teach you."

"Suppose I don't want to learn?"

"I suppose that would be too bad." She grinned up at him impishly.

"This beats all I've ever seen." He was still grumbling as she took his hand and dragged him through the woods and down the long, snowy path leading to the pond. "I have work to do. What will my men think if they see me sashaying around with you, ice skating, of all the crazy things? And why in the hell did you charge the skates to me? If I had wanted a pair of skates I would have bought—"

"Stop being so cranky," she called over her shoulder merrily. "You don't fool me. You're dying to go skating."

"I am not going skating."

By now they had reached the pond, and Gideon sat down to put her skates on. "You'll have fun."

"I can think of a hundred better ways to have fun than getting out there on that ice and breaking my blasted leg."

Gideon sprang to her feet and reached over

to tickle him under the chin. "You won't break your blasted leg." She dropped his skates beside him. "I promise."

Shrugging her hand aside, Tom sat down and watched as she skated out onto the pond. She was an excellent skater, skimming gracefully across the ice.

"Come on! It's wonderful out here!"

Tom shook his head obstinately and reached inside his pocket for a smoke. "What was it you wanted to talk to me about?"

"I want you to build a new schoolhouse!" She giggled at the look of astonishment that appeared on his face. She spun in a tight circle, forming a perfect O. She must have been an accomplished skater in her past life, she thought happily.

"The hell I will."

"What?"

"I said no."

"Why not?"

"Why should I? You have a perfectly good schoolhouse now."

"I have a perfectly insufferable schoolhouse! Why, even the rats don't spend over a few minutes a day there! I've decided that's why the children are so unruly. They don't even have a window to look out, just four drab walls and a roof that's about to fall down on their heads."

"They're not there to look at the scenery. They're there to learn."

"But they don't want to learn, and I think it's because of the terrible surroundings they're forced to endure." Gideon skated passed him, wrinkling her nose as she flew by.

"You're going to bust your butt."

"Fanny! Mr. Lannigan. The other is much too crude!" She whirled and dipped and made faces at him, until he was forced to turn away in an effort to conceal an amused grin forming at the corners of his mouth.

"Come on, coward. Put your skates on, and we'll settle this thing. If I can knock you off your feet, you must agree to build me a new schoolroom—nothing elaborate, just four walls and lots of nice, big, airy windows. On the other hand, if you, by some miraculous stroke of luck, manage to make me lose my balance, then we'll forget the whole thing."

"Ha. You're going to knock me off my feet, while I just make you lose your balance?"

She whizzed by, her skates sending a shower of ice flying at him. "Are you afraid?"

"Suppose I really don't skate? What sort of match would it be?"

"I don't skate either—or at least not very well." She spun around in another tight circle, jumped and landed on one foot and spun like a top. When she stopped, she paused and grinned. "How about it?"

"Forget it. I haven't got the time or the extra men to build you a schoolhouse. The one you've got is good enough."

189

Her grin turned even more impish. "Come out here and tell me that."

"If I come out there, you'll be sorry."

"Ha."

Tom began untying the strings of his boots. "All right, but remember you're the one who asked for this."

She skated past him again, sticking her tongue out this time. Back and forth she skimmed across the ice, waiting while he put on his skates. The snow was falling so hard that visibility was reduced to a mere few feet.

"Tell me when you're ready! I'll come and help you out onto the ice," she called.

"That'll be the day." Tom stood up, and his legs bowed comically as he wobbled on the ice.

Gideon began laughing, the clear, sweet notes filling the crisp air.

"Laugh, you fool. We'll see who's laughing in a minute."

"I told you I would help you." Gideon glided over and latched onto his arm. The would-be helpful gesture sent them both reeling precariously, threatening to spill them both.

"Let go of my arm!"

"Just hush up and lean on me!"

Tom grudgingly put his arm around her waist, and they steadied each other.

"Are you ready?"

"Does it look like I'm ready?"

They made their way cautiously out and took a few, hesitant glides.

"Now, see?" Gideon looked at him and grinned. "It isn't all that hard."

"Damn foolish thing to do. If I break my neck—"

"I'll take full responsibility," she said soothingly as she set their feet moving faster. "Besides, I thought it was your leg you were worried about."

"Wait a minute—hold on—not so damn fast!" Their strides gradually became smoother as they moved slowly around the perimeter of the pond.

"Isn't this nice?"

"It's just wonderful. When do we get the matter of this new schoolhouse settled?"

"Anytime you think you're ready."

"All right. Let me get the rules straight. You knock me off my feet, I build you a new schoolhouse—"

"The children and me a new schoolhouse," she corrected.

"I knock you off balance and we forget I ever took part in this idiotic contest?"

"Correct—but you can't knock me off balance because of your clumsiness. It has to be fair and square."

"We'll see who's clumsy—" Tom's skates suddenly locked with hers and they both went down in a wildly flailing entanglement of arms and legs.

He swore, managing to struggle to his feet first. Gideon was laughing too hard to be any help.

He pulled her up by her arms, and they started out again, taking a second hard spill that sent Gideon skidding across the pond on her bottom. The fall knocked the pins out of her hair, freeing the lustrous mass to tumble loosely down her back.

"Just look what you've done to my hair, Tom Lannigan!" She dissolved in a fit of giggles again as she fell to her side and watched him trying to get up.

He made such a funny sight, all six foot three, two hundred twenty-five pounds of pure muscle sprawled helplessly on the ice.

She finally struggled to her feet and skated over to peer down at him with an air of self-righteous superiority. "Want to concede right now?"

"Concede to you?" He bounded lithely to his feet. "Fun's over, lady."

She skated off, and he came after her. Their feet flew around the pond, the blades of their skates cutting deeply into the frozen pond. The moment he'd begin to gain on her, she'd dart around him, laughing gaily.

"I want pretty pink curtains at the new windows," she taunted, "tied back with lovely satin bows!" She squealed and darted off again as he came flying toward her.

It suddenly occurred to her that he was skating as well or better than she. Skidding to a halt, her hands came to her hips as she watched him race around the pond, skating backwards, sideways, turning, flipping, jumping, *spinning!*

"Tom Lannigan! You lied to me!"

Tom skated by her, deliberately covering the hem of her dress with a shower of ice from his skates. "I did not."

"You said you couldn't skate!"

"I said *suppose* I can't skate. I didn't say that I *couldn't* skate. I was skating," he winked at her, sending her pulse racing erratically, "when you were only a twinkle in your daddy's eye."

He skated to the end of the pond, and flipped around. Gideon's heart sank when she saw the glint of combat filling his eyes now. "Shall we get on with the wager, my dear?"

Squealing, Gideon turned and fled toward the bank, realizing that she was no match for Tom Lannigan, on or off the ice.

Straight as an arrow, Tom came across the ice. With a tremendous lunge, he managed to catch the hem of her skirt just as she was scampering off the pond.

As they tumbled roughly to the ground, Tom's arm came around her waist, cushioning her fall against the broad expanse of his chest.

Gideon broke out laughing as Tom rolled on top of her, pinning her firmly in the snow with his massive bulk. "Help! Someone help me!"

"It won't do you any good to scream for help. There isn't anyone around for miles. Now then," he said smugly, gazing into her eyes, "I believe I have just knocked you off balance."

"You cad! You're crushing me!"

Tom grinned, and two dimples appeared in his cheeks. "And you like it."

"I do not!"

"You do too. I see it in your eyes."

Gideon struggled to free herself as Tom grabbed her arms and pulled them above her head. "Oh no you don't. You asked for this."

"Tom, please." She burst into laughter again.

Their laughter began to recede as their gazes slowly met. Snowflakes lit gently on Gideon's dark lashes and stayed there. Tom's eyes grew lazy as he reached up to trace his finger softly over the delicate line of her cheek.

Gideon lay very still, afraid to break the magical moment as he looked at her through half-closed lids. "I don't want you stirring up trouble over this schoolhouse nonsense," he warned in a voice that had grown strangely husky. Gideon could feel his need pressed tightly against her, firm and pulsing now.

"Ummm, maybe."

He shook her gently. "I want your promise."

"I don't think it was a fair contest. How was I to know you'd take to the ice like a penguin?"

His nearness intoxicated her. The warmth of his breath on her face caused a delicious, warm feeling to stir from somewhere deep within her, and she wanted the moment to last forever.

"Promise me you won't get people stirred up about this. I have enough trouble without taking on more," he pleaded.

"Oh, poor baby," she mocked.

His mouth moved closer to hers. "Promise me."

"Only if you kiss me," she bargained.

His eyes openly caressed her now. "No."

She smiled as her fingers slid sensuously over his shoulders, then trailed on down his neck. She loved to touch him. She watched as his expression changed from mildly amused to one of growing desire. "Yes," she said seductively.

A knowing light passed between them as he gazed deeply into her eyes. "A woman shouldn't be asking a man to kiss her."

She smiled, and her love shone so brightly it caused a renewed pang of guilt to wash over him. "This woman has no pride when it comes to you, Tom Lannigan."

He moved against her in an attempt to warn her that this was not a game they were playing. She was a very desirable woman at his mercy, and he was a man, a hungry man. "You do this to me, and you have no shame," he murmured. "What if I took you right here, right now? Would your pride then be so misplaced?"

"I know it would be sinful, but in my heart I know that it is something I would welcome." Her hands gently cupped his face. "If you're trying to scare me, you might as well stop. It's time you knew, Tom Lannigan." Gideon smiled, and Tom discovered that he was lost. "There isn't anything you could do to me that I wouldn't be in full agreement with."

"Look . . . I don't want you to say that—"

"Why not? It's true. If you want to ravish me—"

Tom stopped her from baring her soul further by thrusting his hands in her hair. It smelled of sunshine and wildflowers, and the fragrance drove him wild as he breathed deeply of it and murmured, "I'm sorely tempted, lady."

She smiled up at him as his mouth slowly lowered to meet hers.

Gideon gave herself freely to his kiss, her body singing with strange new emotions he brought alive in her. She could feel the powerful evidence of his urgent need, and she knew that he wanted her as hungrily as he could want any woman, and the knowledge made her giddy with relief. Soon he would love her as wildly as she loved him, and her life would be complete. She would gladly spend her life with this man, mending his clothes, cooking his meals, soothing his hurts, bearing his children, loving him fiercely until one or the other of them drew a last breath.

When their mouths finally parted, his tongue exquisitely caught at the snowflakes that fell on the soft fullness of her lips.

Murmuring with pleasure, Gideon felt her insides growing weak as his tongue touched the corners of her mouth, her teeth, then his mouth moved on to kiss the pulsing hollow of her throat. "Go home, little one," he whispered as he began to shower urgent kisses around her lips and along her jawline. "Go home."

Gideon wasn't sure she had heard right. She laughed softly, trying to return his almost frantic kisses. "Go home?"

"Yes," he murmured. "Now—tomorrow. You don't belong here . . . go back to Philadelphia and forget you ever heard of Watersweet."

"No . . . no, I have nothing to go back for—" Gideon felt bereft as he suddenly pushed her aside and sat up.

"Go back to Philadelphia and try to put your life back together," he urged again softly. "There's nothing here for you."

"No."

"Yes."

"But . . . I don't want to go back to Philadelphia. I want to stay here," her hand moved to touch the sleeve of his coat, "with you."

Tom shoved himself to his feet, refusing to meet her imploring gaze. "You can't stay here with me."

She shook her head, stunned by his abrupt change in mood. "Why . . . what have I done—"

"Nothing . . . just take my advice and leave." Tom could feel panic closing in on him. The events of the past few minutes had unnerved him. What had he been thinking of? Rolling around on the ground with a woman who was engaged to be married, wishing like hell he could bed her! He had to put a stop to this madness. "Look, let's get out of here. I've wasted too much time as it is," he said curtly.

The unexpected, sharp rebuke caused tears to well in Gideon's eyes, but she quickly turned her head to hide them. "All right," she murmured brokenly.

They removed their skates in strained silence. The memory of his kisses still sang in Gideon's mind, tormenting her. She couldn't imagine what she had done to upset him. She had thought she was finally reaching him, but now he seemed farther from her than ever.

"Are you ready?"

She looked at him as the snow fell silently around them, her eyes brimming with anguish. "Yes."

Refusing to meet her tortured gaze, Tom said brusquely, "Let's go. We're losing light."

"I'm right beside you."

And as far as Gideon was concerned, that's where she would always be, no matter what hateful things he said to discourage her.

11

"**A**nd in conclusion, ladies, I think the only sensible thing to do is to force the men's hand on this matter."

Gideon had dismissed class early Friday afternoon, hoping the mothers of the Watersweet hellions would participate in this very important meeting. She was thrilled to see the response was one hundred percent.

"And how are we supposed to do that?" Gert Tetterson challenged. "I've never been able to get my Tally to wipe his feet before he comes through the front door! How am I supposed to get him to help build a new schoolhouse?"

The discussion had gone on for over an hour. Watersweet was in desperate need of a new teaching facility, and the men had steadfastly refused to build it.

Against Tom's warning not to stir up trouble, Gideon now felt compelled to take matters into her own hands. After all, Tom Lannigan wasn't the one who had to spend ten hours a day in this miserable excuse for a schoolroom. And he hadn't been concerned about her feelings that day at the pond. And he hadn't been concerned enough to even show his face lately. She was getting desperate.

Various murmurs of agreement were heard as Gideon tried to restore order. She knew that what she was proposing was unorthodox, but she knew the ladies of Watersweet were more than capable of carrying it through. "Ladies, please, there are numerous ways of persuading the men to see our viewpoint without bruising their egos."

"Oh, yeah?" Berniece blustered. "Well, how would you know, Miss Yardley? You're not even married!"

Laughter broke out again, and Gideon smiled. "Which makes me all the more dangerous, Berniece. Now, shall we get down to business?"

"What do you suggest we do, teacher?" Selma Miller was more than ready to get on with it. She still had supper to fix, wood to chop, and the wash to gather before her Sherman came home.

"Well, for starters we'll need a good, strong name for our society," Gideon proposed.

The women exchanged puzzled looks. Half of them had never heard of a "society."

"What's a 'soo-ciety'?" Gert asked.

"I guess you could say a society is a group of

interested citizens working together for a common goal," Gideon explained.

The women stared back at her vacantly.

"In our case it means the women of Watersweet are about to take it upon themselves to get that new schoolhouse," Gideon simplified.

Gert looked flabbergasted. "Never heard of a woman doing such a thing."

"It doesn't mean that we can't. I know we, as women, simply take for granted man's self-imposed authority over the weaker sex, but I say it's time we formed a union and put a stop to this nonsense!"

Beulah Morrison sprang from her seat. "I second that!"

"Sit down and shut up, Beulah!" Berniece seized the floor. "I just don't know what we're going to do about all these Philadelphia high-falutin' ideas you've been having, Miss Yardley. You know good and well the man is the head of the household."

"Of course he is, but should that mean that a woman is of no value to her husband beyond having his babies, cleaning his house, cooking his meals—"

"Chopping his wood, mending his socks, emptying his spittoons," Selma chimed in, growing to the idea of women having a little say in things.

Gideon could see she had them thinking now. "All we're asking is that the seed of their loins, their children, have a decent place to learn. I promise you, ladies, if we'll stick together in this matter, we'll accomplish our goal. And I promise each of you will earn your husband's grudging respect in the process."

The women began murmuring to each other worriedly. It sounded mighty risky to them.

"But why us? There are only sixteen married women in camp. Sixteen women can't fight two hundred men!"

"I've already thought about that." Gideon began to pace in front of her desk. "Obviously, those of you who are married will wield the most power. Maybe a nice, tasty apple pie will appear on the dinner table unexpectedly, an extra brush of your hand on his now and then, maybe a smile when he's least expecting it, maybe an extra love pat just before he drops off to sleep. Of course, we'll try to settle this with as much decorum as possible—"

"What's that?"

"Decorum? As much grace and dignity as possible. Remember ladies, subtlety is the name of the game."

"And just what will *you* be doing while we're baking all these apple pies, Miss Yardley?" Beulah inquired.

"I can assure you I will be doing my share. And, if subtlety doesn't work, then we'll just sink lower and use our feminine wiles."

"Well, guess it don't matter none. I don't

have the foggiest idea what subtlety means anyway," Beulah conceded.

Gideon wasn't sure how she knew all these fine words, but they seemed to keep popping out. "To be subtle means to be delicate, elusive, you know. You have to learn to work your man. In the meantime, I will be conducting a campaign of my own with the men in the bunkhouse. I won't have the obvious advantages you have, but I should be able to drop a few hints here and there and hopefully win over Shot Harrison, Jim Carten, and Herb Jenson. Once I have those three ringleaders on my side, the others won't be far behind."

"What about Tom Lannigan?" Berniece eyed Gideon knowingly. "He's gonna have one fit when it dawns on him what you're up to."

"You leave Tom Lannigan to me." *Please,* she added silently. He was her man, but darned if she could get him to realize it. "Now then," Gideon strolled down the row of desks thoughtfully. "We will need a name for our society. It will need to sound strong, purposeful, and be credible enough to make the men take us seriously."

Silence fell over the room as the women began to rack their brains.

"How about Women Hoping for a New Schoolhouse," Beulah suggested. The women thought for a moment, then several shook their heads.

"Sherman would laugh me out of the house," Selma declared.

They all went back to thinking.

"How about The Women's Society for Forming Future Citizens of Watersweet?"

Faces began to pucker and heads began to shake before Gert could even finish. She shrugged. "Sorry . . . I ain't never belonged to one of these women's 'soocieties' before."

"What about Builders of Our Children's Future?" someone suggested.

The women looked at each other and nodded. That didn't sound bad. It was strong, purposeful, and the men would surely have to take a name like Builders of Our Children's Future seriously.

From the back of the room a voice said softly, "Ladies, why should we beat around the bush? Why don't we just call it what it really is? Women Against Senseless, Pigheaded Shantyboys."

Laughter broke out as the women turned to see who would have the nerve to call it what it really was.

Gideon's amusement faded when she saw Echo standing in the doorway. She had been hoping that Echo would come today, yet she wondered how Waite Burne would react to Echo's taking part in such open rebellion. But she could hardly hurt Echo's feeling in front of the other women.

"Women Against Senseless, Pigheaded

Shantyboys? How about it, ladies?" Gideon prompted.

The women in the room applauded their enthusiastic, unanimous approval as Gideon walked to the back of the room to take Echo's hand and squeeze it encouragingly. "It's perfect, Echo."

Echo didn't crack a smile. "Thank you, ma'am. I think so."

Gideon turned back to face the women. "I think we shall just use the initials WASPS when we refer to our society." She winked mischievously. "It shouldn't take the men long to figure out what that means."

The meeting broke up, and Echo waited while Gideon filled the lamp, made the pens for the following day, then banked the stove.

The angry fingers of a cold north wind snatched at their cloaks as they stepped outside. The blustery day promised a blizzard again by dark.

"What do you suppose Mr. Lannigan will say once he finds you've got all the womenfolk stirred up like an old hornet's nest?" Echo teased.

Gideon sighed as she paused to wrap the woolen scarf tighter around her neck. "I don't know. I'd be happy if he'd say anything at all to me." It had been over a week since they had gone skating on the pond together. Tom had steered clear of her since then. She had even stopped going by his office in the afternoon, for he was never there anymore. It seemed hopeless that he would ever warm to her.

"I think you're sweet on him," Echo bantered lightly.

Gideon's mouth curved in a self-conscious smile. "Maybe."

"I think he's sweet on you too."

Gideon scoffed at that. "He is not."

"Oh yes he is. I've seen the way he looks at you."

"Name one time."

"At Menson's store the other day. When you were buying new buttons?"

"He didn't even know I was there."

"Yes, ma'am, he did. He stood over in the corner and pretended he was talking to Walt Mitchell, but he was watching you most all the time."

A smile did escape Gideon this time. "He did not."

"He did so."

They turned and headed for the nearest tote road. "Echo," Gideon decided it was a good time to broach the subject of Waite Burne, "there's something I'd like to talk to you about."

"Yes, ma'am."

"It's rather personal. . . . I hope you won't think I'm being forward."

"I won't think that."

"Well, I know I have no right—"

"Please, ma'am." Echo paused and turned

to face Gideon. "Just say what you need to say. You won't be buttin' in where you're not wanted, and if you do, I'll tell you so."

Gideon smiled gratefully. This was not going to be easy. "Thank you, Echo."

They began walking again. "I'm concerned about your taking part in our efforts to force the men to build a new schoolhouse."

Echo's face clouded. "You don't want me to be in your 'soo-ciety'?"

"I want you to be in it . . . I'm just concerned, that's all."

Echo breathed a sigh of relief. "No need, ma'am."

For a brief moment Gideon toyed with the idea of coming right out and confronting Echo about her husband's drinking. She knew that the other women were in no danger of causing any serious family friction as a result of their harmless crusade for a new school, but she was worried that if Echo's taking a stand in the dispute upset her husband, it might trigger another one of his drinking sprees.

"I wouldn't want your participation in our society to cause you difficulties at home, Echo." Gideon paused, looking straight into Echo's eyes.

Echo met her gaze directly. "You don't think the other women aren't going to have 'difficulties at home' from their participation?"

"I know they will," Gideon hedged, "but . . ."

Echo turned and began walking again, acting as if she hadn't heard the implication in Gideon's tone. "I'm beholden to you for letting me be in your 'soo-ciety,' ma'am. It sure does mean a lot to me."

"Don't change the subject."

Gideon knew she was overstepping her bounds, but she couldn't ignore a potential problem, not where her friend was concerned. Even though Echo had avoided the subject of her husband's drinking and had never asked for help of any kind, Gideon couldn't in good conscience overlook her situation.

"Echo, I think we're both avoiding the issue. You know that I care about you. I just don't want to cause trouble for you, that's all."

"You don't understand, ma'am."

"No, I don't. Help me understand, Echo."

"Waite is my husband till death do us part," Echo said simply.

"I'm aware of your loyalty to your husband —but should he ever mistreat you, you must come to me. My room is tiny, but we'll make do—"

"No, ma'am. I can't do that." Echo stopped her.

"Why not?"

"Because I belong with my husband and because I don't want to leave him." Echo paused again and turned to look at Gideon. "Don't be worryin' about me, ma'am, really."

"He doesn't hurt you, does he? I mean when he's drinking . . ." Concern radiated from Gideon's eyes. She couldn't bear the thought of someone harming this lovely creature. "Because if he ever does, you must let me help you. You're not alone. I will help you . . . Tom will help you—"

"He has never hurt me, ma'am." Echo looked embarrassed, and she seemed to be struggling to find the right words. "Waite's a good man. He drinks a little too much sometimes. He's not mean or anything like that . . . he just likes to relax with his friends and have fun once in a while." Her eyes met Gideon's, then darted away. "You'll see, I'll be just fine. Just please let me be in your 'soo-ciety'."

Gideon sighed, wrapping her arm protectively around the girl's shoulder. How could she help someone who insisted she didn't want to be helped?

"All right, Echo. You can be in our society . . . but you must promise to let me know if Waite gives you any trouble over this."

Echo's face broke out in a happy smile. "Oh, thank you, ma'am! Thank you muchly!"

Gideon wasn't convinced she'd done the right thing. But the smile on Echo's face was worth taking the risk.

* * *

"Looks to me like you're progressing well, little lady." Doc Medifer laid his stethoscope aside and smiled at Gideon paternally. "Any twinges of memory coming back?"

Gideon shook her head. "None." Another week had passed without the slightest sign of her memory returning.

"Well, nothing to be worried about. I'm sure it will return one of these days when you least suspect it."

"Has there ever been a case where it didn't return?" she asked.

"Yes, many such cases . . . and it's a possibility you might want to consider, but it's too soon to tell."

Gideon rose and put on her hat. "I'm not worried."

"You seem to be adjusting well." He flashed her an admiring grin. "I've heard you have the women all fired up to build a new schoolhouse."

Gideon fished inside her purse for a coin to pay her bill. "I certainly have. The one we have is totally inadequate."

Doc chuckled as he waved her coin aside. The little woman had spunk, real spunk. "Put that in your coffer, imp, and don't give up. I hear the women of this town are about to bring the men to their knees."

Gideon grinned. "We're trying our best."

"Well, keep it up. It wouldn't hurt the men

around here to be brought down a notch or two."

Or three, Gideon thought wistfully as she caught sight of Tom Lannigan striding past the window.

"Well, we're close, ladies, very close, but we're not home yet. Next, we move to feminine wiles."

Several pairs of eyes rolled with disbelief as Gideon faced her fellow WASPS the next week.

Feminine wiles! By now the women knew the meaning of the word, they just weren't so sure they had any.

A frail-looking woman rose in the back of the room. Her hands were red and work worn, her dress shabby, and her hair untidy, but she had an honest face. "Miss Yardley, let's talk sensible. I'm all for trying to get my man to help build a new schoolhouse, but we all know it just ain't gonna work. Women don't have any say in such things. Why, just last night my Sherman said for me to shut my mouth, we don't need no new schoolhouse, that the one we've got is plenty good enough for anybody. And he had just polished off three slices of fresh blueberry pie!"

"Well, the school isn't good enough, and we know it," Gideon argued. "If we want our children to learn and become bright, productive citizens, it's up to the community to provide the proper educational facilities. It isn't as if we're asking for the impossible! A large basic room with four or five windows is not an unreasonable demand."

Gideon could see several heads in the crowd nodding in agreement. She knew the ladies' home lives were not completely ideal of late, but they would be proud of their accomplishment once the goal of a new schoolhouse was realized.

"Well, what do we do now?" Freda Davis shouted above the din. "We've come this far, so we can't back down now!"

"No, we can't," Gideon agreed. "We're just going to have to tighten the screws. For starters, you will begin a work slowdown."

There was an audible gasp this time.

"Do you know what that means, ladies?"

They shook their heads fearfully.

"That means you refuse to cook! And if you're forced to cook, be sure that your meal won't be edible. You don't do the wash as often. You don't make the bed or sweep the floor as often. You sit in a chair, stare off into space, and cry a lot." Gideon's eyes narrowed. "This is serious business, ladies. Face it: The only way we're going to win is to outsmart the enemy!"

Berniece shook her head woefully. "Lannigan's going to string you up by your heels."

"I'll take care of Lannigan."

Horror was beginning to creep into the

women's faces as Gideon began to pace again. It always worried them when she started pacing. "Now, at first your men will bluster and blow, but once they get sick of their own cooking and grow weary of having to pick up after themselves, they'll come around to our way of thinking. And in the bedroom? I want you to give a whole new meaning to the word iceberg . . . except you, Echo. Maybe you might just slack off a bit." Gideon felt that there was no use in upsetting Waite any more than necessary. She still thought Echo should drop out of the controversy, but the young girl was so happy to be in a women's society she wouldn't hear of it.

"Ohhhhhhhh." Embarrassed titters filled the room. This Miss Yardley knew no bounds. *Sex* was not a subject to be openly discussed.

"Are you sure you know what you're askin'?" Selma Miller demanded. "You not being married and all . . . you sure this will work?"

"Absolutely. Living with a hundred and twenty-five men has provided me certain advantages. I hear the men talking at night when they think I'm studying."

She moved closer, lowering her voice to a whisper. "The marriage bed is their weakest link, and you're close, ladies, real close. According to my information, some of the men are already tired of haggling over the matter. They want the nice, serene home lives they were accustomed to, but of course there are always the diehards, who keep insisting that they hang on. Those men will never give up unless we make them. Now, I've given this considerable thought, and I'm positive you ladies are smart enough to use any means you have of bringing your men around to your way of thinking," Gideon straightened with a triumphant smile. "And, in order for me to do my part, I must now request a small concession from you. I have a plan—a very unconventional plan that is bound to turn a few heads, but you must bear with me. No matter what you see, or hear, you must go on as if nothing is wrong. I can assure you, no matter how unorthodox my actions may appear to be, I shall be conducting myself with the utmost decorum."

"Oh, Lordy, Lordy," Berniece muttered. "What's she gonna do now?"

"Remember, ladies. We are working for a common goal. As fellow WASPS we are committed to uphold each other in our struggle for equality!"

An enthusiastic cheer went up. She was right! They would bring those ungrateful men right down on their knees! They were close, real close to getting what they wanted. They could not weaken now!

Gideon faced her audience, her face set in a mask of grim determination. "We must stick together in our worthy but humble cause. In the end, we'll have our new schoolroom, or we're not fit to be called WASPS!"

A shout went up, nearly lifting the roof off the tiny schoolhouse.

Fedelia Yardley had stirred up the biggest stink Watersweet had ever seen. And it was bound to get worse.

Hoisting her valises higher, Gideon picked her way up the long stairway behind Menson's store the following night. The full moon illuminated the narrow planked landing where she set her bags down at her sides. Reaching to straighten her hat, she drew a deep, steadying breath.

Before she could lose her nerve, she folded her hand into a fist and rapped loudly on the door. She cocked her ear and strained to listen. Nothing.

For a few frantic seconds, she wondered if Tom might not be home. Fear raced through her. Perhaps he was working late, or maybe he had gone over to Shadow Pine to visit that Marcy woman.

No, she had to get a grip on herself. She was just feeling cowardly. Lannigan was home. He had to be. After all, it was nearly eleven o'clock. He was home all right. He just wasn't answering the door, the inconsiderate slug.

She rapped louder. This time she continued knocking until her knuckles stung.

She could hear a muffled "All right, all right.

Hold your horses!" followed by the sound of feet hitting the floor. Gideon winced as she heard a loud crash, then the door flew open, and a disheveled, disgruntled Tom Lannigan filled the doorway.

"What the—*you*? What's the meaning of this?"

"Sorry to disturb you, but there's been trouble at the bunkhouse."

He reeled for an instant, then rubbed the sleep from his eyes and glanced at the moon overhead. "Trouble?"

Gideon grabbed the leather handles and hefted her valises. "Let's take it inside, shall we, Mr. Lannigan?"

Disoriented, Tom backed up, but not quickly enough, as a corner of one of the hard-shelled valises struck him as she breezed past him.

"Owww, damnation!" He reached to grab his throbbing kneecap. "What are you doing?"

"Stop howling and light the lamp," she retorted as she dropped her bags and hurried to close the door. The icy walk from the bunkhouse had nearly frozen her blood, and all he could do was curse.

After more fumbling and muttering, Tom lit the lamp and turned to face her. "What are you doing roaming around in the middle of the night?"

"I'm sorry I woke you, but you've always indicated that if I needed anything I should come to you," Gideon announced calmly. As she removed her cloak and laid it on a chair, her gaze scanned the room, taking in the washstand, small table, two chairs, nightstand, chest of drawers, pine armoire, and the one narrow, rumpled bed.

She was aware that Tom was glancing anxiously toward the two ladder-back oak chairs and then to the floor, where he had hastily dropped his clothes an hour before.

"What's wrong at the bunkhouse?" he demanded as he padded barefoot across the room. "Where are my damn pants?" he muttered, bending over and pawing through the clothes.

Gideon interrupted her survey of his Spartan furnishings. "Well, they were just horrible," she said.

Something in her tone made him pause, and he turned to face her, gripping his pants by the waistband. "Who?"

"Your men."

"My men? What did they do?"

Gideon met his gaze, then took a thorough glance down his tall frame, clad in form-hugging red longjohns. *Impressive. He would do quite nicely as a husband,* she decided. "They were rude to me."

"Rude to you? What are you babbling about now?"

Gideon finally managed to tear her eyes away from the front of his longjohns. A lady shouldn't look, much less stare. But the sight of him took her breath away.

"Maybe you should put your pants on," she murmured.

Tom cleared his throat and stabbed his foot into his pants leg. Drawing his pants over his hips, he buttoned his fly. "Now, what in the hell is going on?"

Gideon removed her hat. Carefully, she brushed the skiff of snow from the rows of fabric before setting it on the table. "Well . . ." she began.

His annoyance grew as he watched her fuss with the limp feathers attached to the crown of that thing she called a hat. "Leave that blasted thing alone," he snapped. *Waking him up in the middle of the night to fuss with one of her silly hats!*

Lifting her gaze to him, she said coolly, "There's an emergency in the bunkhouse."

"Fire?" It was one of Tom's greatest fears. If fire broke out in the bunkhouse, the building could be a deathtrap.

"Not a fire, exactly." Her indignation returned as she thought of the way some of the men had accused her of deliberately causing all the misery in Watersweet. "For some reason the men are unhappy with me."

Of course their anger could have something to do with the way I walked all the way over to Shadow Pine and persuaded the women there to join the women of Watersweet in their quest for a new schoolhouse.

"Unhappy?" Folding his arms across his broad chest, he looked at her. "What have you done this time?"

"That's not fair! You haven't heard my side, and you're already taking up for them."

"Nobody has heard anything *but* your side for weeks now. So, just turn your little fanny around because whatever the trouble is, you're heading back to the bunkhouse. We can settle this in the morning."

"No!" She braced herself for his wrath. "I am not going back there."

"Oh yes you are." He reached for his flannel shirt.

Her chin shot up a notch higher, and a smugness touched the corners of her mouth. "Ed Holman wrote this on behalf of the others." She reached into her pocket and withdrew a paper and extended it to him. "He told me to give this to you."

Tom strode to the nightstand where unfolded the paper and held it to the lamp to read.

Mr. Lannigan,

Me and the boys has had all we can take.

We left Miss Yardley alone like you said. We behaved ourselves even after she said we could not smoke inside or let our cat in.

Now on the account of her the women in

Shadow Pine won't have nothing to do with us until we build a new schoolhouse.

Enough is enough.

If you try to move her back with us, we quit. And we mean it.

The Men of Wakefield Timber

Tom reread the letter, unable to believe his eyes.

"I can't imagine what I've done to upset them this way," she said sweetly.

Tom released a disgusted sigh. He knew his men. Once they banded together, they were as tight as ticks on a dog and as stubborn as a team of mules. "This is just great." He crumpled the letter and turned around. "Well, I have to hand it to you. In a few short weeks, you've managed to turn this entire camp upside down. I hope you're happy."

"No, what would make me happy, Mr. Lannigan, is to see a new schoolhouse. Now," she said, glancing about, "where will I find some clean linens?"

"Clean what?"

She sighed. "Fresh sheets, Mr. Lannigan, to make up my bed."

"You don't have a bed, Miss Yardley," he said, following the direction of her gaze. "That bed is mine. Besides, you don't really think I'm going to let you stay here."

"You're not?" She crossed her arms. "Then where am I going to stay? From what I understand, you're the only person in camp who has a residence to himself."

Tom edged forward, "Now, wait a minute. You're not—"

"I don't see that we have any other choice," she continued. "You've exhausted all the other possibilities, so until you agree to build a new schoolhouse complete with adjacent accommodations for the teacher, we will simply have to share quarters."

"You're not sharing my quarters," he vowed.

"That's entirely up to you, Mr. Lannigan. However, I *am* staying here. If you wish to sleep with your men in the bunkhouse, you may. Now, about those clean linens—"

"Damn! This isn't a hotel in Philadelphia. Those are the only 'linens' I have! Mrs. Menson does my laundry every two weeks."

"Whether it needs it or not," she muttered as she crossed the room, scooting around him. With a flick of her wrist, she gingerly flipped the top sheet up over the pillow and sat down on the edge of the bed.

His jaw dropped as he watched her begin to remove her shoes. "You're not serious—the women of this community will run you out on a rail!"

Gathering a wool blanket around her shoulders, she covered a tired yawn. "The women of this community and I have a complete understanding."

She turned down the lamp and stretched out on top of the bed. Leaning on one elbow, she smoothed a quilt over her skirt, then lay back on the nice, soft pillow. "Good night, Mr. Lannigan. Pleasant dreams."

12

Gideon spent a miserable night. She tossed and turned on the unfamiliar mattress. She was too hot, then too cold. She didn't see how anyone could sleep through such misery, but Tom had slept on the floor like one of his logs, rolled up in a blanket beside the stove.

Her stiff back muscles screamed for mercy when she rolled to a sitting position as the first light of dawn began to peek through the window.

It had been an hour since Tom had dressed and muttered something about going to his office. She was grateful that it was Saturday; she didn't know what she would have done if she'd had to teach all day.

She lit the lamp and rose to inspect her surroundings. The furnishings were minimal, but they were nicer than those in the bunkhouse. She added a few logs to the small stove, then after she'd dressed, she wandered aimlessly about the room.

She didn't mean to pry, but she found herself peeking inside the chest of drawers, hoping for space to store her things. Tom had clothes in each of the six drawers, but she figured if she consolidated his things, she could have two drawers for her own use.

Before she lost her nerve, she shifted his things to other drawers and placed the contents from one of her valises inside the two middle drawers. Relieved to have that done, she spotted the armoire, and paused thoughtfully. If she scooted his clothes over just a tiny bit she'd have a few hooks in the middle where she could hang her dresses.

That deed efficiently accomplished, she walked to the table where she'd left her hat. Frowning, she realized her creation needed a bit of refurbishing. The snow had matted some of the lace, and the feather looked a little droopy this morning. As she lifted the hat, she noticed how dusty the table was. Glancing around, it came to her attention that the whole room could use a good cleaning.

Noises were coming from the store downstairs, so she knew that the Mensons were probably preparing to open shop. Slipping on her cloak, she hurried outside and down the stairs.

Before she could change her mind, she rapped on the back door to the store. It took two knocks before Mrs. Menson finally opened the door to find the schoolteacher waiting.

"Miss Yardley—is something wrong?"

"No." Gideon smiled lamely. It wasn't going to be easy explaining to a fellow WASPS what she was about to do, but Grace would be the most understanding. "Why?"

"I'm surprised to see you this early in the mornin'!"

"Nothing's wrong, Mrs. Menson. I just needed a few things." Gideon stepped in and a blustery north wind followed her.

"Then come in, dear. We're nearly ready to open. What do you need?"

"I—I" Gideon faltered. Mrs. Menson was looking at her so strangely. Almost as if she knew something was up.

"Come over by the stove, dear, and have a cup of tea. You must be cold from your long walk."

"I can't stay. I just needed some cleaning supplies. You see, I . . ." Gideon's eyes scanned the store, grateful to find that it was deserted. She decided honesty was the only policy at this point. Everybody in town would know she was living with Tom Lannigan before the day was over. "Mrs. Menson, I'm about to embark upon my plan—you know, the unorthodox one I mentioned in our last meeting."

Mrs. Menson's eye skimmed her anxiously. "Yesssss."

Drawing a deep breath, Gideon selected a

mop handle and placed it on the counter. "I've moved in with Tom Lannigan."

Gideon was aware that there was still a possibility that Tom wouldn't let her remain with him. He was probably out right now trying to find other quarters for her. But he wouldn't be successful. The men had taken a stand. She knew they weren't so angry that they couldn't forgive her, but they would never allow Tom to bring her back to the bunkhouse, for the sake of their pride, if for no other reason.

"You've moved in with Tom?" Mrs. Menson repeated breathlessly.

Leaning forward, Gideon said quietly. "Remember, as a fellow WASPS you are to look the other way, and proceed with our plan as if nothing unusual is going on."

"Oh, my," Mrs. Menson said weakly.

"Besides, I really didn't have a choice. The men are angry because I went over to Shadow Pine yesterday and convinced those worldly women they cavort around with that as fellow females it's their duty to become involved in our fight for the new schoolhouse. Since most of them are more than tired of the men's superior attitudes, they agreed to help. Last night the men got wind of what I'd done, and they kicked me out of the bunkhouse. I had nowhere else to go, but to Tom. Everyone else is already overcrowded."

"But you'll be living with a man without benefit of marriage," Grace chastened.

"Grace, I've been living with a *hundred and twenty-five men* without benefit of marriage! Seems to me I'll be cutting my risk down significantly, having to deal with just one man instead of a hundred and twenty-five. Besides, the relationship will be strictly platonic."

"Pla . . . *what*?" Grace repeated blankly.

"Never mind—I won't really be living with Mr. Lannigan—at least not in the way you mean." Gideon blushed when she thought about sleeping in the same bed with big Tom Lannigan. Yet she would bet she could get used to it real quick.

Mrs. Menson still wasn't clearly convinced it was the best way to handle things. "I don't know . . . what will the others say?"

Gideon reached out to touch Mrs. Menson's arm. She was suddenly feeling very alone; she needed a friend, an ally, if she was to carry this off successfully. "Please trust me. If anyone begins to spread vicious gossip, you must remind them of our pact."

Grace eyed her thoughtfully. "You almost sound as if you planned this to happen."

Gideon smiled. "As I've said before, I can be dangerous at times."

Mrs. Menson smiled and reached out to squeeze her hand. "All right, dear. Though I'm not sure I could trust myself alone with a young, randy buck like Tom Lannigan. Are you certain you can handle him?"

Gideon tried to sound more confident than she felt. "I'd better be, or we're all in trouble."

"Grace, are you with someone?" Henry's voice called from the back room.

"No, dear—I mean yes, Henry. . . . Miss Yardley is here."

Gideon heard a disgruntled harumph, then the sound of the door to the storeroom slamming shut.

Leaning even closer, Gideon whispered, "This is war, Grace, and in war, anything goes. Now, I want a large pail, three bars of lye soap, a pair of sheets and pillow cases, and some lemon oil."

Grace glanced at the closed door to the storeroom, then back to Gideon. "Okay, but I hope you know what you're doing."

When the supplies had been gathered, Grace tallied up the bill.

Gideon waited, relieved to find Grace was going along with the plan.

"Oh, and Grace, could you spare some bedding? I want to make a pallet," she added.

"Oh," Mrs. Menson sighed with relief, "of course, a place for you to sleep."

"No."

Grace glanced up again.

"A place for Mr. Lannigan to sleep," Gideon corrected.

Chuckling, Grace ripped the sheet off the pad, and read the total out loud. "Six dollars and ten cents." Glancing up at Gideon, she grinned. "I'll just put that on Mr. Lannigan's bill."

Picking up the bundle, Gideon nodded judiciously. "Now you got it, Grace. Keep up the good work."

That afternoon Gideon surveyed her new quarters with a gleam of pride in her eye. The place fairly shined from top to bottom. She had mopped, scrubbed, and dusted every inch of Tom Lannigan's room.

She had rearranged the furniture to accommodate the pallet she'd made for him near the stove. The place still looked austere, and it afforded very little privacy, but it was clean.

What she needed was a partition of some sort. She didn't know where she'd get a folding screen, but perhaps some fabric could be strung across one corner of the room.

She could really use some material for a hat too. Well, she decided, perhaps it would be rather convenient to live over a store like Menson's.

"Let's see, now . . . five yards of cotton, a spool of white thread, and three cents worth of peppermints." Henry Menson usually dropped a couple of extra pieces of candy into the sack, but Gideon noticed that he didn't today. "Will that be all, Miss Yardley?"

"Yes, thank you, Mr. Menson." Gideon watched Henry wrap the material, thread, and peppermints in heavy brown paper and bind it tightly with string.

Handing the neatly wrapped bundle to Gideon, Henry's customary smile failed to materialize. His thin lips were set in a pinched line as he struggled to be polite. "Right pleasant day we're having."

"It is indeed." Gideon paid for her purchases and turned to leave.

An exceptionally pretty porcelain box that was sitting in the front window caught Gideon's eye, and she lingered to examine it. Her dalliance was merely a tactic to delay leaving. Tom was on the sidewalk outside the store talking to Ed Holman, and she was hoping that if she postponed her departure long enough, she could arrange to accidentally bump into him as she left the store.

She hadn't seen him since he'd dressed and left before dawn that morning.

Her day had been busy but tense. At every moment, she had expected Tom to burst into the room and drag her off to the train station. She had worried herself sick over what he might do next. She'd heard the townspeople buzzing, but no one had said a word directly to her about the events of last night.

The bell over the door sounded, and Gideon glanced up to see Echo coming into the store. Gideon tensed when she saw that Waite Burne accompanied the girl. She tried to put aside her bias as she smiled warmly at her friend.

Echo nodded briefly in Gideon's direction, then quickly averted her eyes as she hurried over to take a seat next to the potbellied stove.

Echo's meek response didn't surprise Gideon. She knew that when Waite was present, Echo preferred to keep to herself.

Waite spotted Gideon. Although he pretended to be interested in a three-bladed cattleman's knife in the front showcase, Gideon felt his eyes moving back to her periodically.

Placing the porcelain box back in the window, Gideon edged closer to the door. She could see Tom was still deep in conversation, and she knew if she left now he would only give her a perfunctory nod, if she was lucky. Moving to the display of calico and muslins, she listened as Sherman Miller wistfully eyed the barrel of apples, good-naturedly complaining to Henry about his wife Selma's cooking—or the lack of it lately.

"Better get you some of those apples, Sherman. They make a right tasty pie," Henry urged. Henry knew full well that Selma hadn't baked Sherman a pie in over a week and that she wouldn't until the matter of a new school was settled, but the little storekeeper enjoyed aggravating Sherman now that the WASPS had swarmed out of hibernation to declare open war on the men of Watersweet.

"Wouldn't do no good, Henry. Those apples would just sit in my kitchen and turn pithy,"

Sherman returned, aware the schoolteacher was hearing the exchange.

Selma ignored her husband's remark and picked up a bottle of Doctor Kilmer's Female Remedy to study the label.

"Yessiree bob, nothing better after a cold day of being out in the woods than to come home to the smell of hot apple pie bubbling in the oven," Henry agreed.

"Yes, a man has a right to come home to that," Sherman made a point of adding, "after he's worked hard for his wife all day."

Selma casually placed the bottle back on the shelf and moved on.

"I like a thick wedge of cheese on my apple pie, don't you, Sherman?" Henry asked. Henry's wife hadn't cooked a hot meal since all this hullabaloo over the schoolhouse had started, let alone an apple pie.

"I don't rightly know, Henry. It's been so long since I had a piece of apple pie I've plumb forgot what I'd put on it."

Gideon wished Henry would just drop the subject. She could see Sherman was practically salivating at the thought of the tasty, rich dessert, and the corners of Selma's mouth were becoming more pinched by the moment.

"Yessir, these women nowadays are something. Don't know their place. That's what it is," Henry decided.

"I agree with you there, Henry. Looks to me like they'd knowed when they're well off,"

Sherman marveled. "I say if a man's good enough to give them a roof over their head and a houseful of kids to run after, looks to me like they'd be grateful enough to make a simple apple pie for him every once in a while."

"Looks like it," Henry sympathized.

"Sherman, you and Henry done been going about this all wrong." A grin spread across Waite's features as he walked over to warm his backside by the stove. Judging from his appearance, Gideon guessed that he hadn't seen a bar of soap or a razor in weeks. "A real man keeps his woman in line. Now, take my little woman, she done been fixing me fine meals lately. Real fine."

Echo glanced up expectantly. "Waite, that ain't so—"

"Hush, darlin'."

Gideon winced as Waite's sharp tone brought the activity in the store to a sudden halt.

Echo's eyes darted pleadingly to Gideon. "But I ain't been—"

"No one asked your opinion." Waite's sharp look silenced his wife. An uneasy silence fell over the store as the shoppers continued to browse.

Gideon wanted to intercede for Echo, but she knew any interference on her part would only make the situation worse.

"A woman shouldn't dispute what her husband says. I think you owe me an apology, my dear."

"I'm sorry," Echo said softly after a moment's hesitation.

"Apology accepted, dear. Now I think this might be a good time for you to tell the little schoolmarm you ain't gonna be in her 'soo-ciety' anymore."

Embarrassment flooded Echo's face. "No, Waite—"

"You don't want to cause a scene now, do you, Echo darlin'?"

"No . . . but don't make me give up my 'soo-ciety,' Waite." Echo's voice trembled, and Gideon could see that she was close to tears. As she took a step forward, Gideon felt Sherman discreetly put a hand on her shoulder to stop her.

"No wife of mine is gonna consort with an unmarried woman living with a man," Waite said quietly. "Now, Echo, don't argue with me. Just you tell Miss Yardley you're not gonna be able to come to any more of her little after-school meetin's. You've got your man to take care of, and you don't have time to be running around rilin' up trouble."

Tears began to roll from the corners of Echo's eyes. "Waite. I'll . . . I'll start cookin' for you again, I promise . . . just don't make me give up—"

"Tell her what I just said." His tone was firm, and brooked no nonsense.

236

Sherman cast a warning toward Waite. "Now, Waite. I think you could settle this matter at another time and place. We've just been ribbin' the women—don't mean no harm, none of it. If they want to have their little society, ain't gonna hurt no one."

"Miller, I won't tell you how to handle your woman, and you won't tell me how to handle mine," Waite said evenly. "Echo?"

Echo's head dropped obediently, and she did as he said in a voice barely above a whisper, "I . . . I can't be in your 'soo-ciety' anymore, ma'am. I'm . . . real sorry."

The front door suddenly swung open, and Gideon went weak with relief when she saw Tom entering the store.

Waite smiled. "That's fine, sugarpie, just fine." Shooting Gideon a smug reminder that he was still the boss in his household, he sauntered back across the room as if the incident had never taken place. "Afternoon, Big Say."

Unaware of what had just taken place, Tom nodded and held the door as Echo fled past him like a shy doe, followed by a confident Waite Burne.

Henry cleared his throat nervously and went back to filling the Millers' order, seeking to lighten the tension that hung over the room like a pall. "As I was saying, Sherman, looks like it's gonna be a spell before any of us get any more pies."

Casting a worried glance at Selma, Sherman

answered. "Well, won't hurt me none to take off a few pounds, Henry."

Gideon felt like stamping her foot. Henry was back on the subject of those darn pies again!

But if Sherman still found the subject amusing, Selma didn't. She quietly moved to the flour barrel.

"Oh, Sherman."

Sherman glanced up. "Yes, darlin'?" He winked at Henry knowingly.

"Would you step over here, please?"

Sherman happily obliged. "What is it, love of my life?"

Selma smiled. "You want an apple pie, darlin'?"

"That would be nice, dear."

Selma dipped her fingers in the barrel, then calmly flipped flour on her husband's face. "Then bake it yourself, dumplin'."

Sherman was floored. He sputtered indignantly, his large hands coming up to wipe the flour away from his eyes, which were rimmed in white.

Recovering from her unwarranted assault, Sherman tensed and spoke in a low tone, "You shouldn't ought to have done that, Selma."

Selma calmly dipped her fingers in the barrel again, then flicked a wad of flour on the front of her husband's red flannel shirt. "Then dry up. Once you and those other baboons agree to build a new schoolhouse, you'll get your pie. Not until then."

Tom had turned to watch the exchange. Gideon could see he was more amused by the marital dispute than concerned. He hadn't expounded on the new schoolhouse issue except to state unequivocally that he wasn't going to build one.

Sherman's hand slowly moved to dip into the flour barrel.

"Don't you dare," Selma warned.

But Sherman's devilish grin assured her that he would dare.

Henry glanced up, and his face paled when he realized what was about to happen. Hurriedly wiping his hands on the front of his apron, he scurried from behind the counter to protect his interests. "Here now . . . we'll have none of this—"

Suddenly, all hell broke loose. Selma screamed as flour fogged the air, and the battle was on.

Tom stepped to the side to avoid getting in the middle of the altercation, but when apples and oranges began flying over his head, he ducked and headed for the front door.

Gideon turned to follow, straightening her hat irritably. Suddenly, she felt herself being lifted off her feet and hoisted roughly over Tom Lannigan's shoulder.

Turning on his heel, Tom hauled Gideon out of the store as she kicked and screamed and

Henry frantically tried to put a stop to the broadening fracas.

"Put me down!" Gideon ordered as Tom carried her outside on the sidewalk.

They could hear pots and pans being flung in anger across the store and Henry pleading at the top of his voice for Sherman and Selma to stop.

"Put me down this instant!"

Tom quickly complied with her demand and turned to face her.

"When are you going to learn to quit butting into other people's business, teacher, especially the marriages in this community!"

"It's time someone tried to improve the quality of life around here!" She picked up her bundle and the hat she'd dropped. With a sigh of disgust, she began dusting off her hat. "And there are some marriages that definitely need improving! Like Waite Burne's, for instance. Why don't you fire him?"

"Waite is one of my best fallers. I don't fire a man just because I don't happen to like him."

"This is different. He's a miserable excuse for a man! You didn't see the way he treated Echo a minute ago! It was disgusting."

"Did he strike her?"

"No."

"Did he threaten to harm her in any way?"

"Well, no. It was just his bossy attitude. I don't like the way he treats her, giving her orders, and then running off to get drunk when life doesn't go to suit him."

"Has she complained about him?" he asked calmly.

"Of course not. Echo is too loyal to do that."

"Unless there's an indication that Waite is mistreating her, you'd better stay out of it. If Echo needs help, she knows she can count on me."

Frustrated, Gideon smashed her hat back on top of her head, and it tilted askew. The corners of Tom's mouth twitched as he looked at her.

"You know, Miss Yardley, the women in these parts have been raised to know their place."

"Is that so, Mr. Lannigan?"

"They're accustomed to taking orders, and they enjoy the security of knowing that someone is looking out for their best interests."

"Whose best interests, Mr. Lannigan? I think that's precisely the issue here. A new schoolhouse would be in the best interest of the entire community. It just seems that it's the women who are farsighted enough to understand that."

"You'd be wise to keep your nose out of things," he said, turning away and ignoring her as if she were some pesky mosquito that he had to keep squashing. "This all started because of you in the first place."

"*Me?* What have I done? You weren't in

there when Waite made Echo drop out of the WASPS society!" she blustered. "It broke her heart!"

She glared up at his towering height resentfully.

Turning, he confronted her again. "Now, you listen to me, young lady. You've been stirring up trouble for weeks over this nonsense about a new school," he charged, "and I want it stopped!"

"What happened in there a minute ago is not my fault! If Henry and Sherman would have kept quiet about those silly apple pies, Selma would never have lost her temper and thrown that flour."

"You have every married couple in Watersweet fighting," he accused. "I can't get anything done for the men running in and out of my office whining about the way their wives won't cook, won't wash their clothes, won't talk, and . . . won't *sleep* with them."

"Ha! It serves them right!"

His hands shot to his hips. "Ha! That kind of fighting is about as dirty as a woman can get."

"If you mean I'm responsible for encouraging the women of this town to use any means they possess in order to have a little say about what goes on around here, you're right, Tom Lannigan! If you and the other men in this town don't have enough pride in your families and your children to see that they have the very best you can give them, then you can just keep your . . . your pants on!"

"No one complained until you showed up." Tom turned and began to walk away as Gideon fell into step behind him. Her hair had come down in the shuffle, and she irritably gathered up the loose strands and tried to shove them back up under her hat. "Don't walk away from me when I'm talking to you! You could put a stop to all this bickering in one minute if you would just agree to take one precious day and ten or fifteen men to build us that new schoolhouse!"

"No."

"Yes!"

"You're not getting a new schoolhouse, so you and your fellow hornets better just fly on back to your nest," he advised.

"WASPS! And just tell me why not!"

"Because I say so."

Gideon was breathless trying to keep up with his long-legged strides. She knew that she should let the subject drop. He was obviously not in any mood to discuss the matter rationally, but she just couldn't. He was being pigheaded and completely unreasonable. "And that's supposed to be a good enough reason?" she demanded.

"It is for most people around these parts."

"Well, it isn't for me."

"Obviously."

They had entered the pines now, and the

path narrowed. "Haven't you ever wanted anything so bad you were willing to fight for it?" she challenged.

"Maybe, but I was always smart enough to know when I was licked." He paused at the foot of a large pine and began to strap on his safety belt.

Gideon peered at the tree's towering trunk, and a knot of fear began to form in the pit of her stomach. It terrified her to see him climb to such soaring heights. "What are you doing?"

"I get paid to work, not to stand around and argue with a wasp."

She ignored his sarcastic comment. "Are you going to cut this tree?"

"No, one of the greenhorns left an ax up there this afternoon."

With rope flying and spurs digging, he began to climb to the top of the two-hundred-foot tree as Gideon clamped her eyes shut and leaned against the trunk to wait for him. She wasn't about to give up yet.

"I know you have your dreams, Tom Lannigan!"

"Not anymore."

"Andre told me that once you had hopes of replanting these pines."

Tom suddenly paused in his ascent and tightened his safety gear. "Andre talks too much." He began climbing again.

"Then it's true, isn't it?" she called.

"You tell me. You seem to know all about it."

"Andre said you and Rutherford Wakefield planned to replant the pines, but Mr. Wakefield died before the dream could be realized." Tom had nearly reached the top now, making it necessary for her to shout to be heard. "Isn't that so?"

She couldn't be sure if he answered her this time.

"If it's true, why is it so hard for you to understand why building a new schoolhouse is important to me? I won't be here forever, but like your dream, I want to leave something for future Watersweet generations. It's important to me!" She thought she was a dismal failure at teaching, so she wanted to leave something behind to prove she'd been there.

Gideon waited a full five minutes until Tom came sliding back down the tree carrying the ax he'd retrieved in his hand. She breathed a sigh of relief when his feet touched solid ground once more.

"Have you heard a word I've said?" she challenged.

"About what?" He disconnected the safety rope and let it drop.

"About the trees and the new schoolhouse. Though my goal isn't as lofty as yours, and it won't change the future to any great extent, it's still a worthy endeavor."

"Then get yourself a little hammer and a bucket of nails and have at it."

She sighed with disgust. "Why must you be so stubborn?"

Tom turned his back on her, and for a long moment Gideon was afraid that he'd simply dismissed the subject. But he asked quietly, "Did Andre mention anything to you about Gideon Wakefield?"

"Well, all he said was that you've tried to persuade Mr. Wakefield's granddaughter to keep the land long enough to complete the planting project, but that she refused, and now she's expected to arrive in Watersweet any day to complete the sale of Wakefield Timber to a rival competitor."

Tom eyes refused to meet hers now. "And?"

"And he said you were roaring mad about the sale, that you think Miss Wakefield is a selfish, conniving, unfeeling little witch who doesn't give a whit about anyone's future but her own."

Tom cleared his throat uneasily. "I . . . uh . . . don't know that for a fact," he admitted.

"Sounds to me like she is," Gideon sympathized. "But I bet if she could only see what's being done to her grandfather's land, she would change her mind."

Tom turned, and she saw his eyes had softened. "Maybe."

"Would it help if I spoke to Miss Wakefield when she arrives? Sometimes a woman can talk to another woman and make her see things differently. And it's quite possible that

Miss Wakefield has never given serious thought to the future generations and what hardships they will encounter if the trees are not replanted now," Gideon reasoned. "I'm sure she wouldn't want to heap any more worries on them than they're already going to have to face. And when you finally agree to build the new schoolhouse, I promise I'll do everything I can to help get the project started." She glanced up to find Tom gazing at her almost affectionately.

"Is that a fact?" he said gently, trying to hide the trace of amusement in his voice. "You think Miss Wakefield might even help us plant the trees?"

Gideon sighed. "Well, I can't speak for her, but I know I will. Of course, there's very little I can do since I don't own the land personally, but I'll ask Miss Wakefield the moment she arrives." Gideon nodded, warming to the thought. "Yes, that's exactly what Tip would want me to do."

"Tip?" Tom suddenly felt a chill wash over him.

Gideon looked up. "Tip?"

"You just said Tip would want his granddaughter to replant the trees."

"Oh." Leaning against the tree, she pursed her lips thoughtfully. "That was what Rutherford was called, wasn't it?"

"Yes, but very few knew his nickname." No one but Rutherford's closest family and friends had ever called him that. "How did you know it?"

"I don't know . . . maybe I heard it somewhere . . . maybe Andre mentioned it . . . oh, well." Waving the coincidence away as unimportant, Gideon stepped closer to him, forcing him to take an involuntary step backwards. "It isn't important . . . and stop doing that!"

"Doing what?"

"Always backing away from me. I won't bite you."

His mouth curved in an unconscious smile.

"And don't do that either!" she added. "When you smile that way, it frustrates me all the more that you don't like me."

"Who says I don't like you?" he countered.

"You have—by your actions, in a thousand different ways."

Reaching out to draw her to him, Tom offered her a sudden, arresting smile. "Well, you're wrong. I was even thinking about asking you to take a walk in the moonlight with me this evening."

"You were?" She drew back from him suspiciously. "Why?"

"Because I want to walk in the moonlight with you."

"Are you going to try and bully me into dropping my crusade for the new schoolhouse?"

"No." He pulled her closer, and her breathing quickened as he brought his mouth closer to hers. Oh, he was experienced! He knew just what to do to make her pulse accelerate like a runaway train. "Can't a man ask a woman to go for a simple walk without her reading some ulterior motive into it?" he said soothingly. "Besides, we live together. A man and a woman who live together should be able to take a walk in the moonlight—wouldn't you agree?"

She drew back from him suspiciously. "You're not going to kick me out in the snow?"

"No, I can honestly tell you I have never kicked a woman out in the snow," he said dryly.

The world spun lopsidedly as Gideon's arms slipped around his waist and his mouth lowered persuasively to coax an answering response from hers.

"Well . . . it wouldn't have done you any good to try . . . I'm seeing this thing through."

"Good for you." His mouth closed masterfully over hers, and she thought she would burst from sheer pleasure. She didn't know what game he was playing now, and she wasn't about to ask.

When their lips finally parted long moments later, Tom looked down at her with a touch of tenderness shining in his eyes. "Let's call a truce, how about it?"

"Do I have to give up my new school-house?"

He smiled. "No, let's just quit nipping at each other's heels for a while."

She returned his smile. "All right."

Looping her arm through his, they started walking back. "I have some paperwork to catch up on. I'll be back at the room later."

"You're not planning to run me out on a rail or make me live in the woods?" She couldn't believe he was giving in this easily.

"No," he chuckled, "though I've considered every other alternative, believe me. Living under my roof is a temporary arrangement. Don't get used to it, teacher."

She looked over and grinned. "I won't. I'm looking forward to moving to my quarters adjacent to the new schoolhouse."

He shook his head. "I wouldn't count on that if I were you." They leaned to kiss again, unhurriedly, savoring the final moments alone. He seemed in no rush to leave, and she wished he would never go.

Finally, he put his large hand at the back of her waist, and they started on again. It was growing late, and the pines were casting their deepening shadows over the earth.

"Are you going straight to the room?" he asked.

"No, I want to stop by and see Echo before I go home. I felt so sorry for her today, Tom. She took such pride in being a part of something worthwhile. Now she has nothing to brighten her life, no cause that she can take pride in, no reason to feel as if she will ever accomplish anything on her own. Waite will always see to that," Gideon added, her voice tinged with bitterness for the man who seemed to wreak such havoc in Echo's life.

She felt his arm circle her waist. "Don't stay too long. You haven't got a lantern with you, and I don't want you wandering around in the dark alone."

Drawing closer to his side, she laid her head on his shoulder as they walked. She felt incredibly safe and contented in the shelter of his arms.

"It's nice to know you'd worry about me if I were in danger," she said.

Tom's eyes grew distant as his arm tightened possessively around her. There was hardly a moment when she wasn't on his mind, and the certain knowledge that he would lose her soon was more than adequate punishment for the part he'd played in the disruption of her life.

13

The night wind was howling as Tom walked home later. He looked up to see a glow in his windows. He found himself whistling as he climbed the long stairway to his room. It was the first time he could remember coming home to a room that wasn't dark, cold, and empty. And Gideon was waiting for him. The thought oddly warmed him. He could admit now he had misjudged her in the beginning, yet he had no way of telling her he had been wrong. Would he now be able to let her go when Talbot Wellington-Kent came to claim her? Tom wasn't sure.

His eyes widened as he opened the door and the warmth of the room surrounded him. A light spilled across the freshly scrubbed floor with a welcoming glow. He could see everything had been moved. His bewildered gaze traveled around the small area, settling on the frilly sheet with rosebuds on it strung up across one corner of the room.

"You like it?" Gideon asked as she moved from the shadows to help remove his coat.

"What have you done . . ." he asked in a dazed tone as his eyes searched what had formerly been a man's domain. There was a fire in the stove, and on top of it a tea kettle was whistling away. On the floor beside the stove was a pallet he'd never seen before. Atop his dresser, instead of his razor and shaving mug, was an assortment of bottles and a silver-handled brush and comb. Sitting on his nightstand, where he'd always kept his cigars, there was a bowl of some kind of dried leaves.

Slipping her arms around his neck, she slowly drew his mouth down to meet hers. "I've been waiting for you," she whispered.

His arms tightened around her as the kiss grew deeper. When their lips parted many long moments later, he gazed at her in the flickering lamplight. "I could get used to this."

"You'd better," she teased. "I don't plan on leaving." *Someday he was going to ask her to marry him, and she would be waiting for him every night.*

"What's that peculiar smell?"

"Oh, these?" Gideon lifted the porcelain bowl she'd fallen in love with downstairs. Grace had dutifully added it to Lannigan's burgeoning bill. "These are dried rose petals. Don't they smell lovely?"

"Where are my cigars?" Tom's brows drew together tightly as he realized his personal belongings were not where he had left them this morning.

"That's a nasty habit. You should give it up."

Gideon smiled to herself. She was going to be good for him. And, she could see he was thinking that this place had never looked or smelled so nice and homey before.

"You've cleaned." The statement sounded more like an accusation than a compliment. He began to walk around the room, trying to assess the damage.

She nodded, grinning. "Took hours, but I've rearranged your drawers, and I threw away a lot of useless things in the process."

His brow lifted. "Useless?"

"Yes. You know, things you had just had lying around. Doesn't everything look better?"

"But I didn't have useless things lying around," he protested. "I use everything."

His distraught gaze searched for his stack of journals beside his bed and found them gone.

"Damn, if you were going to get rid of something, why didn't you throw *your* useless things away?"

Her puzzled gaze followed his to the cluttered table. "My hat-making supplies? Why, I couldn't do that. I have a new creation in progress. It's going to be splendid."

"Just like all the rest."

Following around the room, she began to become concerned that he wasn't pleased with her efforts—or her hats. "Are you angry with me?"

"No . . . where are my cigars?"

"Under the bed—it's really much better to store them there, and they'll be out of sight," she added as if being out of sight would be more worthwhile than being handy. "Is that okay?"

"Sure . . . sure . . . I'll just crawl across the damn floor like a snake when I want a smoke," he muttered.

Her face clouded. "You're angry."

"No, I'm not." His words said one thing, his tone, another.

He looked at the dainty pillows tossed on the hard wooden chairs. *The ruffles were bad enough, but pink rosebuds too?*

Her eyes followed his. "You have to admit the chairs are much softer with cushions on them," she defended.

He looked at the pallet.

"It's really quite comfortable," she added cheerfully.

"Let me guess who gets the pleasure of sleeping on it."

"It's for you," she said. "A gentleman would never ask a lady to sleep on the floor."

"In Philadelphia, maybe not. But in Watersweet—"

"A gentleman is a gentleman, no matter where or when," she reminded, hurriedly stretching out on the bed to stake her claim.

Tom stood, hands on his hips, viewing the renovation helplessly.

Rolling to her side, she lowered the flame of the lamp. She could see this wasn't the time to press the matter. "It's very late, and I've had such a busy day." She stifled a weary yawn. "I hope you don't mind if I don't stay up to keep you company. I didn't sleep very well last night. Honestly, Tom, I don't know how you stand this lumpy mattress," she murmured as her eyes drifted closed. In moments she was fast asleep.

Sighing, Tom walked over and drew the blanket over her. Leaning down, he kissed her softly on her mouth. Desire sprang alive in him, but he forced it aside. This was crazy. He could not fall in love with her.

"Mmmm," she stirred and whispered drowsily. "I missed you today."

"I missed you too, little one. Go to sleep . . . and thank you."

"For what?"

"For trying to make the place look better."

It didn't look better. Tom didn't know how he could live with all these frilly pillows and rosebuds, but he knew she had meant well.

"You're welcome . . . I wanted to do something special for you." She was asleep again before she could tell him how very much she loved him.

Perched gingerly on one of the rosebud cushions, Tom removed his boots, eyeing his bed yearningly. The lumpy mattress looked ten times more inviting than the flat pallet on the hard floor.

Crawling over to the bed, he climbed beneath it to retrieve a cigar. Stretching out on his back in the middle of the floor, he lit the cigar, inhaled, his eyes studying the curtain.

More damn rosebuds. Now what are you going to do, Lannigan?

Damned if I know.

Snow began falling outside the window as the light finally went out in the tiny room over Menson's store a few moments later.

But the room wasn't lonely tonight.

"Owwww, damn! What did you do with the washstand!"

Gideon's eyes flew open. She could see that it was just beginning to get light. As her eyes adjusted to the darkness, she saw Tom bent over in the middle of the room, rubbing his big toe.

"The washstand is in the dressing room," she murmured sleepily.

Tom glanced around the one tiny room. "Where?"

"Behind the screen," she said gesturing to the drape of rosebud fabric, "we have a private area for bathing and dressing."

He was still grumbling as he limped across the room and disappeared behind the makeshift screen. She could hear the slosh of water as he poured it from the pitcher into the bowl. She listened as he splashed his face, complaining with every breath he took.

He stepped back into the room and headed to his dresser. She heard a scrape against wood as he pulled open a drawer.

"Where is my razor?"

"Right there."

"I want my stuff out where I can see it."

Gideon rolled over, covering her head with the pillow. *"I want my stuff out where I can see it"!* she mimicked silently.

He was in a most disagreeable mood this morning.

She felt the pillow being lifted from her head a moment later. "I hate to bother you, but would you care to be more precise than 'right there'?" he asked in a voice dripping with sarcasm.

Lifting her head, she thought for an instant he looked like he really might bundle her up and toss her out in a snowbank.

"Tom," she said quietly. "Your razor is in the second drawer on the right."

"There's nothing in the second drawer on the right but some more of those funny-smelling dried leaves."

"Behind the funny-smelling dry leaves," she said. "Did you look there?"

Grunting, he picked up the lamp and carried it to the table. He crossed the room and gathered his shaving supplies and returned to

the table where with a sweep of his arm he
callously brushed her sewing supplies onto the
floor.

Gideon sat straight up in bed. "How rude!
You have no right to toss my stuff on the floor!"

Ignoring her, he proceeded to lather his
face with soap.

"You don't like my hats," she accused. Never
once had he complimented her on her newfound talent!

"I don't know anything about women's hats,
but I do know that I want my shaving gear left
alone. It is to remain, untouched, on this table,
where I don't have to send a search party to
look for it," he returned calmly.

Lying back down, Gideon rolled over and
covered her head with the pillow again.

When he finished shaving, Tom crossed the
room to his dresser, smacking her on the rump
as he passed the bed. "You going to stay in bed
all day?"

"Leave me alone," she returned in a muffled
voice.

"All right, but the Gabriel horn has blown
twice already. You're going to get hungry before noon."

He reached into the third drawer for his
wool socks and grabbed a lacy camisole instead. Jerking his hand back as if a snake had
bit him, he bellowed, "Good Lord! Don't tell
me you threw out my socks too!"

Throwing the pillow off her head, she glared

at him. "Your socks are in the bottom drawer with your longjohns! And stop yelling at me!"

Giving the drawer a shove, he jerked open the bottom drawer, drew out a pair of socks, and slammed the drawer shut again.

"Like living in a damn boudoir," he muttered as he sat down on the rosebud cushion, jerked on the socks, and then his boots.

"You liked the room last night," she accused. "You thought it was pretty."

A few minutes later, he slammed out the door, and Gideon buried her face in her pillow and bawled.

The rest of the week went more smoothly than Gideon thought that it might. Tom was being reasonably tolerant, in view of the fact he was forced to share his room with her.

At times she couldn't keep her hands off him. She patted and hugged until he would get downright rude with her. She knew she shouldn't be deliberately tempting him, but she couldn't help herself. At night she could hear him tossing on his pallet, aware of her yet determined to remain at arm's length.

Why, she didn't know. But she planned to keep after him until she made him fall in love with her.

After teaching on Friday, Gideon had supper by herself. The cooks fixed her a plate, knowing she preferred to eat alone before the men came in for scheduled meals. It saved her

the embarrassment of eating with hundreds
staring at her, and she thought it probably
made it easier for Tom too. Everyone assumed
that they were living in sin, and though no one
wanted openly to challenge them, it seemed
wiser to Gideon not to invite more speculation
by being seen together in public.

Before going back to her room, she stopped
in Menson's store and bought another several
yards of the rosebud fabric. She was afraid
they might sell the rest of the bolt to someone
else, and all week she'd imagined how different the room would look if she had matching
curtains at the windows.

The curtains would be the crowning touch
to make the room really feel like spring in the
middle of an endless winter.

Tom was gradually accepting most of the
changes she'd made. He still griped about his
back hurting from sleeping on a drafty floor.
And there were times in the night when she
was tempted to invite him to crawl into her
bed.

If he would ever accept, she would object, of
course, but her protests would be perfunctory.
Fantasies of actually living in sin with him
plagued both her days and her nights.

Since she wanted the curtains to be a surprise, she worked on them up until she knew
he was due home each evening. Saturday, she
spent the entire morning finishing the cur-

tains and making a little matching coverlet for the bed.

That afternoon she went back to Menson's to buy a few more things for the room. Andre came in as she was paying for her purchases and insisted she let him carry them upstairs.

"Andre, just set the packages down here," she said as they reached the top landing. "And thank you so much."

"*Non, chérie,* I won't hear of it," he said as he swung the door open for her to lead the way. "Ooo, la, la," he said as his eyes scanned the colorful room. "What is this?"

"You don't think it's too much?" she asked anxiously.

"It's as exquisite as you are," he replied tactfully.

"I'm afraid Tom will think it's too much," she confessed, "and I do want to please him."

"You worry too much, *chérie.*" Andre grinned, imagining big Tom Lannigan planted among all these rosebuds. "Well, I must be on my way." As Andre turned to go, the door opened and Tom walked in.

His jaw dropped when he saw the sea of pink rosebuds that enveloped the room now. His eyes shot to Andre, and he scowled when he saw Andre's amused smirk.

"Tom, I was just admiring your room!" Andre's grin widened. "How lucky can one man get?" He turned, still grinning, and walked out the open door.

Lori Copeland

Gideon clasped her hands together proudly. "Hello—"

"Excuse me. I have to talk to Andre." Without a decent hello, Tom bolted toward the open door as Gideon ran after him.

"Tom! Where are you going?"

He didn't answer her this time.

Sighing, Gideon turned back and closed the door, hoping he had noticed the new curtains.

Bounding down the steps two at a time, Tom reached the bottom about the same time as Andre. Collaring his friend, Tom jerked him into the gathering shadows. "Wait *just* a minute."

Andre drew back with mock surprise. With a supreme effort, he managed to keep the smile off his face this time. "*Oui?* You wanted something?"

"You're damn right I want something," Tom said curtly. "Andre, get that smirk off your face."

"Smirk? I have no *smirk*," Andre denied innocently.

"I'm warning you, Montague. Not *one* word of this. Do you understand? I want your word that you won't tell the other men what you just saw."

"You mean the rosebuds?"

Tom glanced around uneasily. "Yes, dammit, the rosebuds!"

"Ah—such a lucky man. A woman's touch

264

has transformed your humble dwelling into a veritable garden of—"

"Into a disgrace!" Tom snapped. His grip on Andre's collar suddenly loosened, and he slumped against the handrail with defeat. "What am I going to do, Andre? It'll hurt her feelings if I take down all that frilly nonsense, but so help me if I hear the men mention a single pink rosebud, I'll know where it came from, and I'll make your life a living hell." Tom's eyes gleamed with promise now.

Andre's grin gradually began to fade. "Ah, Tom Lannigan, you love her very much, don't you?"

Tom's eyes met his friend's evenly. "I love her very much."

He loved her, and he was going to lose her. A wire had come from Talbot Wellington-Kent an hour ago. Because he could get no satisfactory information from the railroad officials, Gideon's fiancé had decided to come to Watersweet to investigate the accident himself. He would be arriving within the week.

Tom knew he was powerless to stop the inevitable.

"Then Andre will be the soul of discretion, my friend," Andre vowed solemnly.

Straightening, Tom tried to salvage what little was left of his tattered pride. "Andre damn well better be."

Nodding solemnly, the two men shook hands.

A moment later Andre disappeared around the corner of the building.

Tom started back up the steps when his hand suddenly froze on the railing.

He paused, then set his teeth as he heard the sound of Andre's booming laughter echoing over the frozen hillsides.

14

Waite Burne was in another one of his foul moods. He didn't like it when a woman crossed him, and he was still stewing over the way Fedelia Yardley tried to undermine his authority with Echo. She'd been filling his woman's head with a bunch of high falutin' ideas about her bein' equal to a man! If that wasn't the biggest pile he'd ever heard! No woman was equal to Waite Burne, and that was something that would never change.

Kicking the heavy door open, Waite entered the warmth of the one-room shack he called home late the next afternoon. Echo glanced up from the stove, startled by his unexpected intrusion.

"Get off your butt and clean this," he snapped, pitching the frozen carcass of a wild turkey he'd shot earlier onto the table.

Echo obediently moved from the stove, where a large pot of beans and a skillet of potatoes and onions were simmering. The

mouth-watering aromas filtered pleasantly
through the air as she quietly picked up the
bird and carried it to the sink.

Waite sat down at the table, and thrust one
foot out. "Take my boots off."

Wiping her hands, Echo came over to kneel
beside his chair. Her eyes refused to meet his
as she began to untie the strings of his boots.

Staring down at the top of her head, Waite
sneered at her. "You think you're real smart,
don't you?"

By his menacing tone, Echo could tell that
he was still angry at her because of the incident in Menson's store the other day. He was
spoiling for a fight, but she wouldn't give him
the satisfaction of one.

"Ain't you gonna answer me, girl?"

"I'm busy, Waite," she murmured.

"Busy?" He rolled his eyes toward the ceiling and hooted mirthlessly. "My, my, ain't we
talkin' big lately. 'I'm busy, Waite,' " he mimicked. "You learn that from the schoolteacher?"

Echo remained silent. She knew he neither
expected nor wanted an answer. He had been
drinking again. He reeked of cheap whiskey.

"Cat got your tongue?" he goaded, nudging
her roughly with the tip of his filthy boot.

"No."

"Then answer me!"

Echo quietly rose and walked back to the
sink. Mechanically, her hands began stripping

the pin feathers from the frozen bird while she tried to keep her mind blank.

"Am I gonna have to get up and make you talk, little girl?" he threatened in a mildly misleading tone.

"Leave me alone, Waite," Echo said wearily. "Just go sleep it off."

"My boots are still on."

"I untied them," she said. "Just slip them off."

"I don't want to take my boots off myself. That's your job, girlee. Damn miserable, worthless woman. I don't know why I ever put up with you." His breathing became labored, and sweat stood out in heavy patches on his forehead. "You're a pitiful excuse for a woman," he sneered. "I don't know why I should have to put up with you. It it weren't for me, girl, you'd have no one—you hear? No one!"

"You've been drinking, Waite. Please, just—"

"I married you when I didn't have to. I've fed you and put clothes on your back, and what do I get in return?" He got out of his chair, groping for support with one hand. "Nothing back but sass! You embarrassed me in front of Sherman Miller and Henry Menson the other day," he bellowed. "That wasn't smart, girlee. No one embarrasses Waite Burne, least of all a woman!"

"Waite . . . please—"

"I want you to say you're sorry for embarrassing me," he demanded.

"I'm sorry," she repeated obediently.

"You're going to quit that silly 'soo-ciety' you've been going to and stay home and take care of your man liken' you're supposed to, now, aren't you?"

Echo nodded.

"Then say it. I want to hear you say it."

"I won't go to my society meetin' no more."

He wouldn't let up, even as tears began to roll down her cheeks. "Now say you're sorry that you hurt poor ole Waite's feelin's. That weren't a very nice thing for you to do, and you're real sorry, ain't you?"

"Yes, Waite. I'm real sorry."

"And you ain't gonna do that anymore, are you?"

"No."

"And you're gonna stop association' with that Fedelia Yardley. From now on, you're not to see her or go near that schoolhouse unless I tell you you can. You got that?"

Echo shook her head negatively, tears blinding her. He couldn't make her give up Miss Yardley . . . he just couldn't!

"Don't say no to me!"

"Waite . . . just leave me alone." Echo was openly sobbing now. "Don't make me give up Miss Yardley. . . . she's my best . . . friend."

"She ain't no friend! You'll not see that woman again!"

270

"No . . . please." She extended her palms imploringly.

"You say it, Echo!"

She had never seen him so angry. His meaty hands balled into tight fists. "Say it!"

"I—I . . . won't . . . see . . . her . . . again."

"Never!" he demanded.

"Never!"

As suddenly as the argument had begun, it stopped. "That's better," he said in a voice suddenly devoid of all emotion. "If I ever hear of you seeing her again, Echo, you'll be sorry. I mean it."

Echo slumped onto a chair, sobbing quietly.

He pointed toward the sink. "Get that bird cleaned, and my supper on the table before you make me lose my temper."

Echo crossed the room on unsteady legs. Gripping the side of the sink for support, she willed herself to be strong. Waite sat down and propped his feet on the table as he waited to be served.

She felt an ache in her heart. She didn't care about her husband's drinking, his neglect toward her, his drunken accusations. She didn't care about having to drop out of the society, although she had cherished having that small bit of excitement to look forward to each week.

But how would she give up the only friend she'd had in the world? She could endure

Lori Copeland

Waite's infidelity. She knew he visited some women in Shadow Pine. And she could overlook his verbal abuse, but she loved Fedelia, and she couldn't lose her only friend. Her life would be unbearably lonely without her. Echo realized that if Waite was gone she would hardly miss him in comparison. Bitterness rose in her throat at what he was making her do.

"Hurry up, worthless. I ain't got all day," Waite muttered. His back turned to her, he sat with his muddy boots propped carelessly on the cloth that she'd so carefully washed and ironed that afternoon so the table would look nice tonight. "Me and Ben's going over to Shadow Pine and find us a real woman. Lord knows I ain't got one here," he whined.

Whirling, Echo suddenly had had enough. "Then why don't you have your *real* woman fix your supper?"

Waite's eyes widened as his feet slammed to the floor. "What'd you say?" It was the first time the girl had ever sassed him.

Her chin lifted a notch higher. He should never have asked her to give up her friend.

"That Yardley woman has ruined you," he challenged. "You don't seem to care that she's livin' with Lannigan, them not married and all. She's turned the boss man into a regular sissy and you into a sassy little twit!"

"I don't care what you say. She's my friend." It was the first time she'd ever defied him, and they were both aware of it.

272

For a moment, Waite wasn't sure how to handle her. It had always been so easy to push her around. He swayed unsteadily. He needed a drink. A lot of drinks. Maybe if he got drunk and stayed away for a day or so, she'd see what a fool she was being. She'd change her tune then, he thought. "I'm leavin' and I might never come back," he threatened. "Now just what would you do then, Miss High and Mighty?"

"Don't make promises you ain't gonna keep," she said calmly.

"You might not have it so easy without fresh game or a regular paycheck," he sneered.

"I'd manage."

"We'll see, girlee." He shot her a hateful look. "We'll just see." With that he grabbed his coat and stomped out of the house without tying his boots.

Early Wednesday morning, Gideon was trudging to school, her mind still on Tom Lannigan. He'd been a little more benevolent about the new curtains and coverlet last night, listening patiently as she'd explained again how the rosebuds cheered her by reminding her that spring was not far away. Though she could tell he wasn't going to adjust easily to the changes she had wrought upon his life, he had said the curtains could stay.

But not one more rosebud, he'd said. Not even one.

Approaching the schoolyard, Gideon was only dimly aware of the raised voices as her thoughts became more troubled. Tom was falling in love with her. He had never told her so, but she saw it in his eyes every day now. Yet, he rarely touched her. It was as if he was holding himself back from something he longed to have—yet there was no reason. Gideon would welcome his advances. Couldn't he see that in her eyes?

The voices in the schoolyard grew more pronounced.

"Miss Yardley is livin' in sin," King Davis declared. "My pa says so!"

"She is not!" Tirza defended, her eyes bright with unshed tears.

"Tirza, you're such a baby, you don't even know what that means."

"It means you're sayin' bad things about Miss Yardley. And it ain't so!"

"Well, it *is* so if a woman is livin' with a man she's not married to," King tossed over his shoulder arrogantly.

"You take that back, King Davis!" Tirza picked up a stick of wood and reared back to fling it at King's retreating back.

Without thinking, Gideon began to move faster. "Children! Stop this arguing, right now!"

But Tirza was not in a mood for reasoning. King was saying bad things about Miss Yardley, and she wasn't going to stand for it.

274

Gideon calmly stepped between the two to put an end to the fracas. She held up one finger. "I said—" The log intended for King suddenly came sailing through the air and struck the Gideon in the temple.

With a soft moan, she crumpled to the ground, unconscious.

"My Gawd! Look what you done, Tirza!" King accused.

Tirza began sobbing. "I didn't mean to . . . I didn't mean to!"

King dropped to his knees beside the teacher, trying to determine if she was still breathing.

"Tirza's done gone and kilt the teacher," Quinn Morrison whispered reverently. His eyes were round as saucers.

"She ain't dead," King announced. "She's just knocked out."

"Maybe I ought to go git someone to come and see about her," Scooter Wilson said uneasily.

"No, we knocked her out, we'll get her on her feet again. Pud, help me carry Miss Yardley inside."

The two boys carried the teacher inside and laid her on the floor beside the stove. Tirza spread a cool cloth on Gideon's forehead while the others debated about what to do next. The children seemed greatly relieved when Gideon came to, a few minutes later.

"Here, let me help you to your chair, Miss Yardley," Tirza offered.

"No, my name is Gideon," Gideon corrected drowsily. "Gideon Wakefield."

The children looked at one another, shaking their heads sympathetically. "You better rest awhile, Miss Yardley," King Davis said. "That knock on your noggin has got you plumb confused."

"King, help me sit up," Gideon murmured.

King obeyed, lifting her gently to a sitting position. Gideon's eyes traveled slowly about the room as pieces of her memory began to return. Gradually, in bits and snatches, she recalled her life in Philadelphia and Talbot and the moments before the train accident.

"Are you all right, Miss Yardley?" Modeen Menson asked.

"Yes . . . I'm fine, children." Walking to her desk, Gideon sat down, staring vacantly out the window.

I am Gideon Wakefield. I am not Fedelia Yardley—Fedelia was swept downstream with poor old Walter Fedderson.

The teacher was acting strangely, so much so the children sat down at their desks and began working on their math problems without her having to ask them. Every few minutes, one of them would come up to check on her.

"I'm fine, Tirza. Please go on with your work," she'd murmur absently.

Talbot. Dear God, what must Talbot be thinking? He must assume that I was the woman swept downstream in the accident. I must wire him immediately.

A new, more sobering thought came to her as the children worked quietly at their desks. *Tom. Does Tom know who I am?*

With a strangled sob, Gideon fumbled in her coat pocket for a handkerchief.

"Suppose I oughta go get Doc?" Pud finally asked.

"It's starting to snow," King noted. "If you're goin', you'd better start now."

Gideon glanced up, realizing she was too distraught to teach. "That won't be necessary, King. I'm going to be just fine."

"You sure?" She didn't look fine.

"Yes, I'm sure. And children, I'd rather none of you mention this unfortunate incident to anyone." She needed time—time to decide how she was going to handle this startling turn of events.

That was all right with the children. If their folks heard about the incident at school, most likely a few of them would get a whippin' when they got home.

"If you don't mind, I'm going to dismiss school early today. King, I want you to see that everyone gets home safely."

She got no argument there. The children scattered like leaves in the wind.

When the room had emptied, Gideon

dropped her head into her hands. The wood popped in the stove. Outside, the snow fell harder and the wind began to rise.

Tom—oh darling, what would you say if you knew that I am Gideon Wakefield and not Fedelia Yardley? Gideon knew that she wouldn't have the slightest chance of winning his love if the mistaken identity were to be revealed—and she was so close . . . so close.

Lifting her head hours later, she realized it was growing late. She needed to talk to someone. Echo. Echo would help her.

Gideon got up, banked the fire, then closed the door behind her.

The snow was falling harder as the Burnes' cabin came into sight fifteen minutes later. She knew she was acting foolish. She should have gone directly to her quarters. The weather was getting increasingly worse, and it appeared they were in for another blizzard.

The road was completely covered, and Gideon struggled as her shoes sank into the drifts.

The wind was howling, tossing snow about like a demon as she struggled toward the log cabin. Tears were frozen on her cheeks as she realized her life in Watersweet was a sham.

Funny. She had thought she hated the crude logging town, the hard life, the endless snow and the heinous children, but now she wasn't sure.

Tom. My God, how could she return to a colorless life in Philadelphia with Talbot when she had known the sweet agony of falling in love with Tom.

Her hands shot out to break her fall, but she tumbled forward. Lost in thought, she had not seen the log lying in the path. The snow blinded her as she struggled to get up. Her hand gripped for support as a violent gust of wind snatched at her bonnet.

Pulling herself to her feet, she glanced down, realizing that she hadn't tripped over a log; she'd tripped over a body. With a strangled gasp, she recognized who it was. Waite Burne.

Stunned, Gideon reached out to touch him. Drawing back hurriedly, she realized that he was frozen stiff.

"Oh, my God . . ." she whispered, her head beginning to swim. Echo. Where was Echo?

Running now, Gideon covered the last few yards to the cabin. Collapsing against the door, she lifted her fist, and pounded twice.

Echo opened the door, her eyes lighting with delight when she saw Gideon. "What are you doing here on a day like this!"

"Dear God . . ." Gideon's face drained of all color as her hand came up to cover her mouth.

"You look near froze, ma'am. Come in and let me fix you a cup of tea," Echo encouraged.

"Echo . . . Waite . . . he's—"

"I'm so happy to see you, Fedelia." Echo

began bustling around the kitchen, filling the tea pot with water from the pitcher. "But I'd never dream you'd pay me a visit on such a bad day."

"Echo . . . Waite . . ." Gideon's voice was coming in gasps now.

Echo turned to look at her. "Won't be no trouble at all. I was just about to make a cup for myself when you knocked," she said.

Tom—she had to get Tom, but he would be more than a mile away, way over on the south road, working on one of the icers.

The smell of supper bubbling on the stove gave every appearance of normality. A lantern burned on the table, casting its warm rays over the sparsely furnished room. The table was set for two: two plates, two cups, two forks, two spoons, two knives. Coffee perked merrily on the stove, and the smell of venison sizzling in the skillet brought a hunger pang to Gideon's stomach. Everything was as it should be, yet she knew that it wasn't.

"Wind's comin' up," Echo remarked as she carefully measured tea from a jar into two cups.

"Echo, listen to me," Gideon moved hurriedly across the room to grasp the young girl's shoulders. "Where's Waite?"

"Let's see, you take sugar in your tea, don't you?" Echo picked up the porcelain tea kettle to pour hot water into the two cups. "I like three teaspoons—sometimes four. . . . Waite says I have a terrible sweet tooth."

"Echo."

"Waite didn't come home last night," she admitted tiredly. "And I don't care. I just don't care anymore."

"Echo . . . something terrible has happened." Gideon's voice was barely above a whisper.

Echo glanced up expectantly. "What's happened—has Waite been hurt?"

"No . . . it's worse than that. He must have fallen in the dark. And he . . . and he . . . oh, Echo, I think he's dead."

"Dead?"

Gideon nodded. "I'm not sure . . . but he's just laying there so cold." Her voice trailed off weakly.

Echo turned and placed the two cups of steaming tea on the table.

The girl didn't seem to hear or comprehend what Gideon was saying.

"Echo. What do you want me to do? We can't just leave him out there," Gideon said raggedly.

Finally, Echo looked up. "Waite's dead?" she whispered.

Nodding again, Gideon said softly. "He's not fifty feet from the house . . . when did you last see him?"

"A couple of days ago. He got mad and left

the house . . . I thought maybe he was still over in Shadow Pine."

"He must have started home and fallen and hit his head. When did he leave?"

"Couple of days ago," Echo replied again woodenly. "Said he was leavin' me and not comin' back—but I didn't believe him. He's said mean things like that to me before."

Heartbroken, Gideon moved to comfort her friend. "Oh, Echo, you should have told me. Have you been alone?"

"I can manage," Echo said firmly.

Sinking into the nearest chair, Gideon tried to make herself think. She had to call someone . . . she couldn't handle this alone. She felt Echo placing the cup of tea gently between her fingers. "Here, drink this. It'll make you feel better."

The hot liquid seared the lining of her throat, but Gideon drank it anyway. Her mind simply refused to function. Waite Burne lay dead in the snow, and Echo was acting as if there wasn't anything unusual going on.

Finally, Gideon summoned enough strength to push the cup aside and murmur, "I have to find Tom." Gideon rose mechanically to her feet. The entire day had been a nightmare. First her memory returning, and now this. "He's over on the south road—it'll take a while."

"No need to hurry." Echo took an unconcerned sip of her tea. "Waite ain't going no-where."

It suddenly occurred to Gideon that the girl was in shock, which would account for her strange behavior. Laying a hand on Echo's thin shoulder, Gideon prompted gently, "Get your coat, and you can come with me."

"I'll stay here and tend to supper. You go on."

Gideon was shocked by her refusal. "Please, you shouldn't stay here alone. Get your coat, Echo. You're coming with me."

"I'll be just fine. You take the lantern and bundle up real good." Echo stood up and went to the cupboard for a tallow candle. She returned and lifted the lantern's globe to light the candle. A moment later, she replaced the globe and handed the lantern to Gideon. "Tell Tom if he hasn't eaten yet, I have extra to-night."

"Yes . . . all right." Gideon began to edge toward the door. It all seemed like a bad dream.

Echo smiled. "I think I'll just sit a spell and read my Bible."

"Yes . . . that's good." Gideon's hands fumbled blindly for the latch on the door. "I'll be back soon as I can."

"All right, ma'am."

Once outside, Gideon sucked large amounts of bitter-cold air into her lungs. Her head reeled from the shocking events, but she knew she must get help. Her feet began to move in the direction of the south road. Tom—he would know what to do. The soles of her boots flew across the crusted snow as she raced through the darkness. Thick clouds blanketed the moon.

The wildly swinging lantern threw distorted shadows over the path of heavy pine needles. Ordinarily, she wouldn't consider going out at this hour alone, but she barely noticed the grotesque shapes of branches and limbs that eerily reached out and threatened to snatch her away. Her blood pounded, and her lungs filled with the scent of the resinous pine as she raced along.

Poor Echo, poor Echo, poor Echo her mind screamed as she ran faster and faster. What would the girl do now? Waite Burne was a pitiful human being, but he had at least fed and clothed her, and provided a roof over her head.

Up ahead, Gideon detected a faint light and the sound of men's voices. She began shouting, calling for Tom, her voice nearly hysterical now.

Startled, Tom glanced up when he heard her. His brows drew together in a frown as he watched Gideon running toward him.

"Tom! Tom Lannigan!"

Sliding down from the tank on the sprinkler, Tom began walking to meet her. "What's wrong?"

284

"It's Waite!" she gasped. "You have to come . . . now!"

"Waite?" Tom's frown grew more pronounced. "What in the hell has he done now?"

"He's . . . he's dead!"

"Dead?" His rubber-soled boots began to cover the ground with more purpose as he hurried to her. "Where?"

"He's lying in the snow, and he looks so terrible. . . . Oh, Tom, it's just awful!" Gideon's voice bordered near hysteria as she flung herself into the safety of his arms. Hugging him tightly, she let the wonderful feeling of security wash over her. She'd forgotten that she wasn't Fedelia Yardley. She'd forgotten that her memory had returned. She was oblivious to everything except that she was in love with this man, and she wanted him to make everything right again.

Gently taking her by the shoulders, Tom steadied her. "Are you hurt?" he demanded.

"No, no, it isn't me. It's Echo . . . and Waite. He's dead, Tom!"

"Where is Echo?"

"She's back there . . . in the cabin." Gideon broke off sobbing, then took a deep breath and forced herself to go on. "She's acting so strangely . . . she just sits there drinking tea as if nothing has happened!" Closing her eyes, Gideon relived the horror of the terrible scene she had just witnessed.

"Anything wrong, Tom?" Dirk Wilson called from the waiting sled.

"There's trouble at the Burnes' cabin," Tom called back. "You and Joe better come with me!" He turned and set Gideon's feet back in motion. "Are you sure Waite's dead?"

"Yes, yes . . . he's dead!"

"Do you have any idea what happened?"

"He must have fallen."

"One of the men said he saw him over in Shadow Pine last night, drinking pretty heavy."

"Echo said that he'd left her." Gideon broke into tears again.

They began to run, covering the distance back to the Burnes' cabin in record time. Joe and Dirk ran behind them, the sound of their heavy boots thrashing noisily through the thick undergrowth.

When they reached Waite's body, Tom rolled him over and felt for a pulse. "Been dead for hours," he murmured.

Echo was reading her Bible when they knocked on the door and entered the small cabin.

She calmly raised her eyes to meet Tom's, and Gideon thought that she had never seen such pain as she saw in their agonized depths. "Waite's dead," she said brokenly.

Kneeling beside her chair, Tom took Echo's small hand in his. "When did you last see Waite?"

"A few days ago," Echo replied in a small voice. "He said he was leavin' me, but I knew he didn't mean it. I thought he'd come back."

Tom gently reached out to cup her face with his long fingers. "Are you all right, Echo?" he asked gently.

Their eyes met, and Gideon saw a strange but unmistakable message pass between them.

"Yes, sir."

Tom squeezed her hand.

Echo reached out and touched Tom's face gently. "I know you'll be worrin', but you don't need to. I'll make it just fine without him."

Tom nodded and rose to walk to the front porch. "Dirk, you and Joe take the body back to town."

The two men moved off to follow Tom's orders.

"Doc Medifer needs to take a look at her," Tom said shortly. "Joe, you head on over to Doc's house once you've helped Dirk. Tell him to get over here right away."

"Yes, sir. Right away, boss."

Tom helped Echo to the bed, then left with Dirk and Joe to take care of Waite's body.

Gideon gently placed a cool cloth on her friend's forehead.

Echo tried to smile, but tears suddenly began to roll from the corners of her eyes. It was the first emotion she had shown, and Gideon found the sign encouraging.

The dam burst, and Echo began to sob, long, racking sobs that tore at Gideon's heart. Waite's death was finally sinking in, and Echo was trying to deal with it the best she could.

Sinking down onto the bed, Gideon cradled her friend, and they shared a good cry together.

When the heart of the storm had passed, they held each other tightly. Gideon knew Echo was frightened; she had no one now.

"Don't worry, Echo. I'll take care of you," Gideon promised. "You don't ever have to be afraid anymore."

"I . . . love . . . you . . . so . . . much," Echo sobbed, and her voice reminded Gideon of the day that she had held Juice Tetterson in her arms. The young seven-year-old was crying and sniffling exactly the same way on the day that she'd fallen and scraped her knee. "At . . . least . . . now I won't have to . . . lose . . . you," Echo cried.

Smoothing the young girl's hair, Gideon crooned to her softly, "I love you, too, Echo, and you will never lose me," she whispered. "Never."

The sheriff and his deputy in Shadow Pine were summoned. It was late in the morning before the two men finally arrived.

Tom had left the cabin earlier, saying that

he had to check on the crew, but that he would be coming back.

Gideon dismissed school that day so she could stay with Echo. The two sat beside the stove listening to the logging teams passing by outside, their runners squeaking loudly as they cut through the deep snow. It was snowing again, large wet flakes that looked like scraps of cotton filtering down from the sky.

Echo got up occasionally to check the meat she was roasting in the oven. The mouth-watering aroma filled the small cabin. Gideon had tried to persuade Echo to forget about cooking today, but she stubbornly insisted that the sheriff and his deputy would appreciate a hot meal before they made the trip back.

Around ten, Echo got out the flour and sugar, and Gideon helped her bake a chocolate cake from her mother's recipe. Echo, more subdued this morning, said that the cake had been Waite's personal favorite.

The sheriff and his man arrived around eleven thirty. They had been to Watersweet, where they'd determined that Waite's death was caused by a fall and a subsequent blow to his head. In his drunken condition, he never regained consciousness.

"I just don't know what to tell you, Echo. We're mighty sorry your man is dead. We're ruling his death as accidental."

Echo nodded solemnly. "I know you've done your best. I want you and your deputy to take supper with us before you start the cold ride home."

"We sure would be obliged, ma'am," the sheriff accepted wearily. "It's a long ride back."

Gideon and Echo served the men. Tom had returned earlier to help in any way he could. Around four that afternoon, he and three other men built a pine box for Waite's burial. Gideon found the contrast between the two men overwhelming. Tom was a good, honest, hard-working man, and Gideon knew he would never lift a hand to a woman, while she felt sure that Waite had been selfish and unkind.

Gideon deliberately let her hand brush Tom's fingers as she handed the bowl of potatoes to him. Their eyes met and lingered. She could see that he was as concerned for her as he was for Echo, and the knowledge warmed her heart. She smiled, and he winked at her, sending a flush to her face.

She took her place at the table, but discovered that she was still too upset to eat. It seemed like days ago instead of only twenty-four hours, when she had found Waite dead on her way to the cabin. She was thankful that she was numb with fatigue. It made the startling events a little easier to tolerate.

The meal passed pleasantly as the men discussed timber and law. Gideon sipped her cup of strong black coffee and watched Echo. The girl had been a rock all day. The man she'd supposedly loved lay in a pine box, waiting to be buried.

Gideon hated to admit it, but she was glad that Waite Burne was dead. That way, he could never hurt Echo again.

The chocolate cake was served, and all three men went on about Echo's cooking abilities. The deputy said that he'd never eaten a finer meal anywhere, and the sheriff heartily agreed. For someone who was not accustomed to praise from a man, the sincere compliments brought a proud smile to Echo's lips.

It was growing late when the sheriff and his deputy announced that they had to leave. Echo walked the two men to the door.

"Sure am sorry it's turned out this way, ma'am."

"I appreciate all you've done, Sheriff," Echo acknowledged softly. "Now you bundle up tight. The wind is real mean tonight."

Tipping his hat politely, the sheriff opened the door, then paused. Turning back to Echo he said softly, "You're a good woman, Echo Burne. Don't let no one ever tell you different."

The remaining occupants of the small log cabin settled down for the night. The old clock ticked away as if by its continuous labor, it could erase the sorrow that had taken place there today.

Tom sat beside the stove with Gideon,

drinking coffee and listening to the howling wind.

Echo tossed fitfully about on the bed she had once shared with Waite. Gideon was concerned that she wasn't sleeping well, so around one o'clock she warmed a pan of milk and added a small amount of the sleeping powder that Doc Medifer had left earlier. Echo drank the potion gratefully, murmuring her apologies for being so much trouble.

"You should be trying to sleep yourself," Gideon whispered to Tom, as she crept silently back to her chair.

"I'm all right." He stifled a yawn, and Gideon could see that deep lines of fatigue were dominating the corners of his eyes. "We should both try and get some rest," he said softly. "We can hear Echo if she needs anything."

Gideon nodded and got up to get an extra blanket for him. As she handed it to him, she noticed a smile touched the corners of his mouth. She cocked her head. "What's wrong?"

Tom took her hand and pulled her closer, his mouth brushing tenderly over hers. Though he ached to confess how much he had come to love her, the admission would remain unsaid.

His kiss was intense, and it eased the sadness in her heart.

"I'm proud of you," he whispered huskily. His large hand came out to tenderly smooth the loose tendrils of hair around her face.

"For what?"

Tom shook his head slowly. He was consumed with guilt each time she looked at him with so much guileless love shining in her eyes, and he was paid back a thousandfold for his deception.

"You've been good to Echo," he said softly. "She hasn't had much love in her life, and to have a friend like you means everything to her. She'll never forget you."

"I love her, Tom, and there'll be no need for her to forget me. I'll always be here for her." She tore her gaze away.

She'd wanted to tell him that she'd be there for him like that too. But she remembered her life before she came here. She'd made promises, commitments. What of them? She needed time, time to sort things out. She wasn't Fedelia Yardley. She was Gideon Wakefield.

That would change a lot of things. But as she looked at him, she realized that it couldn't change the way she felt about him.

Their mouths touched again and lingered this time, reminding them of desires that ached to be appeased. Reluctantly, Tom set her gently aside, despite her soft murmurs of disappointment. "You need your rest," he said gently. "It will be morning soon."

"But I want to be with you—I don't care about sleeping." She would gladly forfeit a meager hour or two of sleep for the pleasure of staying in his arms. She was uncertain about a lot of things, but her desire for him was not one of them.

He gave her a lopsided grin that caused a familiar flutter in her stomach, then he kissed her briefly again—with enough mastery to make her wish he would change his priorities. When he set her aside this time, she noticed that his breathing was not as even as it had been.

"Go to sleep," he said firmly.

Gideon accepted the dismissal—she had a lot of thinking to do.

A few seconds later, she felt his hand close over hers.

Her eyes drifted shut. She'd seen in his eyes tonight what was in her heart every time she looked at him, but from the depths of her memory came the knowledge that she might never have him as her own, because she was promised to another.

Talbot Wellington-Kent. She strained to recall her feelings for the man. Were they as deep, as tumultuous, as passionate, as the feelings she had for Tom Lannigan? She remembered Talbot's genteel manners, his kindness, his thoughtfulness and patience. She struggled to remember the feelings his kisses had evoked. They had been sweet, chaste, and proper. They hadn't felt like Tom's: they hadn't left her breathless, aching for more.

The sound of sleet peppering against the

window panes lulled her weary body to relax. Logs snapped and popped in the old stove. Though her heart ached for Echo, when she was close to Tom like this, she felt safe.

It occurred to her in that drowsy state between sleep and awareness that she could have adjusted to being Fedelia Yardley. That identity didn't bother her so much anymore. It was as if by fate that she had been born—or reborn—the day of the train accident. Just when she'd begun to hope that her memory would never return, it had come back, sudden and unwelcome and frightening. She didn't want anything to intrude on the love that she had found in Watersweet. Could she just go on pretending that she was Fedelia? The thought was so tempting. If she remained silent, and told no one of the mistake, she could stay here with Tom.

But if she told someone who she really was, Tom would be snatched from her. Her devoted family and friends from her former life would demand that she return to them.

The prospect was too alarming for Gideon to consider. She would never leave Watersweet . . . never.

She might have promised her future to Talbot, but her heart belonged to Tom. If she had to leave Lannigan, she'd suffer a loss more severe than the one Echo was struggling to survive now. Her heart ached. She was torn, torn between the past and the present. The future looked too dismal to consider.

She wanted to avoid the past, but instinctively she suspected that no matter how fast she ran, she couldn't outrun the truth.

As the snow fell gently on the roof of the log cabin, Gideon sighed and snuggled closer to the man who would forever hold the key to her heart, no matter what chains imprisoned her in the past.

"Good night, my love," she murmured sleepily.

"Good night, little one," he returned softly.

15

The touch of a man's lips brushing across her forehead brought Gideon awake a little later. The clock had just struck three.

"I'm leaving now," Tom whispered.

"Mmmm . . . so soon?" Gideon raised her mouth in search of his. He started to turn away, but the temptation was overpowering. As he faced her again, her arms came around his neck, and they kissed with an overwhelming hunger.

It was many long minutes before Tom could bring himself to break the embrace. Squatting in front of her chair, he stared at her, the blue of his eyes openly cherishing her as his hands moved sensuously over her bare arms. "It's getting late, and I want to stop by our room before I get the crew started."

"But you've had so little rest," she murmured. He was calling it *their* room, a big concession from him. She'd realized now how much her efforts to decorate their room had embarrassed him. She wished now that her choice of fabrics had reflected both of them, instead of just her.

"I'll catch up tonight." His lips voluntarily moved back to possess hers. "Why don't you come with me?"

Coming more awake, Gideon glanced over to check on Echo. The girl appeared to be sleeping soundly now. Pushing the blanket aside, she got to her feet.

Tom loaded the stove as Gideon prepared to leave. Returning to the bed, she tucked the blanket around Echo more securely, then leaned down and placed a kiss on the girl's forehead.

Echo stirred momentarily and smiled up at her. "Is it time to get up yet?"

"No, go back to sleep. I'm going with Tom to get a few of my things. I'll be back before the sun comes up."

Echo nodded, then drifted off to sleep almost immediately.

A thick cloud bank was clinging to the eastern horizon as Tom and Gideon stepped out of the cabin. It was still dark, but the snow showed signs of letting up. Only a thin white powder filtered halfheartedly down from the sky. The wind had died an hour ago, and a peaceful silence had settled over the logging town.

Their footsteps left deep tracks in the snow as they made their way around the deep harbor. From somewhere in the distance, a dog barked, momentarily shattering the stillness.

"Do you think you need to stay with Echo a few days?" Tom asked as they moved along in the rays of the lantern.

"Yes, but I want to stay with you."

He paused, and Gideon could see that he wanted to say something, but he seemed to suddenly change his mind, and they began walking again. "I wish that were possible."

So do I, my love.

"We could, you know." Gideon knew she'd never been so forward with a man, but she knew that in her heart she had already accepted Tom Lannigan as the man with whom she would spend her life. All that remained was for them to formalize the vows, and for now she wasn't worried over a piece of paper. She was rushing away from her past, hoping that it wouldn't catch up with her in time to spoil what happiness she had found.

"That's something that can never be, and I want you to stop hoping that it can," he said quietly.

"Why?" It was Gideon who paused this time. "All you have to do is propose to me, Tom Lannigan, and you'll have a wife so fast it'll make your head swim."

Something deep inside filled Gideon with a kind of desperation. If they could marry quickly, perhaps they *could* outrun the past that was slowly eating its way into their lives.

It was foolish to suggest such a thing, but if he didn't marry her, and soon, then Talbot might decide to investigate the accident and come to Watersweet. If she was already married to another man, then he wouldn't be able to take her back with him.

Tom's jaw firmed tenaciously. "I can't do that."

"For heaven sakes, you can! I know it would be next Sunday before the sky pilot would be here to hear our vows, but that wouldn't stop me from becoming your wife today if you'd only ask me. I know it isn't right for a man and woman to be together until they're married but in my heart you are my husband—" A new, more sobering thought washed over Gideon. "Are you in love with that woman in Shadow Pine? Is that it?"

Tom glanced at her dourly. "What woman in Shadow Pine?"

"Marcy Wetlock—the woman Andre told me that you go to see every now and then."

Tom was dumbfounded by Andre's indiscretion. "What has that damn Andre told you about me now?" he demanded.

"Not much . . ." she hedged.

"Oh? Did he happen to mention how often I change my underwear?"

Gideon blushed. "Of course not—I've already found that out for myself."

They began walking again.

"Well?"

"Well, what?

"Are you going to ask me?" A feeling of urgency compelled her. She intuitively felt that if she didn't solidify her relationship with him, it would slip away forever. Her past was breathing close on her heels, feelings of obligation were tightening around her heart like grapevine tendrils. If she didn't make a stab for freedom, the freedom to choose the man she wanted, it might slip away forever.

"Ask you to marry me?"

"Yes."

"I can't."

Though his answer wasn't encouraging, she wasn't completely discouraged. He had as much as said he was in love with her and that he wanted to marry her.

"What are we waiting for?" Gideon challenged. "Shot Harrison to grow hair?"

The tension broken, Tom chuckled and drew her close to his side as they walked along. "The day I can ask you to be my wife, you will be."

"That isn't good enough. I don't have time to wait, Tom." Her voice was filled with a strange sadness now.

"I know you don't."

Gideon waited for him to explain his remark, but he chose not to. They walked in silence.

They were approaching Menson's store and their living quarters. Gideon's hands and feet were already becoming numb with cold. They climbed the long flight of outside stairs, and Tom unlocked the door. When they stepped inside his room, it seemed almost as cold as the outside.

"It'll take a few minutes to get a fire going," he apologized.

Gideon sauntered over to sit on the bed while he loaded the potbellied stove with pieces of kindling and wood. Striking a match, he lit the dry tinder.

Ten minutes later, the stove was putting out enough warmth that Tom could begin to chip the ice atop the water in the pitcher so he could shave.

The growing warmth in the small room soon made Gideon drowsy. Slumping over on her side, she watched the broad band of corded muscles in Tom's back jump and play as he whipped up a foamy lather in a cup. She smiled as he spread the white mixture evenly over the lower half of his face.

"What's so funny?"

"Men."

Eyeing himself in the small mirror, he reached for the straight razor, then absently ran the blade briskly along a leather strop to sharpen it. "You have something against them?"

"No, there's one in particular I find very interesting."

"Only one?" he asked casually.

"Have you ever thought about growing a beard?" Gideon asked, coyly changing the subject.

"I had one for eight years."

"What made you shave it off?"

Tom leaned closer to the mirror, drawing the razor evenly over his cheekbone. "A certain lady I was seeing got to complaining about it." He dipped the blade in a pan of water, then glanced over to wink at her mischievously. "Real good-lookin' woman, blond hair, ruby red lips, with a figure that would make a man shave his head if she'd have asked."

Gideon returned his gaze spiritedly. "And did you?"

"Shave my head?"

"Yes."

He turned his attention back to the mirror. "She really wasn't that good-looking."

"I can't imagine any woman complaining about you," Gideon said with a sigh.

Tom chuckled as he carefully drew the blade down the left side of his neck. "Actually, I got rid of the beard because I got tired of it. It was hot in the summer, and it itched like the devil in the winter."

She smiled, drinking in his handsome features. "Then you were only teasing about Marcy wanting you to shave it off?"

"Did I say it was Marcy?"

"No . . . but she's blond. . . . That's who you meant, wasn't it?"

Tom's incriminating silence made her lower lip sag into an unconscious pout.

"Answer me."

"There's only one woman I'm in love with."

Lifting her head, she smiled. "Say it, Tom."

"No."

"Why?"

"I don't need to say it. You know it."

"Tom . . ."

"Do you like a man with a beard?" he asked.

Sighing, she laid her head back on the pillow. "I don't know . . . I think they look nice on some men."

"Name one."

"Frank Kellier, Lars Rurick, Ed Holman, Dal Hunter, Race Kenniger, Hank Sutherland, Trace Gibson—"

Her seemingly unending recitation was interrupted by Tom's tense condemnation. "Damn, I said to name one."

Gideon laughed. "You needn't worry. I think you are the most handsome, most attractive man in the entire camp—just as I'm sure that you find me the most beautiful, most wonderful, most desirable woman in the territory." She rolled over onto her back. "Even more beautiful and desirable than that poor Marcy Wetlock, who's forced to carry around all that surplus flesh in the front of her chemise."

He chuckled wickedly. "Yeah, poor Marcy."

She pitched a pillow at him, and he grunted

as it hit him in the back. "You find Frank Kellier handsome, huh?"

"Umm . . . yes. Definitely so."

"Even with the one leg?" he prompted softly.

"Of course—it's the kind of man Frank is that makes him attractive."

Tom grabbed a towel to wipe the remainder of the soap from his face. "Do you find Frank and Lars and Ed attractive?"

Gideon grinned. "Why the sudden interest in who I find attractive?"

Turning back to the washbasin, he stripped his shirt off and began to wash. "Just making conversation, that's all."

"Are you jealous?"

"If I am, you'll never know it."

"That means you are."

Hopping off the bed, Gideon removed her cloak. The room was warm and cozy now.

Tom finished washing, then turned his back to her as he reached for a clean shirt.

He turned back around, and Gideon caught a glimpse of his wide, bare chest matted with thick blond hair. Her pulse began to thump. She had seen a man's bare chest before. The men in the bunkhouse were careless at times, but the sight of their bare chests had failed to stir her like this one did.

Moving across the room, she slipped her arms around his waist before he could protest.

Her future was more uncertain than ever, but that seemed to make her only want him more.

"Come on now—we haven't got time for that," he murmured, halfheartedly trying to move her aside.

Gideon held her ground as she laid her cheek against his chest and hugged him tightly. He felt so warm and so male.

"I think I like men with hair on their chests better than men with beards," she whispered.

Her laughing eyes lifted to meet his as she brought her fingers around to explore the soft, silken mat. She felt him tense as she moved shamelessly closer. "Kiss me." She could see in his eyes that he wanted to.

"No. And you'd better not know all that much about a man's bare chest."

"But I lived with a hundred and twenty-five bare chests daily—I peeked once in a while."

"I'll bet you did."

She grinned, deciding to tease him a bit. "I don't know—I was shamelessly weak at times." Her hands brushed lightly through the soft hair on his chest, and she heard his breathing quicken. "I tend to lose my head around a man if I'm not extremely careful."

He caught her hand and stilled it. "You had better be careful, or you are likely to find yourself being ravished by a man, just as you have been asking to be for some time now."

Their eyes met and held.

"I wouldn't care if the man were you," she challenged in the barest of whispers.

His voice deepened. "You're daring me to make love to you?"

"Yes . . . yes . . . yes."

"Lord, you tempt me," his voice dropped to a desperate whisper, and his searing gaze told Gideon that it was raw desire, not simple temptation, that persecuted him.

Pulling her tightly to him, he let her feel the power she had over him. Time was suspended as they stared at each other, their eyes hungrily conveying what their mouths and hands were longing to do.

"I have been this way for weeks. I hope you're proud of yourself," he murmured.

"Most assuredly." Her hand slipped down to touch the proof of his desire, and she felt him shudder with longing.

The sound of the cookee blowing his Gabriel horn filtered through the cozy room, but they were caught up by the promise in each other's eyes.

His hand cupped the side of her neck as his thumb rhythmically caressed the side of it. "A man can stand this kind of teasing only so long."

"I pushed it too far this time, huh?"

"Shoved it, lady. If I were to do what I want to do, we wouldn't leave this room this morning . . . or today . . . or tomorrow."

"Would that be so terrible?"

307

"Yes . . . no . . . I don't know anymore." He sighed, burying his face in her hair. "I just know I want you so damn bad my teeth ache. . . ."

She moved closer, and his mouth dipped lower until their lips teased one another's with just the hint of a kiss. She could see that his resolve was growing very weak. "Then make love to me."

"No . . . if I do . . . we'll both regret it," his ragged whisper came against her lips.

The tip of her tongue sensuously slid along his upper lip. "No, no regrets. We'll make a pact . . . no regrets," she murmured.

He groaned as their lips met with more urgency. Tom knew he had to regain control of the situation. He could not take her . . . it would be madness.

Slowly dropping her head, she let her cheek graze along his naked chest, realizing that he was very near to where she wanted him to be.

The smell of soap, shaving cream, and his manly essence washed over her, making her want him that much more. She wasn't familiar with the strange sensations that were suddenly flooding her whole body, the growing ache from somewhere deep inside her that screamed to be released, but she knew that whatever inferno he was igniting in her, he could sweetly, mercifully assuage.

She knew her thoughts were mirrored in the depths of her eyes as Tom slowly lifted her up to kiss her, but she didn't care. Though her future was uncertain, she was sure of one thing: she loved this man with all her heart.

"Stay here with me this morning . . . today . . . tomorrow," she urged with a reckless note in her voice.

"No . . . I can't do that." Their mouths brushed again, and he groaned, his breath warm against her mouth. "Don't do this . . . I'm only flesh and blood."

Their sighs mingled with one breath as they moved toward the bed. They had been denied too long. Tom knew it, and he didn't have the will to fight it any longer. Not when she was so openly willing to love him.

It came upon them in a rush, the bittersweet ache of passion, the agonizing fires that flared uncontrollably within them, the unquenchable hunger that took reason and crushed it beneath the foot of insanity.

Gideon clung to him with an eagerness that consumed them as the gentle touch of their lips gave way to a heated, insatiable demand. She gave no thought to holding back or denying what had been his from the moment they had first met. His lips coaxed hers open to his thrusting tongue as they lay across the bed, dissolving in each other's arms. The deepening kiss touched the passionate core inside her, spreading a white heat throughout her body. Her heart was aching for the need to give to him, to pleasure him as no other woman could or ever would again.

Cradling her to his chest, he rolled on his back with her. A hand to her hip shifted her more fully atop him, and they were kissing again—tasting, exploring, free to fulfill the craving, the hunger that gnawed at them.

The Gabriel horn blew again, but they were beyond hearing.

As their ragged breathing filled the small room, Tom lifted his head. The blue of his eyes burned into hers, and she could see the anguish of uncertainty in his gaze.

Yes, yes, yes. Her heart and her very soul cried out to him to proceed, to make their love as beautiful and as perfect as she knew it was meant to be.

Incoherent words began to tumble from his lips as he accepted the gift she was offering him. His mouth crushed hers again as his fingers frantically began to work the buttons on her dress.

Waves of pleasure spread through her body as she tried to assist him. Their hands fumbled clumsily, and Gideon heard him swear, followed by the sound of material giving way to his impatience. His fingers searched for the opening of her chemise, and seconds later the fabric parted, exposing the tantalizing fullness of her creamy flesh.

His breath caught as he boldly drank his fill

of her, then his head lowered, and his tongue branded her with its fiery touch.

Her fingers burrowed into his thick mass of blond hair as she was caught up on wave after wave of tormenting pleasure. His mouth returned to take hers again, hot and demanding, tasting her with a hunger they both shared.

They drifted deeper into the bed as his hand found more intimate ground, snatching her breath with his daring.

She was dying, slowly, exquisitely dying in a sea of labyrinthine pleasures. . . . Their future was bleak, but they had now. The memory of the next few moments with Tom Lannigan might have to hold her for a lifetime. She would make each of them count.

Tom's ragged breathing echoed in her ear. He wanted her more than he'd ever wanted anyone, but she was promised to someone else. Whether she knew it or not, he knew it was so. She was engaged to Talbot Wellington-Kent, but with needs raging out of control, he didn't care anymore. She was his, perhaps only for this moment, but he meant to take her, to love her as he had never loved another woman. Her fiancé be damned. She would be his.

He touched her, strumming her desires until he knew that she was ready for him. Gently, he entered her. And after the first moments, she welcomed and encouraged him. Together, they soared the heights they'd denied themselves for so long.

When the world shattered into a million exquisite pieces, she clung to him, murmuring his name, pouring out her love from the depths of her heart.

"Are you all right, little one?"

"Yes," she assured him, drawing him closer when the storm of their loving had passed. "Oh, yes."

A sharp rap suddenly sounded at the door. Startled, Tom raised himself up on his elbow. "Who could that be at this hour?"

Gideon murmured, still dazed from passion, "I don't know. I don't care. Don't answer it," she urged, pulling his mouth back to meet hers. She wouldn't let him go, not now. He moaned, giving in to the kiss, but the second sharp rap on the door and the sound of Andre's voice shouting his name brought him up in bed.

"What is it?" he snapped sharply.

"Please come, Tom. There is someone here who wants to talk to you," came the muffled reply.

"Now?"

"Yes. I'm afraid it's urgent."

Gideon lay on the bed watching as Tom left the bed and began to button his shirt. "Can't it wait until later, Andre?"

Gideon thought Andre's voice sounded unusually grim. "You had better come down now."

Tom glanced at Gideon apologetically. "It must be important, or Andre would not have come here so early."

"Don't go."

His eyes searched hers helplessly. "I'm sorry . . . I have to."

"Then take me with you in your heart."

He gazed at her, his love spilling over in his eyes now. "You will always be in my heart." Moving back to the bed, he took her in his arms as the pounding started at the door again.

"I'll be there in a minute, Andre!"

They could hear the crunch of Andre's boots on the newly fallen snow as he turned and made his way back down the steep stairway.

Kissing her nose, then her cheek, then the tip of her chin, he said softly, "I'm sorry . . . I'll see that we're not interrupted tonight."

She sighed, reaching out to trace his upper lip lovingly with the tip of her finger. "It's all right." She shrugged. "We have the rest of our lives."

A shadow of pain crossed his face. Bending over again he kissed her hotly. "Stop by my office before you leave," he said as he straightened to leave a moment later.

"You won't be busy?"

"Never too busy for you." He gazed at her, and she desperately wished that she could know what troubled him so. "I love you," he said.

Gideon closed her eyes for fear she might cry. "I love you too."

He leaned over to share one last, long, anguished kiss before he slipped out of her arms to see what required his immediate attention so early in the morning.

When Gideon opened the door to Tom's office thirty minutes later, a big, orange sun was just coming over the rim of the pines, promising a lovely day.

She planned to have breakfast with Echo, then ask her friend to accompany her to school that day. Waite would not be buried until late afternoon, and Gideon didn't want her friend to spend the morning alone.

Andre glanced up when he saw Gideon enter. "*Ma chérie.* We've been waiting for you."

"Good morning, gentlemen." Her eyes went immediately to Tom.

He stood at the window, his back turned to her, watching the sunrise.

Starting to go to him, she suddenly noticed that another man was sitting in a dark corner of the room. She stopped and turned to look at him, and her heart stood still.

His city clothes, his new hat, and his high-buttoned shoes with their bulldog toes assured her that he wasn't from the wilds of Michigan.

She blinked until her eyes adjusted to the light.

His face was familiar, too familiar, as he rose from his chair.

"My God . . . it's true . . . you're alive," he breathed. "Gideon . . . my dear . . . you're alive!" The man moved cautiously toward her, his hands extended as if he feared she would suddenly dissolve in a mist. "I was afraid to believe it . . . even though I've dreamed of this moment. I never expected . . . never dared to hope that I might find you here."

Tears of pure joy began to roll from the man's eyes and stream down his cheeks. "I can't believe it . . . you're alive . . . you're alive!"

Gideon's heart seemed to wither. She glanced expectantly at Andre, who purposefully kept his head down and remained silent.

Her eyes darted to Tom. His broad back, tense now, partially blocked the golden rays of sun streaming through the windowpane.

"Tom?" she prompted softly.

As he turned, her heart began to pound as she saw the anguish that filled his eyes. *God, no . . . please no*, her gaze pleaded silently. *Love me enough to fight for me.*

Forcing her eyes to meet his, he said in a shaken voice, "Gideon . . . I'm sorry." His words faltered as he searched for a gentle way to tell her.

It was his tone that told her. He knew.

But had he known from the beginning who she really was? The pain in Gideon's eyes beseeched him to be honest with her. "You've known all along who I am, haven't you?" she whispered.

"No . . . at first I wasn't certain."

"But you went along with the mistaken assumption that I was Fedelia Yardley? Even after you suspected that I wasn't?"

His eyes refused to leave hers. He knew he had a difficult choice to make. He could fight for her. Everything in him wanted to do that. If he asked her to stay with him, she would, Tom knew that. Her love was an unselfish, simple love, and if he lost her, his life would be meaningless. Yet he knew he had nothing to offer her but an uncertain future in a dying land, and a pocketful of worthless dreams.

Wellington-Kent could give her a life of luxury. He could give her everything in life Tom couldn't. Tom had only his love to offer. To Tom, the choice was clear. He had hurt her enough, and he would not let her risk her future happiness to stay with him.

"Yes. I began to suspect who you were when I noticed the strong resemblance between you and Rutherford. Every day it became more clear to me that you were Gideon Wakefield and not Fedelia Yardley, but I still went along with the mistaken assumption."

"Why?" She took a step forward, ignoring

Talbot and Andre's presence. "Why would you do this to me?"

"I've asked myself that question a hundred times," he said tiredly.

"And your answer?"

His eyes lifted back to meet hers, and she saw the torment in their depths. "You were about to sell Wakefield Timber without replanting the trees. The trees were my dream. I wanted revenge."

"Revenge?" Tears stung her eyes. "My God, Tom. Why didn't you just take a gun and shoot me? It would have been more merciful."

Tom drew a deep breath. "At the time, I hated Gideon Wakefield. She was selling a timber business she cared nothing about, selling off the legacy her grandfather had sunk his life into. She cared nothing for replanting the forests. I believed she was a heartless, selfish, shallow fool who'd never done an honest day's work in her life. When I saw the chance to even the score for what she was doing, I took it."

"And now?" she asked softly.

His jaw firmed. "You know how I feel about you now."

"Gideon, my love, I know this is upsetting," Talbot said quietly. "Mr. Lannigan has explained about the loss of your memory—"

Gideon held up her hand to stop him, her eyes going back to Tom. "You have nothing you want to say to me or Talbot? You are willing to let me return to Philadelphia, and go on with your life as if I were never a part of it?"

Drawing a deep breath, Tom turned away from her and said in a voice void of emotion, "Go back to Philadelphia, little one. It's where you belong. There's nothing here for you."

Stunned, Gideon realized he was going to let her go. He wasn't going to fight to keep her.

"Nothing . . . even after what we shared this morning?" she whispered brokenly.

His jaw tightened painfully as he stared out the window. "No regrets, Gideon. Have you forgotten so quickly?"

She began weeping softly as he turned and strode out of the room, slamming the door behind him.

"*Ma chérie* . . . he does not know what he says," Andre consoled. "He is angry with himself."

Lifting her eyes to Talbot, she said in a flat voice, "I want to go home."

Talbot sprang forth to assist her. "Of course, my love. We'll leave on the next train. Once you're back in Philadelphia we can put this whole unfortunate episode behind us."

"Yes, Talbot. That's what I must do," she murmured, still dazed by Tom's cruel rejection. "I must forget all about this unpleasant episode."

16

"Are you comfortable, my dear?"

"Yes, Talbot, thank you."

Talbot smiled paternally and turned his attention to the young girl who sat with her nose pressed eagerly against the train window.

"And you, Echo? Is there anything I can do for you?"

"Oh no, sir, Mr. Wellington-Kent. You've done too much for me already," Echo assured him.

"Call me Talbot, dear, and it's entirely my good fortune to have two such beautiful ladies under my protection." Turning to Gideon again, he coaxed gently, "Perhaps you and Echo might enjoy a pot of hot tea?" He reached for the cord above his head and gave two short pulls. "I'll have the porter bring one immediately."

"If you would enjoy one, Talbot." Gideon's wan smile did little to encourage the offering as her attention strayed back to the passing scenery. The events of the past few days had rendered her numb. Learning that she was Gideon Wakefield and not Fedelia Yardley had come as a shock, but it was Tom's letting her go back to Talbot so easily that Gideon found unbearable.

A hysterical giggle rose in Gideon's throat, but she quickly forced it back down. Well, if Tom Lannigan had wanted to hurt her, he had accomplished his goal. Deceit alone was enough, but the knowledge that he was willing to let her marry another man was beyond the realm of punishment.

Gideon had promised herself one thing: she would never again be the same trusting, gullible fool that Tom Lannigan had proven her to be.

Even his quietly spoken, humble apology had done little to salve her injured pride. The trials he had put her through were too numerous to mention, but one of them was unforgivable: he had made love to her, then let her go.

Gideon knew if he had so much as hinted that he cared for her deeply, she would have swallowed what remained of her pride and stayed. If only he had taken her into his arms and assured her that his confession of love that last morning had not been without meaning, she would have forgiven him. She would never forget what he had done to her, but somewhere deep inside her wounded soul she knew that she loved him more than life itself and that she wasn't willing to let him go. She had never wanted to give him up.

Biting her lower lip until she tasted blood, she vowed that she would not let Talbot see her cry again. The poor man had listened to her sniffling for days now, and shown incredible patience, even though he'd completely misunderstood the reason for her abject misery.

Gideon was sure that Talbot had seen the love in her eyes when she'd looked at Tom Lannigan, but he had far too much breeding to question her about it. She was just grateful that Talbot had arrived before she'd talked Tom into marrying her. Of course he wouldn't have married her, she realized that now . . . that miserable . . . insufferable cad. She still loved him so much—she sniffled loudly—she would have him on any terms.

Get a grip on yourself, Gideon! Her inner voice warned her sternly, but her control was on another downhill slide. A loud sob escaped her, bringing Talbot and Echo's conversation to an abrupt halt.

Echo leaned over and cooed sympathetically as Talbot quickly extracted his handkerchief from his breast pocket and thrust it at her. "Are you all right, dear?"

"Fine, thank you . . . *sniff* . . . Talbot. I must be coming down with a cold."

Talbot and Echo exchanged helpless looks. Leaning forward, Talbot placed his hand consolingly over Gideon's fingers. Staring at Talbot's hand, Gideon was reminded how different his slender, pale fingers were from Tom's large, nut-brown, work-callused hands.

"I know how all of this has upset you, my dear, but once we reach Philadelphia and you resume your normal life, I'm sure you'll enjoy yourself again." Talbot peered at her hopefully. "Do you remember your life in Philadelphia?"

Gideon nodded. "It's coming back in bits and pieces."

"Then you will forget all this misery since your accident. And you will enjoy life as you did before."

Talbot had spent hours filling her in on her childhood, the deaths of her parents, how he had been appointed her legal guardian until she reached the age of eighteen, and their subsequent engagement, but Gideon felt detached from it all. She could remember the past, but she didn't feel that it had any relevance to the present.

Talbot hesitantly withdrew his hand, drawing a deep sigh as he settled back against the seat. "Well, you're not to be concerned. I will see that you have the finest physicians money can buy. I'm sure the superb medical facilities we have at our disposal will help to ease you through this crisis."

Gideon's tearful gaze studied the bare third finger of her left hand as she vaguely recalled what had happened to the engagement ring she had been wearing the day she'd left for Watersweet.

"I'm sorry about your ring, Talbot."

"My dear, material possessions are the least of my worries. My only concern is that you are well and happy. We shall always be able to replace a ring." Turning back to Echo, he smiled. "And we're going to provide both you and Gideon with new clothes, young lady. Entire wardrobes: coats, hats, shoes, dresses, lingerie, and anything else that you might decide you want. You and Gideon shall make a holiday of touring the stores to your hearts' content!"

"Oh . . . I just don't know what to say. . . . I know I'm going to wake up some morning and find that this has all been a wonderful dream!" Echo exclaimed.

Gideon could see the girl was in complete awe of the generous carriage maker. Talbot seemed to have taken to Echo immediately, and they had formed a close friendship already. She listened as the two began to rattle on about the proposed shopping expedition as if they were two children planning a trip to the circus together.

Gideon sighed, returning her gaze to the window. Talbot was no more than a polite stranger to her, yet in a matter of weeks she would be his bride. The unnerving thought sent the handkerchief to the corners of her eyes again. She knew she should be grateful that such a man of wealth and prestige would want her for his wife.

Through the past few dark days Gideon had found Talbot to be an honorable and gentle man. He had been there for her to lean on when her world had fallen apart in Tom's office. She had ached for Tom to take her into his arms and beg for her forgiveness, but he had stood aside, letting Talbot dry her tears of disbelief. Talbot had then informed her that once they reached Philadelphia, after a reasonable time of adjustment, their wedding would proceed as planned.

When Gideon had told Talbot about Echo and how she had come to love the girl like a sister, he had insisted that Echo accompany them back to Philadelphia. Once Waite received a proper burial, she had eagerly accepted his invitation.

It helped Gideon to see Echo smiling and happy again, looking forward to a bright new future, but she herself had dreaded the hour when she would board the train and leave Tom. A familiar wetness began to slide down her cheeks again as she recalled this morning.

Tom hadn't even come to see her off. Her eyes had searched for him in the blinding snow until they ached, but as the train began pulling out of Watersweet, he still had not arrived.

As the cars had passed through a grove of

dense pines, Gideon had seen him standing at the side of the tracks, watching from a distance.

He'd stood alone, following the train with his eyes as it left Watersweet. Deep inside, she still believed that he cared for her. Yet he'd stood there and done nothing to stop her from leaving.

Racing to the back of the train she had caught one final glimpse of him. She still prayed for a sign of his remorse.

He had stared back at her, but shown no sign of relenting.

The icy air had frozen the hot tears to her cheeks, but she had stood there in that cold caboose until his tall, achingly familiar features had long faded from her sight.

Tears had blinded her, and Talbot had stepped out and helped her tenderly back into the coach. She remembered thinking that she had no idea how she would live without Tom Lannigan, and, at that moment, she hadn't even cared to try. Fumbling for the handkerchief that Talbot had given her earlier, Gideon found that as usual it was wet with tears. A moment later, Echo quietly pressed a clean one into her hand.

Smiling in mute gratitude, Gideon discreetly dabbed at the moist corners of her eyes. Drawing a deep, ragged breath, she willed her mind to cease functioning as the train made its way to Philadelphia, a home that held no comfort, a home that promised marriage to a man she no longer knew or loved.

"Isn't it the loveliest thing you've ever seen!" Echo entered the study and whirled about the room gaily, modeling a stunning silk gown of federal blue for Gideon.

Winter was finally coming to an end and the first tender buds of spring were popping out on the trees lining the old cobblestone street in front of the Wellington-Kent mansion.

Turning from the window where she'd stood looking at the tiny crocuses that had pushed their heads above the ground to make their first appearance, Gideon smiled at the young girl.

The past few weeks had brought about a miraculous change in Echo. Under Talbot's dedicated care and tutelage, she had become quite a lovely young woman. Her earlier gauntness had disappeared into nubile curves, and her sallow complexion had taken on a warm, healthy glow. Gideon had never seen her friend looking more beautiful.

"It's breathtaking, Echo. I see you and Talbot have been shopping again this afternoon."

Echo's smile rapidly turned to one of immediate concern. "Yes, I hope you don't mind."

"Don't be silly—of course I don't mind. Now, show me what you've bought." Gideon's closets were already overflowing with clothes she couldn't hope to wear even if she lived to be a hundred.

"Well, okay, but Talbot wants me to remind you that the seamstress has arrived for the final fitting of your wedding gown. You simply must see the rose crepe de chine we found in this marvelous little shop near the center of town. You're simply going to adore it!"

"I'm sure it is in excellent taste."

"We must hurry, though. Talbot says he is taking you to the opera tonight!"

"I'll be along shortly. I just have this letter that I want to finish." Gideon returned to the Louis Quatorze writing desk and resumed her seat while Echo continued to pirouette happily around the room, trying to catch occasional glimpses of her gown in the large gold-framed mirror suspended above the fireplace.

Gideon brought her hand up to her forehead and murmured, "Echo . . . I was wondering if you would mind accompanying Talbot tonight. I seem to have come down with this dreadful headache."

"Oh?" Echo's dancing came to a halt, and she became instantly sympathetic. "Another one?"

Gideon made her smile as wan as possible. "Yes, I'm afraid so . . . would you mind terribly going to the opera in my place?"

"No, not if Talbot doesn't mind."

Gideon knew Echo would do anything she asked, and she felt a twinge of conscience that this was the fourth time this week she had asked the girl to fill in for her, but she simply was not up to another outing tonight.

Since her return to Philadelphia, her social schedule had been exhausting. With the balls and the formal teas and the endless succession of parties and social gatherings held in honor of her forthcoming marriage, Gideon had not been able to catch her breath. She realized that she had been wretched company for poor Talbot. A constant feeling of depression was hanging over her, and she knew that he was puzzled by her continuing despondency.

He had casually brought up the subject of Watersweet at dinner one evening and encouraged Gideon to talk about the weeks she'd spent there, in an effort to confront the problem, but Gideon had quietly refused to talk about it. The thought of Tom Lannigan was still far too painful even to think about, let alone discuss. She had excused herself from the table early and had gone to her room without dinner that evening.

She hated to hurt Talbot's feelings again. He had done everything he could to make her happy, but nothing seemed to ease her sorrow.

If it hadn't been for Echo's company, Gideon knew that Talbot would have been as lonely as he had been when he'd thought she was dead.

The door to the study opened again, and Talbot entered. "There you two are. Miss Perryworth is waiting in the solarium for you, darling."

Gideon nodded without glancing up. "I shall be along soon, Talbot."

Strolling toward the fire, Talbot and Echo exchanged shy smiles. "You look lovely in that color, little one," he said softly.

A flash of pain seared through Gideon, and she saw her hand begin to tremble. *Little one* —Tom had called her little one in that magical time an eternity ago . . . or had it really been only eight weeks since she had left him standing beneath a pine with the snow falling heavily on his broad shoulders? She wondered if he ever thought of her, if his nights were endless with her memory as hers were with his.

Echo smiled and dipped demurely, a rosy blush flooding her cheeks from Talbot's compliment. "Thank you, sir."

"Echo, why don't you run along and change for dinner," Gideon suggested. "I would like to speak to Talbot alone for a moment."

"Yes, ma'am." Echo hurriedly curtsied again, then ran happily out of the room.

"There's something you wanted to discuss with me, dear?"

"I wanted to make my personal apologies to you, Talbot. I fear I have this dreadful headache again, and I have asked Echo to go to the opera with you tonight."

"Oh. I'm sorry. Shall I have Freda bring you some headache powder?"

"No, I plan to retire early. I'll take something later."

"I do hope you're planning to have dinner with us tonight. You've grown extremely thin lately."

Gideon smiled. "You worry too much about me."

Talbot's expression softened. "I care very deeply for you, Gideon."

"I know . . . as I do for you, Talbot."

"I don't want to push you, but there are so many wedding gifts flooding in." Talbot shrugged. "They must be opened and tagged soon."

"Can't the servants do that?"

"Of course . . . I just thought you might want to open the gifts personally."

She nodded modestly. "I shall try to oversee the opening of gifts very soon."

"Thank you. There are those in my family who would be deeply hurt if they thought that someone other than the bride had opened their gifts."

"Of course. I shall take care of it as soon as possible."

"Mother wishes our company this Sunday for brunch. She has invited a few of her closest friends to have tea with us."

"Very well."

"Was there anything else?"

"Yes." Gideon folded the letter she had been writing, then slipped it into an envelope with her initials embossed in silver. "Some days ago I received a letter from Sven Templeton, asking that the sale of Wakefield Timber be completed."

"Yes, I'm sure Mr. Templeton is eager to get on with his plans."

"Yes . . . I'm sure he is," Gideon murmured, remembering the unspeakable carnage she had witnessed under the hand of uncaring timber barons like Sven Templeton. "I've just written to inform Mr. Templeton that I shall be keeping my grandfather's business after all."

Surprise flashed briefly across Talbot's face, but he recovered admirably. "That is entirely up to you, but do you think it is wise?"

"Yes, I plan to start a program of replanting the pines as soon as possible." Gideon's chin firmed. "There shall not be another tree cut from Wakefield land that isn't replaced immediately."

Talbot met her determined gaze thoughtfully. "Quite a large undertaking, wouldn't you say?"

"Yes, but it will be done."

"And Tom Lannigan? Will he be in charge of this vast replanting?"

Gideon's gaze dropped guiltily back to the letter in her hand. "I have no idea what Mr. Lannigan's plans are."

Talbot continued to study her. "And if he

should refuse to stay on as foreman of Wakefield Timber?"

The pain was there again, deep and searing as ever. "That will be Mr. Lannigan's decision. He doesn't consult me on such matters."

Talbot sighed. "I see." He hesitated a moment, and Gideon wondered if he would demand that she fire Lannigan as he'd insisted that awful day in Lannigan's office. Talbot cleared his throat. "Let's not keep Miss Perryworth waiting any longer."

He crossed the room and leaned down to kiss her. Gideon casually averted her face, and the kiss landed benignly on her temple.

"I am no longer a virgin, Talbot." Gideon knew he would have to know.

The room grew suddenly silent.

"I suspected as much. Lannigan?"

"Yes," she said softly.

"I assume there shall be no lasting repercussions for your indiscretion?"

"No, I'm not carrying Tom's child, if that's what you mean."

Drawing a deep breath, he said quietly, "Very well. We'll not speak of this matter again."

"Thank you, Talbot." She knew she should say she was sorry, but she wasn't. The memory of the morning Tom had made love to her was the only thing that had carried her through the past eight weeks.

"See that you don't delay Miss Perryworth."

"I'll be along soon, I promise," she murmured.

"See that you do." Talbot straightened, then moved gracefully to leave the room.

The moment had passed, and Gideon suspected that Talbot had let the issue drop because he didn't want to upset her. She knew he simply wanted to forget that horrible chapter in their lives. But she couldn't forget.

17

"*D*ammit, Tom! Have you had some sort of death wish lately?" Andre's hand snaked out to jerk Tom back to safety as another pile of logs broke loose and spilled out into the icy waters of Lake Huron.

The spring river drive was on, and the time had arrived for the shanty boys to discard their shoepacs and rubbers for their corked boots and peavey poles. The logs that had been harvested that season were broken out and driven by the white-water men down the crowded strip of water to the sorting booms at the booming ground.

The fingerlike tributaries of the Saginaw— the rivers Molasses, Salt, Tobacco, Pine, Tittabawassee, Bad, Shiawassee, Cass, Chippewa, Cedar—and their tributaries and branches were jammed with logs, riverhogs, equipment, cooks, clerks, and wanigans.

The pandemonium of thousands of logs dumped into the streams from neighboring

logging camps—all massed together and floating down rivers and streams—was a nightmare to the unexperienced, but to the sea-
soned sorters at the booming grounds, whose
job it was to separate company logs bearing
the same marks into individual pocket booms,
the job was handled with skill.

"I'm sorry, I wasn't thinking," Tom murmured.

The uncharacteristic meekness recently
sounding in Tom's voice fueled Andre's anger
more. "You have been guilty of that a lot
lately," he snapped.

"Let it drop, Montague."

"I cannot let it drop, Tom! *Mon Dieu!* You're
going to get yourself killed if you don't snap
out of it!"

Tom started to walk off, when Andre
grabbed his arm and spun him around, his
eyes meeting Tom's angrily. "If you can't get
Gideon out of your mind, then do us both a
favor and go after her!"

"I can't go after her."

"Why not? She's not married to Wellington-
Kent yet, is she?"

The facade Tom had been struggling to
carry for weeks was momentarily discarded,
and for the first time since Gideon left Watersweet, Andre heard Tom's voice falter with
emotion, "I . . . don't know."

Tom had been agonizing over Gideon
Wakefield's departure, and Andre knew some-

thing had to be done about it before the man got himself killed.

"Then find out."

"No. It would only make it worse if I knew for certain."

Andre gripped his friend's shoulder tightly, his eyes locking with Tom's in mute understanding. "Then I beg of you, go after her."

"If it were that simple, I would never have let her get on that train." Andre flinched as he saw bright tears well in Tom's eyes. It wasn't a pleasant sight, and Andre realized it was a privilege few would ever witness.

"It looks to me like you're making it harder than it has to be." Andre softened his tone, wanting to ease the haunted expression he saw in Tom's eyes. "My friend, you love the woman, so what's stopping you?"

The muscle in Tom's jaw tightened stubbornly. "I've done enough to disrupt her life. I refuse to do any more."

"Don't you think she's grieving over you too?"

Angrily shrugging away from the hand Andre had placed on his shoulder, Tom picked up a pike pole and started toward the river bank.

"Don't be a fool, Tom. It's not too late."

Tom continued on, ignoring Andre.

"Lannigan, you're not thinking straight—go back to the office. I'll take care of things here."

Andre muttered one heated obscenity after another under his breath as he watched Tom

337

hop on one of the churning logs, ignoring his suggestions.

"No one does my job for me, Montague," Tom shouted above the roar. "Get to work, or I'll dock your butt."

Andre viewed the lake's unusually great head of water from the melting snow and heavy rains, and his face grew more somber. A riverhog's job was most hazardous this time of year, and though Andre knew Tom was the best in the business, he was worried.

Tom hadn't been himself lately. He was taking too many chances. It was as if he thought that by deliberately asking for trouble, he could somehow bring some missing ingredient back into his life.

Andre's eyes narrowed as he saw a large jam begin to form at the sharp bend leading out into the channel. One of the men shouted for Tom, and he went bounding lithely across the rolling logs to locate the key log causing the problem.

The roar of the logs breaking away from the bank was deafening as several of the old-timers started working to break up the jam. Their poles rolled and jabbed and hooked logs on top of each other in an effort to break up the stubborn mass.

Overhead the sky was a bright blue, though the air still had touches of the last vestiges of winter.

Andre hung around to watch the men trying to free the logs to move them downstream. He was powerless to shake the niggling feeling that something was not right.

Suddenly, the log causing all the trouble broke loose and shot down the river, followed by hundreds of logs under the immense pressure of the moving water. Andre began tensing again as he watched Tom jump back to regain his footing, but the log his foot had been aiming for had moved to join the others in its mad rush downstream.

Andre took an involuntary step forward, aware of what was about to happen, but powerless to stop it. "Lannigan!" he shouted.

Distracted, Tom glanced up as his foot slipped, and he dropped into the roiling water, immediately sucked out of sight beneath the churning mass of pine.

"Oh, *mon Dieu*!" Andre started running, cupping his hands to his mouth, shouting frantically. "Man down! Man down!"

Men started running down the banks with poles poised, watching for the victim to surface between the milling logs.

Suddenly, a red woolen cap bobbed to the surface, but its owner failed to follow.

Andre's heart began to pound erratically as he raced along the icy banks. Abruptly, he turned and plunged headlong into the swirling mass of water and logs.

Dent Milligan immediately plunged in after

him, blocking his efforts to reach the approximate area where Tom had gone down.

"Let me go!" Andre screamed. "Tom's out there!"

"You can't help him, Montague!" Dent shouted above the roar of the churning water. Andre begin to swear as he fought to loosen the other man's hold, but Dent was equal to any giant's strength, and he hurriedly dragged the two-hundred-twenty-pound lumberjack through the icy water as if he were a sack of grain and flung him up on the shore.

The men gathered around, their eyes anxiously searching the milling logs for signs of their boss.

"Maybe he'll wash up downstream somewhere," someone murmured.

"He might make it to one of the wanigans . . ." The men's eyes moved to watch the long row of scrows chained together, waiting in the middle of the lake. The rafts with raised decks and a pine slab shack perched on top would serve as kitchen, office, supply room, dining shack, and camp store, while the drive was on.

But there was no sign of Tom on any of them.

"No . . . he's a goner," someone else in the crowd said, voicing what every man there was silently thinking.

"No!" Andre said tightly, his eyes refusing to

leave the churning mass of logs. "Please, Tom," he urged softly, "hang on, my friend."

The soft strains of organ music filtered beneath the study door of the oldest Methodist church in Philadelphia, Pennsylvania, on Saturday afternoon, the twenty-first of April. It was a beautiful spring day, and if Gideon were to judge from the sounds of the birds' merry chatter coming in through the open window, everything was right with the world. But nothing at all was right with hers.

She stared listlessly back at the image of the stranger magnified in the floor-length mirror and wondered for the thousandth time what her beloved Tom was doing that day. Was he well? Was he eating properly? Was he dressed warmly enough?

An angellike apparition stared back at her in a lovely tulle and lace wedding gown of the purest pristine white, adorned with thousands of tiny pearls. The creation had been handsewn by one of the finest seamstresses in all of Philadelphia and would be the envy of a queen.

Gideon thought the woman in the mirror looked familiar, but surely it wasn't her—about to walk down the aisle with a man, who, though very, very kind, was not the one she wanted to spend her life with.

And if this was supposed to be the happiest

day of her life, why did she feel like running out and flinging herself off the nearest bridge?

The door opened, and Echo entered the room. The cloying, sweet smell of chrysanthemums and asters followed her into the room.

"I have never seen so many people in my entire life," Echo confessed. "Such fine carriages and fancy clothes. I do declare it's like living with royalty. You can absolutely smell the money packed into those pews."

Sighing, Gideon picked up her wedding veil and slipped it carefully on her head. "That's nice."

"Oh . . . you look like an angel," Echo said admiringly as she hurried over to assist Gideon in the final moments before the ceremony was to begin.

"I don't feel like an angel," Gideon grumbled.

"It's just wedding-day jitters." Echo fussed with her veil, trying to get everything just right. "Talbot will be so proud of you."

"Talbot deserves better than me."

"That's not true. Talbot's the luckiest man in the world to have someone like you."

A soft tap at the door of the study warned the two women that the ceremony was about to begin.

Echo looked at Gideon, and her smile became radiant. "Try to be happy. I know your heart still yearns for another man and I ache for you, but Talbot loves you so very much

. . . and he is such a good man. He will do his very best to make you happy."

Gideon was surprised by Echo's quiet declaration. She'd never dreamed that the girl perceived the real reason for all of Gideon's tears of late. As close as she felt to Echo, Gideon had never confided her love for Tom to her. Reaching out to touch the tip of Echo's nose gently, Gideon said softly, "Talbot would be far better off with someone like you."

"But he doesn't want me," Echo said simply.

"And if he did?"

Echo's gaze softened. "Talbot is a wonderful man. You are very lucky he loves you."

The strains of the organ grew louder, and Echo hurried to open the door as Gideon's stomach suddenly tangled in a million knots. "Hurry now . . . Talbot is waiting for you."

Taking a deep breath, Gideon lifted the train of her dress in her hand and stepped into the foyer.

The dimly lit hallway was teeming with five giggling, breathless young women all dressed in long flowing gowns in various hues of the rainbow, wearing matching wide-brimmed hats.

The women were all her close childhood friends, but Gideon felt worlds removed from them now. Smiling at the women faintly, Gideon moved on to stand at the head of the sanctuary doorway.

The massive old Methodist church was, as

Echo had said, filled to overflowing. All of
Talbot's family, friends, and business associ-
ates were there to witness the exchanging of
vows between Miss Gideon Wakefield and Mr.
Talbot Wellington-Kent.

"Miss Wakefield?"

Gideon glanced up to find one of Talbot's
manservants extending a wire to her. "This
just came for you. I thought it might be important."

"Oh?" Debating whether to open the wire
or not, Gideon finally decided she should.
Handing her bouquet to Echo, she ripped the
envelope apart, her eyes hurriedly scanning
the brief message from Andre.

Gideon lifted her eyes slowly, and the letter
fluttered lightly to the floor as the first of her
bridesmaids started down the aisle.

The room began spinning, and Gideon
thought she was going to faint. One by one,
each of the girls were stepping out now to
walk with measured grace behind the other,
smiling as the procession of dresses moved
down the aisle. Blue, yellow, pink, green, violet.

The organ music swelled, and Echo's tur-
quoise gown blurred as she moved to take her
place at the doorway.

"Are you all right?" Echo asked expectantly.
Gideon's face was as white as the paper that
lay discarded at her feet.

344

Gideon shook her head, unable to find her voice.

A chord was sounding Echo's clue to begin her slow walk down the aisle. Glancing at Gideon, she started out hesitantly, peering over her shoulder occasionally to see if Gideon planned to follow.

The music changed in tempo. The crowd came to its feet as the organ pealed out the bride's entrance.

Staring sightlessly ahead of her, Gideon began moving woodenly. Her slippered feet moved silently down the polished floor leading to the altar, as she felt tears begin to roll from the corners of her eyes.

The music expanded and filled the large cathedral, and her tears came even faster. She could barely make out Talbot standing ahead of her, looking so fine and handsome in his wedding finery. His best man and childhood friend Frank Lawson flanked his right side, and beyond them stood five more groomsmen.

The seven men smiled as they watched the vision of loveliness coming toward them.

It seemed like hours before she reached the end of that incredibly long aisle. She was vaguely aware of Talbot smiling as he stepped forward, extending his arm to her.

The music slowly died away, and the minister in his long white robe began to pray. "Most heavenly and divine Father . . ."

The orchid bouquet in Gideon's hand began to tremble.

"We are gathered today to ask your blessing on this man and woman. . . ."

Gideon's whole body began to shake, and her tears flowed like wine.

Talbot glanced worriedly at her from the corner of his eye, and he reached out to squeeze her hand reassuringly.

"This holy and sacred union is not to be entered into lightly, but . . ."

A loud sob tore from the depths of her soul, and Gideon began to weep openly, long racking sobs that shook her small frame and filtered softly throughout the hushed audience.

The guests began to shuffle uneasily and whisper among themselves, mystified by the strange outbreak.

The priest glanced expectantly at Talbot, and Talbot held up his hand to interrupt the service.

Heaving a resigned sigh, he tenderly turned his bride, lifted her veil, and tipped her tear-stained face up to meet his.

"It's Tom Lannigan again, isn't it?"

Speechless, Gideon nodded, horrified that her face was wet with tears and she had no handkerchief.

Talbot calmly reached into his breast pocket and handed her his, a gesture that had become almost habitual between them now.

"Are you that deeply in love with him?"

Gideon nodded shamefully, realizing what an embarrassment she must be to him. His friends and family were looking on, completely at a loss as to what was taking place.

"I—I just found out that he was hurt very badly last week in a logging accident," she said.

Talbot's eyes closed briefly. "I see."

"He's—he's not a bad man, Talbot."

"Maybe not, but is he the man you really want to share your life with?" he asked in a tone that clearly indicated that he didn't believe Lannigan was worthy of her.

"Yes. Oh, Talbot, I love him more than anything or anyone in my life. I ache to be with him."

"And does he return your love?"

"I don't know . . . but deep in my heart I believe that he does. He just knows that I belong to you . . . and he knows he hurt me."

"And you would give up everything I offer you to be with this man?"

Gideon's tearful eyes gazed at him. "I don't care about things, Talbot; I just know that my life is miserable without him. I would rather spend one hour living in squalor with him, than live the rest of my life spending your money." She caught herself, not wanting to hurt him. "I realize that wasn't put very diplomatically, but it's true."

"Then go to him," Talbot urged softly.

A sob tore from Gideon's throat as she dabbed at her eyes again. "Wht about you, Talbot? I love you in so many ways, but I don't think I could ever make you completely happy. You deserve better."

Talbot gazed at her affectionately, and Gideon could see an understanding in his eyes. "I knew the day I brought you home that this hour would come."

"Talbot—I'm so sorry. I don't want to hurt you."

"Then you must go to the man you love, my dear. And may God bless your union."

Smiling, Gideon rose on her tiptoes and placed an affectionate kiss on his lips. "Thank you, Talbot." She whirled away, then hurriedly whirled back and leaned closer to whisper something into his ear, and he smiled.

"I would be most honored."

Gideon nodded, then turned to smile at Echo. Turning back to face the sea of stunned faces in the crowd staring back at her, she murmured sheepishly, "I'm sorry . . . if you'll just keep your seats, the ceremony will continue in a few moments."

Fleeing back down the long aisle that had seemed endless only minutes ago, her decision was crystal clear this time: she was going home.

Talbot looked at the faces of the stunned bridesmaids and smiled as his eyes met Echo's.

The young woman's face was pale as she stared back at him, wide-eyed and uncertain.

Clearing his throat, Talbot began. "Echo, it has just been brought to my attention that you would make a more suitable bride for me."

Echo's mouth dropped open. "Me . . . sir?"

Talbot cleared his throat nervously, and continued, "I know this might seem a bit out of the ordinary, but I must admit that the thought has occurred to me on more than one occasion, even before Gideon brought it to my attention again, that you are an exquisite creature . . . one with whom I would be extremely pleased to spend the rest of my life."

After a deep breath, he blurted, "Echo, my dear, would you do me the honor of becoming my wife?"

"Me, sir?" Echo repeated vacantly, refusing to believe her own ears.

Aware of the gasp of disbelief coming from his mother's pew, Talbot grinned and winked devilishly at his latest choice in brides.

"Yes, you, ma'am."

18

"Watersweet, comin' up!"

As the conductor sounded the call, Gideon sprang to her feet and ran to the back of the car to watch the train pull into town. Stepping onto the back platform, she felt the warm, southerly breeze brushing her cheeks intimately as if to say, "Welcome home, little one."

Drawing a long, appreciative breath, she let the pungent smell of the white pine embrace her. She had missed the sights and the smells of this wonderful logging town. Every morning while she'd been away, she had awakened long before sunup, long before the household servants rose, to lie beneath the rose-colored canopy above her lonely bed and listen for the sound of the Gabriel horn to call her to breakfast.

At times, she had longed so badly to hear the familiar sound that she'd imagined she could make out quite clearly the long, doleful bale echoing across the frozen hillsides.

Closing her eyes, she would fondly relive how she had woken each morning to find Tom sleeping on the pallet near the stove. When she would ask for water, he would bring a fresh pitcher to her without complaint. A smile surfaced when she'd recall what a gentleman he had proven himself to be. One morning he had risen fifteen minutes earlier to warm the water, but it had grown cold again by the time she had finished thanking him for his thoughtfulness.

The engineer gave a couple of loud toots on the whistle, and steam belched from the train's smokestack as Gideon ran back inside the car to gather her belongings. She could hear the wheels on the coach begin to screech loudly against the rails, and she wanted to be first in line when the train finally ground to a halt in front of the old D.S.S. & A.R.R. depot.

After stepping down from the coach, Gideon hurried across the street. She saw few familiar faces, and the town appeared to be nearly empty.

She spotted Berniece Trucksmore coming out of Menson's store and she eagerly began waving to get her attention.

Berniece paused, stunned to see Gideon Wakefield again.

"Miss Yardley . . . uh, Miss Wakefield . . . what on earth has brought you back here?"

Gideon set her valises down on the planked sidewalk and tried to catch her breath. "Hello, Berniece. Where is everyone?"

Berniece glanced around expectantly. "Who?"

Gideon smiled as she reached up to remove her hat. She couldn't recall the sun ever feeling so warm. "The men . . . where are they?"

"The men—or most of them—are gone now," she said, making Gideon's smile widen as she detected an immense note of relief in Berniece's voice.

"Gone?"

"Yes—cutting season's over. Most of the roughnecks have gone back to their families. The ones who haven't are over in Shadow Pine drinking liquor that'd grow horns on a horse and recklessly gambling their hard-earned money away. If they can't get that accomplished, they'll be spending it on those loose women they have over there." Berniece sniffed self-righteously. "Bunch of heathens."

"Where's Tom Lannigan?"

"Tom?" Berniece's forehead drew into a frown, and she clucked her tongue sadly. "Poor Tom."

Gideon edged forward. "Where is he, Berniece? He isn't worse, is he?"

Her heart started to pound. If anything had happened—if he had died from his injuries—she couldn't bear it, she just couldn't.

"No, he isn't any worse. The doctor says he's going to make it, but he's in a pitiful state."

"Is he at home?"

"Oh my, no. He's not up to that yet. He's still at Doc—" Berniece's explanation fell on deaf ears as Gideon suddenly darted off in the direction of Doctor Medifer's house.

"Miss Wakefield—your luggage!" she called.

"I'll get it later!"

"But don't you want to hear about the accident?" Berniece demanded, but Gideon was already out of earshot.

Heaving a sigh of disgust, Berniece picked up the two discarded valises and hauled them inside Henry's store for safekeeping.

It didn't take Gideon long to cover the ground to Doc Medifer's house. She bounded up the front steps and pounded on the doctor's door, still trying to catch her breath. Panic seized her as she pounded again, more loudly this time. What was taking so long? Why didn't someone answer the door?

She pounded loud enough this time to wake the dead, and the door was suddenly pulled open by an irate Doc Medifer.

"What in the blue blazes is goin' on out here?"

Gideon rushed past him, nearly knocking the elderly man off his feet. "Good morning, Doctor Medifer. I'm here to see Tom Lannigan, please," she demanded all in one breath.

The doctor took a startled step backwards. "Miss Yard—Miss Wakefield?"

"Please, where is Tom? I have to see him."

Pushing the door closed behind her, Doc studied her flushed features with growing amusement. "My goodness, young lady, have you run all the way from Philadelphia?"

Gideon's hand flew self-consciously to her hair. She knew she must look a mess. She was still carrying her hat, and her hair was stringing down the sides of her face. "I'm sorry. It's just that I've traveled a very long way to see him." Her eyes suddenly filled with bright tears. "It's very important that I be with him." Gideon could vividly recall the last morning they'd shared together in his room.

Willis Medifer's smile was so kind that it made it even harder for Gideon to control her urge to cry. "My dear, the whole town had been thinking that you would be very good for Tom right now. Follow me. I'll take you to your young man."

He turned, and she followed him down the long hallway to the room that she had occupied only a few months earlier.

Andre was just closing the door behind him as they approached.

Gideon began to cry when she saw the tall, good-looking Frenchman. With a smile, he held out his arms, and she gratefully went into them. "I came as soon as I could," she sobbed.

"I am most grateful, *ma chérie*."

"How is he?"

"Not so good, *petite fleur*. His heart is very sad."

Gideon quickly pulled from his embrace. "I want to see him."

Andre gently restrained her, his eyes troubled. "I do not know if he will let you, *ma chérie*."

"But why not? I love him . . . he needs me."

"It will come as a great shock to him to see you here," Andre confessed. "He believes you are on your honeymoon with your new husband."

Gideon searched Andre's eyes for some sign of hope. "He doesn't know about the wire you sent?"

Andre shook his head. "No, and he will be most upset when he learns what I have done, but I felt certain that you would want to know."

Her face softened. "I am so happy you did. But now I must go to him and tell him how very much I love him."

"But—your fiancé?"

"I'm no longer engaged, Andre."

Andre closed his eyes, his handsome features flooding with relief. "Oui, this is good. But Tom is a stubborn man, *ma chérie*. I fear he will be hesitant to accept your love now . . . but perhaps just the sight of you will give him the will to live again."

"What do you mean he will be hesitant to accept my love?" Gideon flared. Nothing could keep her from Tom Lannigan now!

"His leg was injured in the accident, and infection has set in. It's possible the leg will have to be removed. Doc isn't sure. You know Tom. He's proud, and he feels if his leg is taken, he'll be less of a man," Andre said gently.

"Less of a man . . . Tom Lannigan? That's nonsense!"

"We have tried everything we know to help him see it that way," Doc interjected. "But he is a stubborn man."

"Is he strong enough to go home yet?"

"He has the strength of ten men, but the uncertainty about his leg has defeated him," Doc admitted. "I'm afraid he thinks his life is over. He refuses to eat or to wash or even to get out of bed. Nothing we say has helped. He has simply made up his mind that he wants to die."

Gideon's back stiffened with resolve. "I'll get him out of that bed."

"He is very unmanageable, *ma chérie.* It will take a firm hand to pull him out of it."

Gideon would have to show her love by being tough with him, but could she carry it off? The answer came swiftly. She knew if it meant losing him otherwise, she could do anything.

"Just let me handle him from now on."

Andre breathed a sigh of relief. "Gladly."

"I'll go in and tell him that you're here," Doc offered. "I fear that he won't be happy."

Gideon's hand came out to block the doctor's entrance into Tom's room. "I'll tell him I'm here." Her chin lifted. "I can match Lannigan stubbornness any day of the week."

Andre grinned. "You are very brave, my little friend. He's not in the most sociable mood."

Gideon reached for the doorknob and turned it. "Good. Neither am I."

The room was dark when she entered. Although the window was open a crack to let in the balmy air, someone had drawn the shade.

Gideon allowed time for her eyes to adjust to the dim light. She could see Tom lying on the bed with his eyes closed.

Taking a deep breath, she let her gaze move to the area beneath the sheet where he was resting his injured right leg. Catching her breath softly, she bit her bottom lip as compassion coursed through her.

Drawing another deep, cleansing breath, she moved silently toward the bed, relieved to have the first shock of seeing him over with. She had known it wouldn't be easy. He looked so pale and beaten.

He had always been such a vital force, so tall, so proud, so very much his own man, but he would be again; she would see to that. The task that lay ahead would not be easy, but she

knew, now more than ever, that she would be
his unending source of strength.

"Who is it?" The familiar sound of his voice
sent goosebumps spreading along her spine.

"Come to empty yore slop jar, sir," she
teased in a soft drawl.

Tom's eyes slowly opened. "Gideon?"

She moved to his side. "Yes, my love?"

Taking his hand, she gazed into the depths
of the most troubled blue eyes she'd ever seen.
For only the briefest moment, he allowed her
to see his love for her.

"What are you doing here?" he whispered.

"Where else would I be?"

As she watched him shake his head, she was
heartbroken to see tears begin rolling from
the corners of his eyes. "Why . . . why did
you come back now?"

"Because we are in love, and we should be
together."

"No." He turned his head away.

She turned it back gently but firmly. "Yes."

"My God, I'm going to lose my leg. I don't
want you to see me like that."

"Listen to me, Tom Lannigan, that wouldn't
matter to me—do you understand? No matter
what happens, we will go on."

"Go back where you belong," he said brokenly. "I don't want you here."

"I am where I belong."

"There's nothing here for you now."

"You are."

Rolling to his side, he turned his back to her.

With a sigh, she pulled a chair up beside his bed. It was clear that he thought that he had had the final word. "All right. I'll put up with this maudlin act just so long," she warned. "I know the accident has been a terrible shock, but I won't let you just roll over and die, Tom Lannigan. Someday very soon we will have to get on with our lives."

"Go away."

"Not as long as there is breath left in my body."

He refused to answer—for days he refused to answer, or to eat, or to bathe. And when the days turned into a week, Gideon began to lose patience with him. He was drowning in self-pity, and she knew she had to take matters into her own hands.

On Monday morning, she entered his room with a tray loaded with bacon, eggs, flapjacks, and hot coffee. The aroma drifted pleasantly through the small room as she set the tray beside his bed and went to open the window. "Good morning, darling."

He barely glanced at her before he rolled over and presented his back to her again.

She walked back to the bed, smacked him on the rump, and taking him firmly by the shoulders, she flipped him over onto his back. After tucking a napkin under his stubbled chin, she brought the first forkful of food up to his mouth. "Open up!"

He refused, staring back at her with a stoic, silent resentment.

She deliberately poked him in the ribs, hard.

As he opened his mouth to swear, she quickly stuck the eggs into his mouth. At that point, he was forced to chew or strangle.

Before he could catch his breath, a forkful of pancakes entered his mouth, followed by more eggs, then a wedge of bacon.

"Dammit, you're choking me!" he sputtered.

"I've given it serious thought," she agreed, "and you're not out of the woods yet, but if you'll eat three more bites without me having to manhandle you, I'll spare your life—today."

"Damn miserable pest!"

"Just eat."

The food tasted far better than Tom had expected. He heard his stomach growl as she brought another bite of pancake to his mouth. "See how good this is? Ummm," she offered temptingly.

"Put some more butter on those things," he grumbled. "I've had hay that tasted better."

She smiled. "Put it on yourself."

Entering his room the next morning, she carried a basin of water and fresh towels.

"Good morning, sweet thing."

As usual, she was met with his stony silence.

She walked to the window and released the shade. It zipped to the top with a noisy clatter.

Tom's hand shot up irritably to ward off the deluge of bright sunshine. "Good Lord! Don't you have anything else to do but torment me?"

"No, I've made that my life's goal." She suddenly loomed over him menacingly. "Guess who gets to give you a bath this morning?"

His eyes widened with alarm.

"Yes, me. The doctor tells me that you refuse to do it yourself."

"Over my dead body," he vowed.

"I'm not looking for trouble, but if you want it, you got it." She reached over and began to unbutton his nightshirt as his hands shot out to stop her. She was surprised to find that his strength had not diminished over the weeks of convalescence. He was just as the doctor had said—strong as ten men.

"I would hate to floor you, lady."

"Not half as much as I would hate to be floored." She shoved his hands aside and continued with her work as he stared at her in disbelief. "What happened to the schoolhouse?"

She knew he wasn't going to answer her, so she thumped him soundly on the ear and asked again, "What happened to the schoolhouse?"

"King Davis burnt it to the ground the day you left," he snapped.

"Well, good for King. Now you'll have to build a new one."

Peeling off his shirt she let her eyes linger momentarily on his broad chest. If he had been able to feel the swift tightening in her stomach, he would have been assured that her attraction to him was not in question.

After dipping the cloth into the warm water, she lathered it with soap, then brought it to his chest.

Once more, his hand moved quickly to block her efforts, and their eyes locked in a stubborn duel.

"You are not going to wash me."

"You're too sick to stop me."

"The hell I am!"

"You're an invalid. You can't even get out of bed," she taunted.

His expression turned to hurt. "I can get out of bed; I just don't happen to want to get out of bed."

"Then you will have to endure being bathed like a little baby each day," she said simply. "You're not going to make everyone else suffer just because you're too lazy to wash." She slapped the cloth to his chest with enough force to take his breath away, and her eyes openly defied him to stop her. "And if you don't shut up and let me get this over with, tomorrow morning I'll start with your bottom first."

His face flushed with anger. "Where is Andre—dammit, tell him to get in here!"

"Andre is busy."

"Doing what?"

"Running *my* business! Since you're too irresponsible to do your job, he has to do it."

"You're letting Andre do *my* job?"

"Well," she shrugged, "someone has to see that Wakefield Timber runs smoothly."

Speechless, he watched as she began to wash him like an infant. When she went to draw the sheet back, he swore and reached out to jerk it back angrily.

Steeling herself, Gideon grabbed it back and hung on until she dislodged it from his deathlike clutch. Thrusting it aside, she laid bare the neatly bandaged leg he had been trying so hard to hide from her.

A tense silence fell between them as she stared at his swollen right leg. The sight was one Gideon would gladly have forfeited, but she knew that it was just one more milestone that had to be faced. Willing her features to remain expressionless, she began to carefully clean around the bandage.

"It serves you right," he accused.

"What serves me right?"

"Seeing . . . my leg. . . . Are you happy now?" She realized that he was embarrassed, and she ached for him.

"I wish it was well," she said softly, "but since it isn't, we have to deal with it. If it can be saved, so much the better. If you lose it, well, it will only make me love you that much more."

"I don't want your pity, dammit!"

She calmly draped the sheet neatly back in place. Meeting his accusing gaze, she said unemotionally, "You might as well get used to it; I'm all yours: my hopes, my hurts, my fears, and most of all, my love. Now, I can wash the remaining area, or you can. Which will it be?"

"If it's washed, honey, you'll wash it," he dared sarcastically. He was sure she wouldn't go that far.

She shrugged and flipped back the sheet again. After drawing his nightshirt over his head, more for her protection than his, she began washing away.

When she lowered the sheet again, her face was bright red, and he was fit to be tied. "I don't have to put up with this!"

"Oh, but you do. You're helpless, remember?"

"So help me God, if I could get out of this bed—"

"God helps those who help themselves, so I doubt that He has time to listen to a man like you whine all day. He has been very good to you, Tom. He's given you a fine strong body, and a woman who loves you more than anything on earth. You really should be ashamed of the way you're acting." She picked up a container of cornstarch and opened it. "This should make you more comfortable during this warm weather." White powder fogged around his head as she dusted away.

"Good Lord! Stop putting that girlish crap all over me—you *read* to Frank Kellier when he was injured! Why are you torturing me?"

Ignoring his temper tantrum, Gideon gathered the basin and towels and walked out on him, leaving him to rant and rave for as loud and long as he wanted.

When she entered his room on the next day, he was sitting on the side of the bed waiting for her. He was cleanly shaven, and everything on his breakfast tray had been eaten.

"Good morning, my love."

"Just give me the pan of water and leave."

"Sorry, I can't do that."

"You aren't going to wash me again today."

Her eyes locked pointedly with his. "Does this mean you're offering to do it yourself?"

They glared at each other. Finally, he gave her a brief nod and turned his back again.

"Good." Gideon walked over to arrange the basin and soap, then turned and busied herself straightening the bed. "Looks like your appetite is coming back."

"I'm only eating to get enough strength to get away from you."

"You couldn't possibly eat that much."

Tom picked up the washrag and stared at it.

Walking to the other side of the bed, Gideon absently lowered his hand down into the basin of water. "It won't bite you."

Grumbling under his breath, he began to wash.

"It's a lovely day. Why don't we go outside after your bath? A little sunshine will do you good."

"How am I suppose to get out there? Crawl on my belly like a damn snake?"

Gideon turned to look at him. "What are those wooden things propped next to your bed?"

His eyes snapped fire as he reached for the despised sticks propped beside his bed and flung them angrily across the room. "Crutches! But I'll not use them!"

Gideon calmly walked across the room, picked them up, and brought them back to stand beside his bed. "Yes, you will."

The days passed slowly, but eventually Tom began to regain his will to go on. His pride was slower to heal, but Gideon began to see small signs that that too would mend. They spent their mornings sitting in the sun talking while she sewed. They still had their minor skirmishes, but they came with less frequency now.

"You know it really burns me the way you keep doing that to me."

"Doing what to you?"

"Tom, you're going to eat—no, I'm not—yes, you are. Tom, you're going to wash—no, I'm not—yes, you are. Tom, you're not an invalid—Tom, use your crutches—what a hell of a way to treat a man in my condition! What did you do, leave your precious fiancé again and hop a train to ride clear across the country just to rub it in that I'm a cripple?"

Gideon sighed. "Am I that transparent? Well, you've guessed it. That's exactly what happened. The moment I'd heard you might lose your leg, I broke my engagement and rushed right back here to make fun of you."

He glanced at her sourly. "I don't find that amusing."

"Stop feeling so sorry for yourself," she continued. "You could be in worse condition. What if you were in danger of losing both legs? And while we're on the subject of what's amusing, I didn't happen to find it very funny when I was the one involved in an accident, and I was the one who lost her memory, and you told me that I was the new schoolteacher," she reminded.

"I didn't tell you that."

"You didn't bother to tell me otherwise."

His eyes refused to meet hers now. "I've already told you I'm sorry for that. It was a rotten thing to do, and you have every right to be upset."

"Tom, I think you should know why I had decided to sell my grandfather's business."

"It's no skin off my nose if you wanted to sell and invest your money in ridiculous hats. The land is yours, not mine. I just had that mixed up for a while."

"You really don't think I have a gift for making lovely hats, do you?"

"Gideon, I think you should take up gardening," he said dispassionately.

Ignoring him, she continued. "I didn't really know my grandfather, except through the letters we wrote to each other. I had only met him once, when I was a very small child. Mother was in ill health, and she could never make the long trip again to visit her father. I grew up aware that Tip owned a timber business in Michigan, but I didn't have the slightest idea what that meant.

"When he died, I had already accepted Talbot's marriage proposal, and since I knew nothing about running a logging camp, Talbot thought it best to sell the company and reinvest the money in my hat shops. Had I known what I know now, I would have willingly kept the land. I share your dream to replant the pines, Tom. I've seen what man is doing to the land, and it saddens me."

Tom stared off into space, but she could tell he was listening.

"I'm sorry I didn't know. It might have made things different between us," she said softly.

He shook his head slowly. "We would have never met if you had not come here to finalize the sale."

"True, but sometimes I wonder if that would have made any difference to you. I can't seem to reach you, whether I'm Fedelia Yardley or Gideon Wakefield."

"That isn't the way it is."

"You didn't even come to see me off that morning," she said quietly.

"I couldn't." His voice turned oddly uneven.

"Why not? Because you were afraid it would hurt too much?"

"Dammit, it hurt—more than you'll ever know."

"More than I'll ever know? Are we ready to talk about hurt? Because if we are, let me tell you how much I've hurt the past few weeks. Every time the mail came, and I didn't hear from you, I hurt. Every time I thought about the way you just let me go that morning, I felt incredible pain. Every time I remembered the way you looked as you watched that train pull out of town—"

"Do you think I *wanted* to let you go?"

"I don't know, Tom. Did you?"

"You know better than that."

"No, I don't." She gazed at him, her eyes pleading with him for the truth. "*You* tell me what you felt that morning."

His face clouded. "Pain . . . because you belonged to someone else. I felt helpless, angry, and guilty."

"I've belonged to you from the moment we

met. Wasn't I willing to give myself to you in order to prove that?"

"You didn't know you were engaged to another man. I did. I should never have lost my head and let things get out of control that morning."

She willed his eyes to meet hers. "Do you ever think about what happened that morning?"

His eyes slowly traveled back to confront hers. "Yes."

"Often?"

"More than I care to."

"I'm glad you made love to me that day."

His eyes moved away again. "It shouldn't have happened. I had no right to take what belonged to another man."

Gideon sighed, and her attention returned to her sewing. "Talbot's a good man."

His grunt told her he didn't care to hear about Talbot.

"He would have made me a fine husband."

"I suppose he had a good laugh when he heard about my accident. Probably thought I got what I deserved."

"Talbot doesn't like to make fun of people like I do," she mocked. "I suppose Talbot and Echo are somewhere in Europe, honeymooning right about now."

Tom's gaze lifted incredulously. "Talbot and Echo?"

Gideon nodded with a sigh. "When I told

Talbot that I couldn't marry him because I loved you, he married Echo. Isn't that romantic?"

He sat up straighter. "He broke the engagement?"

"No, I broke the engagement." She drew the thread through the cloth mechanically.

"Because of me?"

"Because of *me.* I didn't love Talbot—not the way I should have."

"How do you know for sure . . . your memory?"

"My memory returned the morning I found Waite's body in the snow. I'd accidentally gotten hit in the head that morning at school. My memory has been returning bit by bit ever since. But whether I'd ever gotten my memory back or not, I couldn't possibly love another man the way I love you."

Tom rolled his eyes in disbelief. "You *knew* you were Gideon Wakefield when we made love?"

She nodded. "What I couldn't be sure of was if you had known it all along."

"Well, now you know. I knew—or at least I suspected who you were, and I didn't do a damn thing to help you. In fact, I hurt you. I took your virginity when I knew it belonged to another man."

She lifted her eyes, and found him staring at her. "But you see, Tom, *I* knew exactly who I was when I asked you to make love to me, so you took nothing. I gave it to you."

Their gazes held, softly caressing each other. "That afternoon was a mistake, Gideon. It's only made things worse."

"No, it wasn't a mistake. We made love because we both wanted it, and because neither one of us could bear the thought of my going back to Philadelphia without knowing what it was to truly belong to each other."

"But I lied to you."

"Yes, you did, and I didn't like you very much for a while. But I've never stopped loving you. Not even once. Nothing you can do or say will ever change that."

Shaking his head, Tom said softly, "Did Talbot know about that afternoon?"

"Yes—I told him weeks before the wedding."

Sighing, Tom settled back in his chair, finding it all very hard to believe. "And Echo married Talbot?"

"That's right."

"Gideon, if I didn't know you better, I'd swear you were making that up."

"Well, I'm not. It was apparent to me after a few weeks that Echo was meant to be Talbot's wife. You should see them together, Tom. They laugh and giggle like two adolescents. Talbot isn't even stuffy when he's with Echo, and I've never seen Echo so happy."

Tom stared off thoughtfully, trying to absorb

the strange turn of events. "Lord knows she deserves a little happiness."

"Echo is wealthy beyond her wildest dreams, and she has a good, kind husband who will give her the love and respect that she deserves."

"And just when was all of this decided?"

"The day of the wedding—at the altar."

Turning his head, Tom looked aghast. "Where?"

"At the altar." She shrugged, then flashed him a sheepish grin. "Well, better late than never."

When he continued to just look at her as if he really didn't understand, Gideon leaned over and laid her hand on his. "Stop fighting it, Tom. It's all really very simple. Fate and the B&O Railroad gave me to you."

Tom grunted disagreeably. "What do you people do up there in Philadelphia? Change fiancés like we change socks?"

"No." She took his face in her hands to meet his gaze. "We listen to our hearts."

It was dark when she slipped into his room later that night. They had spent the day together, but tonight she felt lonely, so she had left her bed at the hotel and walked back to see him.

"Are you asleep?"

"No . . . what are you doing here?"

"I miss you."

Smiling, he patted a place on the bed beside him. "Come here and keep me company, little one. I can't sleep either."

Little one. Ever so slowly, he was returning to her. She scurried quietly across the room to settle down on the narrow bed beside him.

"We have to be quiet. We don't want Doc to hear us." She giggled. It felt like they were doing something naughty.

"Doc couldn't hear anything if they reenacted the Civil War in his backyard. Listen." They lay still and Gideon could hear loud snores coming from another part of the house.

They turned on their sides and gazed at one another in the moonlight that was streaming through the window.

"Why can't you sleep?" she whispered.

"Because I lied to you again. I *am* glad I made love to you that morning," he confessed softly.

Her fingers reached out to trace the contour of his face lovingly. She longed to kiss away the pain and the fear she still saw shining from deep within his eyes. "I know that. I didn't believe a nasty word you said to me."

"Go back to Philadelphia, Gideon. I can't marry you," he said raggedly.

"Why not?"

"I have nothing to offer you. I'm not even sure I'll be a whole man anymore."

Her hand moved below his waist. "I thought

it was your leg you were afraid you might lose."

Catching his breath at the touch of her hand, he shook his head. "It might as well have been. I can't ask you to be my wife when I may not be able to provide for you."

Tom was stunned to feel the first stirring of desire as her hand began to caress him. Somehow, he'd thought that he would never feel that way again.

"Not good enough. I have enough money to last us the rest of our lives," she reminded.

"I couldn't take your money."

"It would be our money."

"And what happens if you find yourself saddled with a cripple? You'll regret giving up Talbot and his Wellington-Kent fortune, and you'll end up hating me." His breathing grew more ragged. "Will you stop that?"

"Why?"

"Because—"

"Because why, Tom Lannigan? Because it feels good, and you like it, and it makes you realize that you're still very much alive and very much a man?"

"Don't do this to me."

Her mouth moved to meet his, and he closed his eyes, growing weak with wanting as her hands continued to drive home her point. "Marry me and take me back to our room and make love to me until we both have our fill."

"No."

"Yes."

"It wouldn't work."

"Why not?"

"Because I might lose my leg, Gideon. Don't you understand what that would mean? If I lost my leg then I couldn't harvest timber. And if I can't do my job, I can't support you, and if I can't support you, I would never consider myself a man."

"You don't need to support me. You're all the man I'll ever be able to handle. We'll have all the money we'll ever need, and we'll let Andre run the crew."

"No. I could never be happy letting another man run your company."

"Our company." Her tongue brushed his, and he groaned as he moved against her to make her more aware of his building need. Every fiber of him wanted to take her, and the thought that he still could made it even sweeter. "Don't kid yourself, Mr. Lannigan. You will be so busy replanting trees and loving me, you'll have no time left for all this self-pity," she warned.

His eyes opened slowly to meet hers. "Are you serious . . . you want to replant the pine?" he whispered.

She nodded, rubbing her nose against his affectionately. "Every last one that Wakefield Timber has harvested over the years—but I'll need your help. I know nothing about running a timber business, and you know everything.

You'll have to marry me or else I shall be forced to run off and marry Sven Templeton."

He chuckled, his voice breaking as he thought about what she was offering: the chance to see his dream fulfilled. He wanted it almost as much as he wanted her.

Moving closer, he eased her on top of him.

"Oh, my. Is this my old Tom Lannigan?" She sighed, wrapping her arms around his neck.

"Watch the leg," he murmured.

"I'll be easy with you, darling," she teased.

Raising her dress, he began to remove her pantaloons. "You're shameless, lady, but you've worn me down."

Grinning, she gazed up at him lovingly. "Not yet, but I plan to. Welcome home, darling."

Their mouths met greedily as his hand took on a new, exciting boldness.

"Gideon, I love you. I want to marry you, but it wouldn't be fair to you or our children. I love you too much . . . too damn much," he whispered when their mouths parted a moment later.

"Okay, then I'll strike a bargain with you. You consent to overseeing the planting of the trees, and I'll leave you alone."

"Alone?"

"That's right. I won't come around or bother you anymore until you've had time to come to grips with your injury. Deal?"

It was tempting, so very tempting. Tom

gazed at her, turning the thought over in his mind. "You would be content to step back— give me room to think about what's happened and where I'm going?"

She nodded. "I would."

His eyes narrowed with suspicion. He wasn't sure that he liked her backing off that quickly, yet she was offering him a reasonable compromise.

"What if I decide I can't marry you and I eventually go back to my father's business— it's what both he and my mother want."

"That will be up to you."

"All right," he said finally. "I accept your terms, but I can't promise anything. I'll see that your trees are planted, but it may be a long time before I can think about the future."

She smiled, and he had the unsettling feeling that she had just tricked him.

"What is going on in that mind of yours?" he challenged.

"Nothing, darling." Her face sobered instantly. "I'll wait for you—for however long it takes."

"All right," he conceded, entering her with a tantalizing slowness. "I'll hold you to your word." He drew her mouth slowly back to meet his, whispering, "First thing tomorrow morning."

Epilogue

Exactly Two Days Later

A soft rain pattered on the eaves of the hotel roof as Gideon turned and presented her back to her new husband.

Leaning on his crutches, Tom patiently began to undo the strings to her corset. "Why do women go to all this fuss?" he chided.

"To please a man." She tilted her head and winked at him. "Aren't you pleased? Why, Thomas, you're getting pretty good with those things." She noticed that he had become quite adept at using his crutches lately.

His voice held just a touch of impatience. "You'll see just how good, once you and this bear trap have parted company."

"Patience, darling." She sighed as his large fingers struggled to free the restrictive garment. "Wasn't the ceremony beautiful? I'll never forget the way you looked at me when the minister pronounced us man and wife

. . . almost as if I hadn't tracked you down like a hunted animal."

The corset gave way, and his fingers released her undergarments, freeing her breasts to his waiting hands. His breath was warm against her cheek, a whisper so soft that it sent shivers racing down her spine. "I wasn't running."

"It would have done you no good," she murmured. "You're mine, Tom Lannigan."

Tom drew in the scent of her intoxicating French perfume as he drew her closer. "Do you hear me complaining?"

"You don't think I'm still that greedy, conniving woman from Philadelphia who—" He turned her, and his gentle kiss stilled her playful repartee, assuring her that he knew he had been wrong.

"We both made a mistake," he admitted when their lips parted a few moments later.

"I didn't make a mistake."

"Now, come on. I'm sure you didn't like me at first," he reminded her.

She shook her head. "I have loved you from the moment I opened my eyes and saw you standing over me in Doc Medifer's office on the day of the accident. I knew somehow you were mine. From there, it was only a matter of convincing you."

"Oh, is that so? And I wasn't to have any say about it one way or the other?"

She picked up his left hand and placed a

feathery kiss on the shiny gold band she had slipped onto his third finger a little more than an hour ago. "Absolutely nothing."

"What if I told you I had already made up my mind I wanted you first."

"I'd say you sure had a funny way of trying to get me. By the way, what took you so long to marry me?"

"Two days? You tricked me. I had the feeling that's what you were doing, but I thought surely you wouldn't do that to a man in my condition."

"Yes, I can see you're in pitiful state," she murmured as her hands began to take shameful liberties with him.

He chuckled as her fingers grew even more audacious. "You knew I could never stay away from you." It had taken Tom exactly twenty-four hours without the pleasure of her company to make him realize that all he really wanted was her. He had come crawling back like a whipped pup.

"Was it only two days?"

"A day and a half," he corrected himself sheepishly.

"It seemed more like two eons." Turning, Gideon slipped her arms around his waist, and their lips met with a fevered eagerness that continually amazed them. "Hello, my darling husband," she whispered against his mouth.

"Hello, my love." His mouth moved to her shoulders, then down her bare arms, teasing, exploring the silkiness, then dipping lower again to taste the creamy swell of flesh he cupped in his hand.

Her fingers entangled his mass of dark blond hair as she drew his head closer to her breast. The naked heat of their bodies fused them tightly against each other, and she could feel his passion, firm and ready to take what was now forever his.

It had taken only a moment for her to help him out of his clothes, and they had gone hungrily into each other's arms.

They stood in the darkness, listening to sound of the rain falling gently outside the window, exchanging long, heated kisses.

This moment was to be savored and cherished and built upon. The shifting lantern light coming from the window boldly revealed him as a most splendid man, her man.

Their lips parted, and Gideon lifted a hand to his cheek. "No regrets?" Her eyes appealed to him in humble supplication as her earlier confidence was beginning to dim. She realized how brazenly she had worn him down until he had consented to marry her, but deep within her heart she also knew that he loved her every bit as much as she loved him, and he had left her no other choice.

He spread his hand over her nubile curves, nudging the searing proof of his words along her bare stomach. "Regrets? Maybe when I'm a hundred years old, and you've grown into a nagging, wrinkled old woman," he teased.

"But not now?"

His eyes lowered. "Not now . . . not ever." His lips brushed over hers, allowing the kiss to deepen until they were both drowning in it. He was all steeled muscle, and touching him made her weak with longing as they stood body to body, mouth to mouth. There was a sweet ache growing in the pit of her stomach, and with the tantalizing knowledge that he would soon appease it, her body grew limp with anticipation.

"You're no longer afraid of the future?"

"No. I will always take care of you and our children, love. You're my life now." He paused, and his eyes grew troubled. "Gideon . . . my leg . . . I know that you say it doesn't make any difference what happens, but I have to know. Are you saying that only because of the love we share? I would understand. . . ." His gaze openly pleaded with her for the quiet assurance he so desperately needed at that moment. His virility was not in question, but his ego was still very fragile.

"No, my love." She raised her hands to gently cup his face and shake it lovingly. "It doesn't bother me, but it bothers you, so we shall do something about it. I received a letter from Talbot this morning, and he wrote that he has heard of a marvelous doctor who is using some new drugs to cure all sorts of infections. I know your leg is steadily improving, but he wants us to come to Philadelphia right away. The doctor believes he can help you."

Moving steadily toward their marriage bed, she removed his crutches and laid them aside as he whispered in her ear, sweet hoarse murmurings that only a man and woman in love can share. They drifted onto the downy softness that would be the cradle of their love.

"You're cold," he whispered as he gathered her slender fingertips in a gentle grasp and brought them to his mouth. His weight was heavy, but she welcomed its comfort.

She gazed up at him with all the love she had stored in her heart for him. "You will warm me."

Their mouths met again, this time hungering to consummate their vows. Hands touched and explored and grew increasingly more impatient as desire became master.

Gideon had never dreamed there could be so much to discover about this man she loved, so many new sensations, so much pleasure. They had come a long way together, and she knew that they still had a long way to go, but they would make it. Together, they had discovered that they had to give to receive. And by offering everything, they had found it all.

As their pleasure heightened to exquisite torture, Tom whispered her name, and he, too, understood the oneness that they shared.

Gideon wanted to both laugh and cry with joy as she whispered back her undying love.

Easing his weight from her slightly, his hands slowly undid the pins in her hair. The fragrant mass tumbled about the pillow as he caught it and buried his face for a moment, overcome by his love for her. Lifting his gaze, their eyes met again. This time Gideon could see in them a love that would sustain them not only for the days to come, but for the rest of their lives.

"I love you, Gideon Lannigan . . . today, tomorrow, and for eternity," he vowed huskily. His hands reached up to grip the iron railing above her head, allowing him the leverage needed to join his body with hers. She could feel him trembling as he willed himself to take her gently.

Closing her eyes, Gideon allowed the beauty of the moment to enfold her; she was his now, completely, fully, and forever.

And like the pines they would sow together, their love would live on for generations to come, a silent, lasting tribute to the love of one very stubborn woman and one giant of a man, Gideon Wakefield and big Tom Lannigan.

Reckless abandon.
Intrigue. And spirited
love. A magnificent array of
tempestuous, passionate historical
romances to capture your heart.

Virginia Henley
☐	17161-X	The Raven and the Rose	$4.99
☐	20144-6	The Hawk and the Dove	$4.99
☐	20429-1	The Falcon and the Flower	$4.99

Joanne Redd
☐	20825-4	Steal The Flame	$4.50
☐	18982-9	To Love an Eagle	$4.50
☐	20114-4	Chasing a Dream	$4.50
☐	20224-8	Desert Bride	$3.95

Lori Copeland
☐	10374-6	Avenging Angel	$4.50
☐	20134-9	Passion's Captive	$4.50
☐	20325-2	Sweet Talkin' Stranger	$4.99
☐	20842-4	Sweet Hannah Rose	$4.95

Elaine Coffman
☐	20529-8	Escape Not My Love	$4.99
☐	20262-0	If My Love Could Hold You	$4.99
☐	20198-5	My Enemy, My Love	$4.99

At your local bookstore or use this handy page for ordering:

DELL READERS SERVICE, DEPT. DHR
P.O. Box 5057, Des Plaines, IL . 60017-5057

Please send me the above title(s). I am enclosing $_____
(Please add $2.50 per order to cover shipping and handling.) Send
check or money order—no cash or C.O.D.s please.

Ms./Mrs./Mr._____

Address _____

City/State _____ Zip_____

DHR-9/91

Prices and availability subject to change without notice. Please allow four to six
weeks for delivery.

Experience the Passion and the Ecstasy

Heather Graham

☐ 20235-3 Sweet Savage Eden $3.95

☐ 11740-2 Devil's Mistress $4.95

Meagan McKinney

☐ 16412-5 No Choice But
Surrender $4.99

☐ 20301-5 My Wicked
Enchantress $4.99

☐ 20521-2 When Angels Fall $4.99